A DOSE OF
Insulin

KEITH C PAYNE

*To Sarah Clarke,
a wonderful friend.
Keith*

authorHOUSE®

*Keith C Payne
25 . 2 . 2020*

AuthorHouse™ *UK*
1663 Liberty Drive
Bloomington, IN 47403 USA
www.authorhouse.co.uk
Phone: 0800 047 8203 (Domestic TFN)
   +44 1908 723714 (International)

© 2020 Keith C Payne. All rights reserved.

This is a work of fiction. All of the characters, names, incidents, organizations, and dialogue in this novel are either the products of the author's imagination or are used fictitiously.

No part of this book may be reproduced, stored in a retrieval system, or transmitted by any means without the written permission of the author.

Published by AuthorHouse 02/07/2020

ISBN: 978-1-7283-9831-0 (sc)
ISBN: 978-1-7283-9832-7 (hc)
ISBN: 978-1-7283-9830-3 (e)

Print information available on the last page.

Any people depicted in stock imagery provided by Getty Images are models, and such images are being used for illustrative purposes only.
Certain stock imagery © Getty Images.

This book is printed on acid-free paper.

Because of the dynamic nature of the Internet, any web addresses or links contained in this book may have changed since publication and may no longer be valid. The views expressed in this work are solely those of the author and do not necessarily reflect the views of the publisher, and the publisher hereby disclaims any responsibility for them.

If you know Reading, Berkshire, then read on, and even if you don't read on anyway.

This novel encapsulates a special bond between two sisters living in Caversham on the outskirt of Reading.

Eventually, the elder sibling comes to see her life as one without the rewards she believes she so richly deserves; maybe her experience of different traumas will now result in something else, possibly something worse.

Elsa, the youngest of these sisters, has diabetes. Could her diabetes provide the solution to another problem?

Acknowledgements

As always, Doreen L Payne for her support, patience and encouragement when I write, also my entire family.

And of course, Diabetics and Medics everywhere.

Chapter 1

Bulbs are struggling to push their way through the soil, new leaves appear in the trees and much to our joy, the weather is improving.

Warmer and brighter than the last few dismal months; everything feels so much better.

Alice was pleased the days were getting warmer and especially looked forward to the months ahead, and whatever was in store for her and her Mum.

Mum, Jennifer, was expecting another child.

It was a happy time, but now Alice wished so much that she possessed foresight as the future certainly wouldn't be what she would have chosen!

Shortly after my sister was born, Dad left us, and the times were difficult.

Without another grown up in our lives, it must have been a lonely life for Mum and undoubtedly dispiriting.

I didn't think much about the reason until a few years later when I eventually discovered why she had experienced such a sad existence.

It was something so cruel minded that most people would find it challenging to believe Mum's story.

Although I was only six years old, I did try to help Mum as best I could.

It was fun feeding my newborn sister, and sometimes I helped change her nappies and other essential responsibilities associated with bringing up a baby.

As a result, during our early years, the relationship between me, and my younger sibling, Elsa, was more like that of a parent and child. In later years, an exceedingly strong, and loving bond would develop between us.

Being six years older was a massive difference, but as we grew up, mentally, the age gap disappeared entirely.

Elsa would think in depth; much more profound than me before reacting, and her thoughtful opinion was always worth considering.

Once Elsa had made her mind up about something, she certainly wasn't backward in coming forward with her opinion.

Without a partner, Mum attempted to ensure Elsa, and I enjoyed those earliest years. She put us before anything else. However, please don't think it was easy going, as Mum didn't let us get away with anything unacceptable.

These times were tough for us all, but Mum always attempted to provide something interesting to occupy us.

Often she walked us to the local parks, where Elsa and I would play on the swings and the slide or chase after dogs as we attempted to beat them to specific points around the park; mostly without success. Sometimes, when Mum wasn't looking, we paddled and even chased after the waterfowl in the duck pond.

In the Autumn months, we would kick through the

massive piles of leaves, swept together by the park keepers. It was fun but looking back, today, neither Elsa nor I can understand why we believed that.

Knowing why we were told off by Mum for destroying the park-keepers efforts was much more understandable.

We were encouraged to save money whenever we received it for Birthdays or as presents for one reason or another. I could never understand why Mum persuaded us to do this; a quick trip to the shops and I'd soon know what to do with the money!

During our school holidays, the Market day would be a special treat.

We would open our money boxes, count how much we had saved and then walk to one of the local Markets.

However, spending the money was always under Mums watchful eye.

She would even add the extra cash if there were something special we wanted and we didn't have enough money to buy it. Bless her.

Other times when we had little money to spend, and for something to keep us occupied, Mum would walk us to Reading Railway Station, where we would enjoy a drink and something to eat in the Station's café. Nothing special but this trip provided a physical activity for Elsa and Me.

Other memories came flooding back like a summertime trip to the seaside.

Thinking about Mum and how much she must have struggled to find sufficient cash for our trip to Bournemouth.

For Elsa and Me, it was going to be an incredible adventure.

Recalling that particular holiday, I remembered it being a significant time, but somewhat upsetting for Mum.

We enjoyed building sandcastles and making moats around them by digging out pots of sand with our shovels and buckets.

That experience was a pointless exercise.

As we kept filling the moat around our castle, with buckets of seawater, the water immediately drained away.

The Seagulls were prettier looking creatures than the pigeons at Reading Railway Station. But unlike the pigeons, they didn't wait to be offered our food; they just took it!

When we least expected it, they would swoop from anywhere and snatch whatever we were holding in our hands whether it be crisps, sandwiches or ice cream. They were bold creatures!

I thought it was funny, but Elsa, my little sister, was frightened, so sometimes, either Mum or I would hold her treat until it was safer for her to eat it.

Elsa's mood would immediately change from one of fright to laughter when the seagulls then tried to steal the food from Mum and me.

Especially on the occasion when I was holding Elsa's ice cream cornet.

Trying to escape from the seagulls, I ran and tripped over the remains of our sandcastle and covered my face with sand and ice cream! I must have looked a sight, but a funny one!

A man standing nearby, about Mum's age and with his son, also found it amusing. Telling Mum, any food no matter what it was must be eaten indoors where the gulls can't get hold of it.

I remember he was a pleasant man and showed us how to build moats around our Castles. Unlike ours, the seawater he poured, didn't drain away into the sand!

"Come and have a look at this." He said.

He took us all, including Mum, to the sandcastle he'd built for his son, who he introduced as Ray.

There was a castle, professionally designed, with perfectly square walls around which was a circular moat, full of water. We stared with puzzlement as the seawater didn't drain away.

Ray was happily pushing a small boat around this waterway.

The lad's father told us to take a closer look and asked us to guess why the water wasn't disappearing.

I had no idea, although Elsa exploded with joy, believing she was smarter than Mum or me. "I know mister, underneath the sand is a water tap."

"Unfortunately not, young lady, it would be so much easier if there were a tap!"

Impatiently I waited for him to explain the answer as by now I was genuinely mystified.

Desperately trying to find the answer, Elsa interrupted again and told us all it was a trick, a magic one!

"No, I'm sorry young lady; let me tell you the answer.

I level the sand as flat as possible and then cut a large plastic water ring in half, like the type you use when swimming in the Sea.

Then, I place half of the plastic ring on the flat sand and mark the sand around it with Ray's spade.

I dig a circular and shallow trench in the same shape as the outline of the plastic ring, and then inside the ditch, I place one half of the plastic ring and fill it with water.

As you can see, the water doesn't flow away, and there's your moat!"

It was impressive, and Mum told him what a clever man he was.

Elsa just stared.

The two of them, Mum and this companionable Man, chatted amiably for some good while.

Later, Mum reminded us it was time to go, as dinner would soon be ready to eat at the hotel.

As she said goodbye to the young lad and the Man, who had already introduced himself as Graeme, spelt 'aeme' he had specified, he would meet us all tomorrow morning.

He had the other half of the plastic water ring and would help us build a castle and moat of our own.

While Elsa and I cleaned the grains of sand from our bodies and clothing under a beachside water tap, we talked about Mum and this chap Graeme, spelt 'aeme' I noted with amusement.

Eating Dinner, Elsa and I continued to joke about Mum and how this chap made sure we understood the accurate spelling of his name.

Mum dismissed our comments although after continual bantering she accepted that he was a clever and interesting man and she would be pleased to meet up with him tomorrow.

For long periods, Mum was quiet, and it made me think that despite our jokes, she was thinking, quite seriously, of this Man, Graeme.

Typically, as far as clothing went, Mum was organised, but today she tried on several outfits of clothing and made every effort with her makeup.

I wondered why all the fuss as we were only going to the beach?

Meeting on the beach, as arranged, Graeme and Mum were exceptionally polite and formal for a while; gradually, they began to talk more naturally, as they had the day before.

Graeme helped Elsa and me, and his son, Ray, to build our sandcastle with a waterproof moat.

While we continued to play, Graeme and Mum walked down the beach and paddled in the sea.

Continually I watched Mum closely, in case things changed for her and she found it more challenging than she could cope. However, I was pleased to note everything was fine as Mum and Graeme, laughed and joked, although I was never quite sure what about?

At lunchtime, Graeme suggested that we eat in a pleasant beach café he knew of; "No scatty seagulls in there." he said with a grin.

It must have been a fifteen-minute walk, at least, but it was worth it as us three children played different ball games along the beach.

Elsa often put her hands on her hips and complained loudly each time Ray or I accidentally kicked the ball into the sea and teased her about fetching it!

Her expression was most humorous, and as you will understand, sometimes, just sometimes, it wasn't an accidental kick!

We selected something to eat from the shelves and drinks from the counter and chose a seat by the window which faced the open sea. It was a picturesque view, and we could see a large ship sailing in the distance.

The shopfront door was open, and as Elsa was drinking from her can of Cola, a seagull flew into the doorway, settled on the step and then looked around a few times to make sure it was safe.

Confidently the Seagul stared at each one of us in turn, and then walked to the lower shelves and boldly grabbed a packet of food in its beak and disappeared outside. It all seemed so natural to the gull.

With amusement, Elsa, chocked while drinking her cola and spread it all over her pretty beach outfit.

Mum turned to Graeme and asked with a huge grin on her face, "And what did you say about safe from seagulls and eating indoors?" Everyone laughed except Ray and Elsa, who were probably too young to understand Mum's humour.

The day continued like this, with laughs, jokes and pleasant conversation.

Mum and Graeme strolled towards the shoreline, probably a final chat and another paddle in the sea before we returned, our last night in the hotel.

The empathy between them seemed most natural.

"They got on well Elsa; for once it's so nice to see Mum and a friendly man having a pleasant conversation.

And we're all meeting up again tomorrow. Do you think anything might come of this?"

"It would be nice. I can't ever remember seeing Mum with a boyfriend. Mum's been by herself ever since we were babies." Elsa replied.

I couldn't resist the opportunity and reminded Elsa she was still a baby!

Returning from the water, Mum asked Elsa to pass her a towel and wiped her feet but found it challenging to remove the irritating grains of sand from between her toes.

What seemed her final attempt to remove the sand and she lost her footing landing heavily beside Graeme's startled son Ray.

As she apologised profoundly, Graeme assisted Mum to her feet. Just the look in their eyes told me how much they had enjoyed each others company.

Mum then told Elsa and me, with a controlled look on her face, tonight would be a good night as both families would be enjoying dinner together in our hotel restaurant.

Mum was the first in the shower, and she was in there so long, I wondered whether the water would be cold when Elsa and I wanted to wash. I knew I needed a shower soon as, despite all my efforts, I could still feel those grains of sand; they were everywhere.

Elsa pushed in between me and the shower room and asked Mum to hurry up as she also wanted to *look good for dinner*. I thought of a brilliant comment but decided that perhaps this wasn't the best time.

"I'll be finished soon, Elsa. I'm just finishing my make

up; perhaps you'd like to help me and tell me whether I look beautiful."

"You always look beautiful Mum; you are the prettiest Mum in the whole wide world," Elsa said with extreme pride.

The door eventually opened, and as Elsa had said, she did look beautiful; She had made such an astounding effort!

Elsa and I looked at each other, and Elsa mouthed the word "Yessss!"

We were early and already sitting at the dinner table when Graeme and Ben arrived.

As we were seated either side of Mum, Graeme and his Son had no choice but to sit opposite.

Graeme remarked how elegant Mum looked, and she replied accordingly.

We talked about our many pleasant and amusing experiences during the weekend and how nice it was to meet others of a similar disposition. Although, it was Mum and Graeme who seemed to be doing most of the talking.

The evening was most amiable, and as we finished our sweet courses, Graeme leant forward in his seat and inquisitively asked Mum when she would be returning home.

Mum said, "Unfortunately, tomorrow morning."

Mum and Graeme were getting on so well, and I wished we were staying longer.

"Oh, that's a real shame." He replied briefly in a softly spoken voice.

"Are you staying longer, Graeme?" Mum asked with

increased interest and probably a little hope for the future. Maybe this was it!

Graeme responded immediately "Not much longer; we're only staying until tomorrow evening; anyway, it's been pleasant meeting you and your family. Maybe we'll meet up in Bournemouth some other time. Also, it would be pleasing to introduce you all to my wife, Karen.

She's coming to collect us; she's spent the weekend in Poole with her Mum who's suffering badly from Arthritis; her Dad, the poor soul, he used to care for her, but died a few years ago."

I couldn't face Mum; since the time Dad left us, I couldn't remember Mum being so upset. She was distraught.

I'd hoped something good would develop with Graeme and knew Mum felt precisely the same. I could understand how she must have felt and wanted to cry for her.

No matter our age, none of us ever forgot the amusing times and the friends we always made while playing on the beach or paddling on the seashore. That one exception, even today, is still most upsetting.

The weather was always excellent, as, in later years, our minds still prevented us from remembering the wet and dismal days.

Now and again, on the train journey home, I could sense Mum was reliving her experience during our dinner with Graeme. Despite the humour between Elsa and me, Mum said nothing and looked extremely pallid.

I took her hand in mine and asked whether she was ok.

"I'm fine thanks, Alice and you must stop worrying

about me. Anyway, I've got his contact details, and before you ask; Yes Graeme's."

It was difficult to know what to say in reply. I was pleased but wondered what to expect from Mum and Graeme further down the line?

Whenever I asked Mum whether she had heard from Graeme, she claimed there had been no contact between them and on one occasion she told me to stop asking about him.

I complied with this request, but her attitude seemed strange. Was there something she wasn't telling me?

Whatever, Mum said nothing more and I stopped asking questions.

Chapter 2

It was only later in life that Elsa and Alice realised Mum had worked three different jobs, apart from the time she spent looking after us.

This exceptional amount of work was to ensure we had somewhere to live, money for food and days out; they must have been long and tiring days for her.

Weekday, Mum would wake up at 5 am, clean a rich man's house, anytime from 6 am until 8 am, return home to cook our breakfast before we travelled to school.

We never told her, although Elsa and I guessed she knew, that often when she had left for her second job, we would climb back into our beds and sometimes go back to sleep.

Elsa and I would walk to school, occasionally late and as you would expect, suffer detention at first break!

Mum then worked in a shop between 9.30 am and 4 pm. All this before arriving home to cook our evening meal and looking after one of my classmates, Michael, or as we all called him at School, Mickie.

She did this for his Father until he returned home from his prestigious job in London.

Mum looked after Mickie for a couple of years, until the day when she suddenly ceased to care for him. At the time, my classmates also noticed he wasn't attending school.

Neither, the School nor my Mum explained why this was, and under intense questioning, from my school friends and me, we were all told to stop asking about this particular matter.

During this time, I had become Mickie's best friend, so naturally enough, I was upset; it was such a mystery to us all.

This instruction left everyone with even more questions, and crazy theories developed accordingly.

Mickie's father was one of the '60's Great Train Robbers, and he had escaped to South America. He was one of the Beatles *Minders* and had travelled abroad with them; he was a member of one of the notorious gangs of the time and was now on the run and so on.

Whatever the story, it was never a trivial explanation!

We all agreed that talking about Mickie's disappearance was more fun than School lessons, although we never did find out what happened to him or his family. Even the early years of social media provided no answers.

Both Elsa and Me had school friends, but never friends as close as Elsa and I were to each other.

It just seemed natural for the two of us to spend our free time in each others company.

Mum mentioned this on several occasions, saying it would be good for us to established other friendships which we eventually did, but never the special bond us sisters had for each other.

Even her attempt to register Elsa to the Brownies and me to the Girl Guides didn't work.

A Dose of Insulin

One evening while eating our dinner, we discussed a few ideas or hobbies which might interest us and also involve ourselves and others.

It wasn't as easy as you might think it would be, and it was Mum who eventually pointed out that Elsa was good at running short distances and at School sports days, I had the ability for the long jump and even the high jump.

It was Elsa, who initially confirmed enthusiasm for the idea when she shouted "Athletics; how about joining an Athletics club, Sis?"

"Excellent Elsa," said Mum as though it had initially been Elsa's idea. "Caversham Athletic Club is only a few Streets away and who knows either of you could become British champs!"

Within a couple of days, Mum had obtained two registration forms from the Athletic Club.

"Now fill in your details and of course in your neatest handwriting."

We were soon attending Caversham Athletics Club, and the various meetings, at weekends and midweek evenings.

It had been a fantastic idea, and the two of us developed friendships with some of the other members.

I remained a member until I became interested in boys and other things of interest although on occasions I would return to watch Elsa perform her athletics.

Elsa continued as a member of the Athletic Club for much longer than I had expected.

She also became keen on racquet games such as Squash, Badminton and Tennis at which she did seem to excel.

I was useless at anything that involved a racquet but did

enjoy watching Elsa, although that was more likely because I just enjoyed spending time with her.

However, she laughed each time I called Badminton, Shuttlecock.

"Alice, Shuttlecock's a stupid name, and the correct name is Badminton so, please talk like a grown-up!" She said, quite seriously.

I laughed, but now and again, I couldn't help joking with her and deliberately repeating the word shuttlecock!

Whatever, our dear Mum, only ever seemed to think of Elsa and Me and what was best for us during the early stages of our life; in fact, until the day she died.

Like Mum, Elsa was always there for me, her older sister, especially so when I met my first true boyfriend, David.

I was settling down to my first working role as a shelf stacker in a local supermarket; it was a monotonous occupation, but it paid the bills I reasoned.

Once again, the gift of foresight would have been an exceptional asset!

The building was clean and everything well structured with sufficient staff to deal with all the daily tasks of which there were more than the customer's realised.

When I first joined the Supermarket, a staff member, Penny, took me on a tour of the facilities and in particular, the Canteen.

Penny was a friendly girl, average height with dark hair. She treated me in such a manner that I immediately warmed to her.

Chapter 3

"We have a drinks machine, tea, coffee and hot chocolate and another machine with tins of cold drinks. Over there you can buy snacks, but if you want something filling to eat, you'll have to bring it to work with you."

We sat at one of the several tables to drink the hot chocolate and coffee we had bought from the machine, and Penny told me more about the business.

After a few days, my only complaint was the constant cold in the warehouse; when I mentioned this, my Supervisor said I wasn't working hard enough to keep myself warm!

A humourous comment I questioned although Penny caused me concern when she told me "That woman doesn't have a sense of humour!"

One Monday morning, it was as much as I could do to stand in front of the bathroom sink and brush my teeth. No matter which way I positioned myself, no matter which way I stood, the pain in my back was agonising.

Should I go to work, I questioned.

I had been brought up by my Mum to believe that one always sought the reason why you *should* carry out your responsibilities rather than finding a reason why you *couldn't*.

Through many years it had developed as a family trait, this, was not surprising as Mum was such a hard worker!

That was the answer, so with great difficulty, I prepared myself for the short journey to work, although understandably the whole process took much longer than it usually did. Frequently I had to stop and lean against something to ease my pain!

The supervisor, known as the Bull, because of her overbearing size and temperament, was not impressed when I entered the building eight minutes later than the official clocking on time of seven.

To make matters worse, when attempting and failing to load a package of coffee jars onto the warehouse trailer for distribution to the relevant shelves in the shop, the supervisor warned me again that my job was at risk.

"Miss Edwards, you are unable to arrive on time, and now you struggle to do your job and load the shelves. Perhaps we should, in turn, struggle to pay your wages, or even better, fire you!" The supervisor continued with no sympathy whatsoever.

Before I could reply, the giant carton of coffee jars was lifted onto the warehouse trailer by a fit and able young man.

He explained to the Supervisor, "This young lady, despite the pain in her back, has at least made an effort to get to work, so that should count in her favour, and it is obvious she's suffering intense pain, so if you don't mind, I'll assist her to stack the shelves."

I was still in pain and therefore exceedingly grateful of this young man's intervention.

With that, and despite the Supervisors protestations, the young man introduced himself as David. He was dark-haired, not far short of six-foot, lean and handsome.

Unlike everyone else, he didn't seem to possess any fear for this deplorable Supervisor.

All of a sudden, my painful back was not the focus of my immediate attention.

However, I did decide it would be a good idea to demonstrate my suffering and inability to load the shelves, just a little longer; in fact, as long as David was nearby.

The shelves were extensive and looking extremely bare; everywhere gaps appeared where tins or types of one product or another were missing.

David finished loading the coffee jars onto the shelves and then apologising for leaving me alone, departed back to the warehouse to continue his tasks.

Several times during that particular day and despite the back pain, which continued to trouble me, I sought an excuse to wander into the shop's warehouse.

Despite the effort, I was disappointed not to see David again.

'Where was he?' I continually asked myself.

The working day seemed to drag.

Not only because of my bad back, which I now decided was a result of my strenuous dancing at the local nightclub during the weekend but also because at any moment, I expected David to re-appear.

And he didn't.

Much to my relief, the shop's closing time finally arrived,

and as I walked towards the clocking-off machine, I hoped David would be there. Once again, I was to be disappointed.

Walking home, I could only think of this delightful young man and how much I longed to see him and that handsome profile once again.

Unlocking the front door and entering the living room, it was immediately apparent to Mum Jennifer and Sister Elsa, that during the day, something out of the ordinary had seriously captured my attention.

No persuasion whatsoever was required for me to reveal the day's events.

However, young Elsa appeared by far the more interested party and the one with all the related advice.

"What time does he clock-on? You must be there just before he arrives. Do you have a works canteen? You can plan to meet him there, some time or another. Maybe even wait by the clocking-off machine when the working day finishes."

Each evening I returned home and had to inform a most interested and subsequently disappointed Elsa, that there had been no contact.

That special tingle in my heart was now beginning to fade and fade quickly.

Later, I heard that David, the day after he had assisted me with the shelves, had moved to another of our firm's branches as Warehouse Manager, after an already agreed promotion.

Therefore it was, unlikely he would ever return to this businesses location. I reflected on the adage; *There's always more fish in the sea!*

Chapter 4

Some weeks later, Elsa welcomed me home, but before she could say anything, I asked her "Well, what do you think happened today?"

There was no pause before I continued excitedly, "When I left the shop, David was waiting for me outside. We are meeting up tonight for a drink at the Hare and Hounds."

After a considerable time, I emerged from my bedroom, looking impeccable, or so I believed!

My hair hung in perfect waves, my eyelids also perfectly lined, and the makeup on my face made the presentation one of absolute perfection; especially when dressed in my latest brands of designer clothes.

While so pleased for her precious sister, Elsa couldn't help but remark amusingly on the time and effort Alice had made for this special evening and the man she would be meeting!

The evening went well for them both, and Alice remarked to David that the conversation had flowed so naturally that it was as though they had known each other for years.

"Perhaps we have David; do you believe in reincarnation?"

"Not really once you're gone, that's it," David replied succinctly.

This particular subject continued for a significant percentage of our evening's conversation although, hands up, he won this specific argument by a mile!

"Incidentally David, I asked, what is your surname?"

"Wilson, he responded, David Wilson. And yours?"

"Officially Oliver but since my father disappeared, we have used my Mum's maiden name of Edwards."

"So it's Alice Edwards, and your father disappeared? It sounds mysterious; do you want to tell me about it?"

"Not now, thank you; perhaps some other time!" I replied as the history was all too personal and although a pleasant chap, I didn't know David that well.

Alice accepted David's request that they meet up again but settled on a date, perhaps much sooner than David had initially intended.

Arriving home, Alice's intention to tell all of this evening's adventure was cut short.

Elsa was spread-eagled on the kitchen's wooden floor amongst some broken crockery, cutlery and furniture scattered around the room.

What had happened?

At first, I panicked, and then it became evident, Elsa had suffered a hypoglycaemic fit! Totally out of control, hence the damage. Now she lay, seemingly unconscious on the kitchen floor.

Mum, Jennifer was attempting to place various forms of sweetener into Elsa's mouth, in an attempt to bring her back to consciousness and normality.

Nothing appeared to be working, and Mum was explaining to Alice that she would probably have to call for an emergency ambulance service as Elsa wasn't responding.

In my head, everything seemed much worse than perhaps it was! Whatever, it wasn't good.

Elsa had contracted Diabetes when she was two years old and suffered the most severe kind, type one.

As a result, she injected insulin twice daily and on rare occasions accidentally gave herself more insulin than she needed. Or to explain it more accurately, she ate less than she should have considering the amount of insulin she had injected, hence the fit.

Alice had witnessed this severe reaction a few times during Elsa's young life. Her responses were always so frightening.

Suffering from a hypo, sometimes Elsa lost physical and mental control, and anything in her way was at risk, hence the kitchen mess and disruption.

I attempted to help Mum by cleaning up the broken crockery and generally tidying up the kitchen, while she continued to try and bring Elsa back to normality.

There was no improvement whatsoever in Elsa's comatose situation, and I could tell Mum was most concerned.

Alice realised, with horror; this was, by far, the most serious of all the hypoglycaemic episodes she had ever witnessed.

Mum, shouted for Alice to pass her the jar of honey from the kitchen cupboard. With her fingers, she gradually wiped the honey around Elsa's mouth; taking care that Elsa didn't clamp her teeth onto her fragile fingers.

I hoped this intensely sweet nectar would do something to help Elsa recover quickly.

There was still no positive reaction at all, and at this point, I realised just how much I treasured my dear little sister.

Mum picked up the phone and called the emergency services. Elsa had ceased to writhe on the kitchen floor and now just lay motionless and unconscious.

Although it couldn't have taken long, it seemed an absolute eternity before we heard the Ambulances sirens and witnessed the emergency vehicle with its blue flashing lights pulling up outside our house.

Between them, the ambulance technicians, known as medics; two men and a woman carried various items of emergency medical equipment into the room with them; some bulky, some not so large.

The lady medic checked Elsa's pulse but couldn't locate any when checking her wrists and then her temples. Resting her ear over Elsa's heart, there was no sound of a beat.

She shouted something at one of the male assistants who then started to place electrical wires connected to sticky pads to Elsa's legs, arms and chest.

He switched the machine on and glancing at the monitor for what seemed ages, then diverted his attention to the Lady medic and without saying anything, just shook his head negatively.

I knew what this meant and couldn't bear this intolerable situation any longer. I ran outdoors with tears streaming from my eyes.

Despite the very late hour, many of the neighbours

were drawn by the ambulance and gathered outside. Some cuddled Alice; asking whether everything was alright.

A stupid question which Alice was unable to answer as once again she just burst into floods of tears.

One of these neighbours then pointed Alice to her front door where her Mum, Jennifer, was calling her.

Without further ado, Alice rushed inside her home, and there was Elsa, sitting on a chair and answering the Medics different questions.

Her date of birth, whether she had any brothers or sisters, the name of her Mum and much more.

I knew these various questions were the general practice for the medics, to test just how conscious and aware Diabetics were. Although I didn't care, I was so relieved to see my little sister recovering.

Gradually Elsa answered the questions in turn. The lady medic handed me a paper tissue to wipe my tearful eyes, and took Mum to one side and said with concern: "It was close, we thought she'd gone."

A bottle of fluid was still being held above Elsa by the other male medic, and thin plastic tubes hung from the bottle and were somehow, inserted into Elsa's arm.

Later I was told this bottle held a concentrated glucose solution, it was called a drip, and it was this solution which had saved her life.

I was overjoyed and for many years afterwards, affectionately referring to Elsa in conversation as my dear *little drip*.

Chapter 5

It was later the following day, while Elsa rested in bed recovering from her Diabetic fit that Mum explained to Alice the signs of an approaching *Hypo* and what she should do immediately she witnessed such a possible situation.

Whether it be Elsa or anybody else she knew to be Diabetic.

Mum advised that too much insulin in a person's body could be a killer.

"So what you're saying Mum is that anybody whose, not a diabetic could end up suffering if their body produced too much insulin?"

"No Alice what I'm trying to explain is that Insulin occurs naturally in our bodies to clear unnecessary levels of sugar. Sometimes our Pancreas stops working, and that's when people, like Elsa, develop diabetes.

What you're probably thinking is that somebody whose Pancreas is ok is not a Diabetic and therefore doesn't need to take insulin.

However, if they did, or somebody injected them with insulin, it could most likely kill them.

And as it's created naturally in our bodies, it's therefore

unlikely that initially, anybody would be able to understand why they died! It's not like something as visual as a knife wound or a gunshot wound.

If however, somebody like Elsa with type one diabetes doesn't ensure that the amount of food they've subsequently eaten, balances with the insulin they've taken, then that's when they experience a hypoglycemic fit.

You'll have noticed that sometimes when Elsa is what we call *low on sugar*, I often give her sweet things to eat. As explained, this quickly stops her hypos.

Elsa would have known the debilitating effects of such low blood sugar levels, but on occasions like this, she had passed the point of no return, when it happened.

Therefore she needed immediate professional assistance. Physically, she wouldn't have been able to do anything at all to help herself.

It only takes an hour or two, and unless somebody intervenes, whoever it is, the relative person could be on their way out. Mum stated graphically. Whatever Alice, Diabetes and bad control is a big worry.

Unsatisfactory control of Diabetes, as well as excess insulin, can be dangerous!"

Mum's explanation or rather her lecture was interesting although I'm sure I'd heard it beforehand; on more than a few occasions.

The following morning, having showered, Alice joined Elsa in her bedroom.

Elsa was her usual jovial self, and Alice thought nobody would have believed in a worst-case scenario, she had been so bad and could have died 24 hours previously.

While they chatted about nothing in particular, Alice suddenly stopped talking. Elsa asked her whether anything was wrong.

"I just think that three women together could do with a man around the house; especially in emergencies, like yesterday."

"You mean David!" Elsa responded with a mischievous grin on her face.

"No, I was thinking about our Father and why he left us; when we were younger, Mum had always said 'they didn't get on', and that was it. But you and I were there the day it happened Elsa!

My friends up the road often said they saw him with other women.

Whatever our Dad never cared about us, the bastard spent all his money on these women, and our poor Mum struggled to support us; as we've previously discussed, we owe her so much Elsa."

"Tell me about the day it happened. I can't remember anything." Elsa said.

"I recall, it was leading up to Christmas when he finally left us; while Dad was at work, or so we thought! Mum shopped for our Christmas tree and beautiful decorations. I remember the fairy which she bought from the local market; it looked so beautiful at the top of the tree, with silver tinsel flowing prettily from the Fairy's feet.

It amazed me how Mum managed to carry the Christmas tree home. When the string bindings, securing the tree, were cut, it appeared taller and much broader than she was.

Dad dealt with the Christmas tree lights as each year, one or two of the bulbs consistently failed.

Up until that point in time, I adored Christmas. Different presents bought and wrapped by Mum, sat beneath the tree. These weren't the gifts Father Christmas, brought us on his sledge during the early hours of Christmas Day but chocolates, chocolate coins, packets of sweets, drinks and small games or puzzles she knew we'd both appreciate.

Mind you, Elsa, you were so young that you would have eaten anything, wrapped up or not! I can remember Mum panicking, a couple of times when you tried to swallow some of the presents in one go, wrappings and all, whether it was chocolate or not.

Do you remember the joy we experienced counting down the days and then the hours before Father Christmas arrived? Our home was so festive, and we were thrilled.

Not just our house, but everybody's home; Christmas lights hung around front garden trees and in peoples windows. Some along the High Street walkways, and in shop windows. Some white, some beautifully coloured. Also, brightly coloured paper chains hung everywhere.

All around was the beautiful sound of traditional Christmas classics.

The Salvation Army played their musical instruments and sang as people walked along the high street and smiled at each other; everyone was happy and looking forward to the Christmas break." I remembered it was glamorous.

"Yes, it was great fun, Alice, although I was so young, I can only remember that Christmas briefly, or I think I do.

Whatever I can't remember specific events!" Elsa remarked joyfully.

"Well on this particular Christmas Eve, Mum had taken us out shopping for a few extras she had thought we needed for Christmas day dinner.

Returning home, we suspected nothing, but when Mum opened our sitting-room door, our Christmas tree had vanished, as well as all the presents Mum had bought for us and so carefully displayed underneath the tree.

Me and you Elsa, we just stared at the open space where the tree had been.

Except for pine needles scattered everywhere and a paper note, it was barren.

Mum cried! Even more so when she read the letter left on the floor where the tree and presents had been.

Dad wasn't coming back – ever!

That was my worst Christmas, and indeed Mum's as in between the continuous tears she attempted, with great difficulty, to comfort you and me."

"It sounds awful, Sis!"

"It was Elsa. The whole Christmas, poor Mum was in a complete daze. Anyway, it didn't take her long to find out what happened; Dad had been given an ultimatum, by this *other woman* and so he moved in with her on Christmas Eve!"

"Can you believe that Elsa, Christmas Eve; the heartless bastard, and he had even taken the tree and all its decorations with him. Christmas gifts as well!"

"What else do you remember Alice?"

"That particular memory is the one imprinted on my

brain, although I was also so young, I can't even remember what he looked like; Mum destroyed all her photographs of him."

"Destroyed all her photographs! I'd have destroyed him, the bastard, and his girlfriend. Mum must have hated him." Elsa said with unbridled anger as though it had only happened yesterday.

"I'd never let a man treat me, or you like that, Alice!"

"Well, I'm pleased to say, David's not like that; he's lovely," Alice replied.

"He'd better not be like that, or else he needs to watch out." Elsa emotionally responded. "When are you seeing him next?" She enquired.

"Tomorrow night; he's taking me out for a curry."

"Well, I hope it's a *hot* one, and you can then tell me all about it," Elsa said as she chuckled to herself.

Typical little sister thought Alice.

Chapter 6

Tonight was *the* night. Alice dressed in her new cotton stretch black trousers and skimpy bra and pranced in front of the full-length mirror attached to the door of her wooden wardrobe.

She liked her reflection and then tried on an assortment of different blouses.

Eventually, she decided on the white top with a patterned neckline as it presented her exceptionally well, especially when she draped a black cashmere cardigan around her shoulders.

She had already decided on the most suitable shoes for this occasion; the printed leather pumps, which she had recently purchased.

The artistic patterns on this footwear showed exceptionally well against her plain coloured clothing.

The thought went through her mind that wearing her new shoes; she would stand nearly as tall as David.

Having satisfied herself that her clothing was perfect for the occasion, she partially undressed and commenced the other significant task, her hair.

There was a double knock on the bedroom door

immediately followed by the sound of Elsa's tiny voice. "It's me, Sis."

"Go away; I'm busy Elsa."

The knocking continued at an irritating level as did Elsa's pleading for me to open the door, which I eventually did.

For a good few seconds, Elsa just stood in the doorway with her mouth wide open before saying "Wow Sis. You look gorgeous! David's gonna be well made up."

Alice stepped towards her enchanting little sister and hugged her.

"Go and show Mum," Elsa suggested, "She'll also think you look great!"

Walking up the stairs carefully, I could hear Mum talking, but as I entered her room, she said 'goodbye for now; we'll talk later.' Finishing her phone call to whoever it was on the other end, most abruptly.

"Who was that Mum?" I asked with interest.

"Just a friend." She briefly replied.

Mum was never secretive, so I wondered who it was? Why hang up when I entered her room?

Downstairs there was a knock at the Front door, and before Alice could answer, Elsa rushed past her and opened it.

There was David, dressed in a smart, dark, pinstripe suit and an open-necked shirt and looking equally impressive in his attire as did Alice.

"She couldn't wait for you to arrive and has tried on nearly everything in her wardrobe." Elsa blurted.

David smiled and commented, "You look brilliant

Alice." Before asking whether there was a specific Curry House she liked?

"How about *The House of Tandoori*, you told me the other night you'd been there before, and the food was good," Alice replied.

"Excellent, then the House of Tandouri it is." He responded.

"That's settled then, and just in case, it's only a few minutes from St Olives Hospital," Alice said with a broad grin on her face.

Elsa and Mum, smiled accordingly, although I wasn't too sure that Elsa understood my humorous quip.

"You both look extremely nice, have a wonderful evening together." Mum wished as they hesitantly took each other's hand and walked away from the house.

Elsa also responded briefly, saying "Have a great time Sis."

Alice noticed the smile of amusement on David's face and explained; "She's such an exceptional sister and always wants the best for me. She's extremely kind, and I genuinely believe she thinks more about my happiness than her own."

"You are so lucky having a sister like her! Unfortunately, I don't have any brothers or sisters." David commented.

"And my Mum," I added, "she's also an incredible woman."

Arriving at the Curry House, it was approximately 7.30 pm, and the restaurant was packed. "An excellent recommendation!" remarked David.

Entering, the restaurant, the spicey aroma was exceptional; you could almost touch it. The chatter wasn't deafening, but a constant hum and the clatter of cutlery and china also added to the atmosphere.

A waiter greeted us and pointed upstairs where he said: "I think there might be a table available."

There was, and we relaxed while viewing the menu with so many choices, that it was difficult to make an easy decision.

"Next time I think it would be better to book a table beforehand!" David said, believing we had been lucky on this occasion.

"So there's going to be another time, is there?" Alice humorously remarked.

The walls displayed interesting pictures of Asian scenery, people working in their villages and towns and close-ups of individuals, some sewing, some making tools for their work and some caring for their children.

David seemed uneasy about what to say. It was fortunate the pictures provided an alternative topic of conversation.

However, it was a more confident Alice, who started the conversation.

"What's the matter, David, when we had our drink the other night, everything was so spontaneous, but tonight you seem to be saying much less?"

"I'm not sure, Alice; perhaps you're too good for me."

"Oh, yes, that old line. Just tell me you don't want this friendship to develop any further David! At least you could have waited and said it after we'd finished the meal!"

"No. Oh Alice, sorry I mean, yes, Of course, I want our friendship to develop. It's just that you seem such a confident and pretty girl and I do believe you could find somebody much better than me. I'm just worried that we formalise this relationship and then you dump me!"

Demonstrating David's point, a confident Alice responded. "Well, it's you I'm having this curry with David, *not* somebody else!"

Following that comment, the evening flowed in a more natural and thereby relaxed manner.

Alice explained that her immediate family and dancing were her fundamental interests. "Although after my painful back, I'm giving dancing a rest for a while. Oh, and don't forget shopping, in particular, clothing." She said with a laugh. "What about you?"

"Nothing, in particular." he responded, "I suppose I like sport, particularly football. When I was younger, I played regularly, but now I only watch it on T.V.

Films, I like movies and sometimes visit the cinema to watch them on the 'big screen' with the cinematic sound. It's sensational and makes you feel as though you're there, in the middle of the film's scenery and alongside the actors. Tell me what type of movies you like, and I'll take you to see one."

They talked about their upbringing, their families and just about everything else one does on such a significant date.

Finishing their meal; David opened his dilapidated wallet and paid the bill, leaving the waiter a generous tip.

"This wallet's a hundred years old and belonged to my Great, Great Grandfather.

Whatever, he worked in India, in fact, Calcutta, for many years, for an important and well known Maharaja, and when he returned home to England, he was given this wallet as a thank you for his services.

You and I wouldn't think it much of a thank you gift, but it was from the Maharaja's own house and therefore a privileged possession.

Anyway, as you will understand Alice, it's not about what it's worth financially, although I expect today that's absolutely nothing, but about the memory of a family member and his days during the British Empire; such exciting times."

David escorted Alice home; as slowly as he could walk without making it too apparent. At the front door, there was a lingering kiss, and another meeting was agreed; tomorrow!

Alice stepped indoors, and Mum casually walked from the sitting room; her lackadaisical step was intentional, Alice guessed.

"I've sent Elsa to bed; you know what she's like, she wanted to stay up and find out what your evening was like."

With that explanation, there was the sound of quick footsteps descending the stairs and Elsa was there, standing immediately in front of Alice and tugging on her sleeves.

"So what happened Alice, was it a good night, are you seeing him again……?"

"Whoa, Elsa. Yes, it was another excellent evening, and we're meeting up again tomorrow night."

"Jeees Sis, you must be keen."

"Yes, he's so nice but off to bed *my little drip* as that's all I've got to tell you and I need some sleep."

Chapter 7

Early the following morning, Elsa was predictably knocking on the bedroom door before Alice had awoken. "Was it a good night, what did you have to eat, was the food good, what did you do after the curry, what happened next?"

"Yes Elsa, as I briefly told you last night, like our first date, it was a fantastic evening, and we are meeting again this evening, *and* I don't want you lurking in the background when he calls. Do you understand?"

Alice was pleased to attend work as she escaped the multitude of questions she knew she would have suffered all day or certainly when Elsa returned from school.

Alice's back was much improved, although she was now so wary of how she lifted the various products while working.

As always, the Lunch break was a welcome relief.

While carefully peeling back the foil protecting her lunch parcel, dutifully prepared by Mum and the contents always a pleasant mystery. Alice is joined at the table by Penny.

"Haven't seen much of you for a few days, Penny remarked. What have you been up to?"

"Not a lot, well that is apart from one major event! Do you remember David, the tall, dark-haired lad that used to work in the warehouse?"

"What you mean David Wilson, the tasty looking one, who recently left to work somewhere else?" Penny responded.

"What you even know his surname!" Alice said with surprise.

"Well, it was plastered all over his chest; or should I say his plastic nametag Alice!"

"Whatever, that's him, and we're dating!" Alice crowed, like somebody who had just won the *big one* on the national lottery.

Laughing, Penny jealously commented, "Well Alice, you lucky git! I think you're much too good to associate with me any longer,"

"Apart from that Penny, not so long ago, I thought I'd lost my little sister Elsa when she had a severe Diabetic fit.

It got me thinking about how fortunate I am to have such a wonderful little sister; she's so loyal, and I trust her implicitly.

Elsa always knows what's important to me." Alice concluded with her glowing tribute.

While continuing to eat the remainder of her sandwich, Penny said: "She sounds a little treasure, Alice."

"That's pretty much what David said, and despite her young age, 12 years old, she doesn't care about what others think of her - It's about who *she* is, that matters to her if you know what I mean.

Everyone knows she's a real joy to be with although sometimes she can be a little irritating.

However, no matter what she says or does at the time, I adore the funny little brat."

"You are extremely fortunate, Alice, but you must keep me updated on your relationship with David."

They finished their lunch break and returned to their respective duties.

Alice's concentration was now only focussed on tomorrow and her forthcoming date with David and whether it would develop further.

Chapter 8

At the pre-arranged time, much to Alice's emotional delight, David promptly arrived. Promptness, a characteristic she appreciated.

It was mid-morning Saturday.

Mum invited David inside and offered him a seat.

As you would understand, it was only a matter of seconds before Elsa had placed a kitchen chair between her Mother and David.

"So what're you both doing tonight? She asked, not another Curry!"

"The choice will be your Sister's." was his courteous response.

"Well, what is it Sis, are you going back to David's?"

"Don't be so rude Elsa, it's none of your business what they do!" was Mum's pointed comment.

With that remark, Alice grabbed hold of David's hand saying "Right we're off Mum and please make sure the *little drip* isn't around when I get home!"

There was an "Arghhh" from Elsa. David and Alice, hand-in-hand, stepped outside.

"Well, exactly where *are* we going?" Alice questioned.

"I've been thinking about my place. You haven't seen it yet, and we could get a pizza delivered, perhaps even watch a film and spend some time together; just the two of us."

"Ok". Was Alice's sole response, although the thought travelled around in her mind that she had also been thinking about somewhere alone!

They had walked only a short distance when David spotted a black cab and hailed it to stop.

"Richfield Avenue please." He requested.

David lived in a flat overlooking the River Thames at Caversham.

As the taxi pulled to a stop outside a row of what looked like Victorian houses, Alice was looking forward to seeing just what type of flat he lived in; presumably rented or maybe he owned it. And whether or not he was a clean and tidy householder?

Having climbed several stone steps, David unlocked the front door and stood back for Alice to enter. "It's a climb, he said as my flats on the top floor."

Alice didn't notice the climb as she was thinking more about the flat itself.

Once again, David unlocked the door and invited Alice to enter before him.

Alice had only gone a few paces when she announced: "It's lovely." Perhaps this was a formal response, often repeated without any real thought when entering somebody else's premises for the first time!

"Would you like to have a look around before I make a cup of coffee or whatever it is you'd like to drink?"

"Love to." Alice instinctively replied.

"Well this is the sitting room; come over and look at this vista. It's exceptional."

David eased back the patterned curtains, so Alice had an uninterrupted view.

She stared out over the River with the odd boat and barge, travelling up and down the river while a vessel was also manoeuvring to moor safely alongside the bankside and a wooden walkway.

"Hey David, this view is lovely, and it reminds me of the background view when watching TV's Meridian news."

"No, Alice the Meridian News view, is of Henley Bridge, although it also reminds me of Caversham and the constant flow of traffic crossing this Reading Landmark," David remarked. "Anyway, I don't care. I love living here, and the scenery is always spectacular."

Whatever he was right. The view from his window was a prodigious setting.

David was so fortunate to live in a dwelling that overlooked the River Thames and the gateway to Reading. I knew the sight from his flat window would appeal to Mum and Elsa and certainly Penny.

A pair of Swans, probably protecting their young, had also caught Alice's attention, as they swam, wings raised towards a group of small ducks; the Swan's flapped their giant wings as a warning, and the odd white feather fluttered into the air.

The feather's drifted out of sight with the River's flow as the gloom of a spring evening fully set in.

Daylight was beginning to fade and viewing through a

drizzle of softly falling rain, the street lights sparkled and captivated, this spectacle even more.

Now and again, a few of the street lights seemed to flash as they regularly switched on and off. "Possibly a weak or faulty connection somewhere," David mentioned.

It was then she felt David's arms moving around her waist.

Momentarily she slightly turned her head towards him with expectation and a smile on that picture-perfect face of hers.

"I just don't want you to fall out of the window." He said, with a grin.

The sitting room looked comfortable with what was a new coffee table, probably oak and a slightly larger size than usual.

Undoubtedly it was instead of a dining table and big enough to hold plenty of food and drink while we sat alongside each other in comfort.

The carpet looked dusty but also more than a little threadbare. Possibly bought from one of the local *We buy and sell it all* shops, of which there are several around this area of Reading.

David noticed Alice's stare and stated. "Yes, the carpet badly needs replacing but the Landlord says if I want a new one, I must replace it myself."

At least that answered one of my questions without me having to ask him directly.

However, it did leave me thinking about my home; Did we own it, was Mum, the owner? I'd never thought about it beforehand.

"Right, let me show you the rest of the flat. There are only three other rooms, a kitchen, one-bedroom and somewhere to shower and relieve myself, whenever I need to."

The tiled kitchen was small, so small that it was challenging for David and me to move.

In the corner, surrounded by a replicated marble surface was an electric ring for cooking and alongside an electric toaster and kettle.

Not great but it did the job for him. At least it was clean and tidy.

David opened the cupboard doors which hung obstructively above the *marble* surface and probably made the kitchen look even more claustrophobic than it was.

"Ok, is it Tea or coffee?" he asked.

"Black coffee please David. But aren't you going to show me the bedroom?" I innocently asked.

"Later." He said with another of those cheeky grins on his face.

There was only a small Setee in the sitting room and thereby no other option for Alice than to sit beside David; not that she was complaining!

Sipping her coffee carefully as it was piping hot, Alice noticed once again that there was a pause in the flow of conversation and wondered whether this could be a natural characteristic of David's?

The silence was, however, broken by David when he reminded Alice that they should order the Pizza they had talked about eating earlier.

"Thank you, David, but I'm not that hungry," Alice replied.

"Me neither, then how about a biscuit with that coffee, I've got a couple of choices in the cupboard."

"It's very kind of you, David, but I really couldn't eat anything at the moment!"

David then talked more about the Reading area and its local history. Not only was he knowledgeable, but he also made everything sound spectacular.

I had lived in Caversham all my life, but I was unable to create anywhere near as much enthusiasm as David.

Alice moved her position on the somewhat restricted two-seater sofa and felt a little comfier. She then felt David's arm slowly slide around her shoulder, at which point he pulled her even closer; looked directly into her big blue eyes and spontaneously kissed her full on the lips.

Alice's response was predictably reciprocal. Gradually there was a different sensation when he undid the zip on the back of her dress. Indeed a different experience from when Elsa or her Mum helped her with a sticky zip!

Momentarily Alice was lost for words and then just said the first thing that came to mind. "So you've had plenty of experience of this David."

David said nothing and gently peeled down the top of her dress and then casually unclipped her Bra with consummate ease.

As expected, she then felt the soft touch of David's hand on her left knee and panicked.

"I'm not on *the Pill*!" She exclaimed.

With that, in his right hand, David produced a packet of

condoms, which he had obviously, placed down the side of the sofa just in case he got lucky.

"Are you comfortable here or would you now like to see my bedroom?" He said with a certain amount of enthusiasm.

Alice was still thinking about her answer when David stood up from the sofa, took Alice in both arms and carefully carried her to his bedroom, kicking open the door with his freestanding foot.

In the bedroom, David unwrapped Alice's dress which had curled around her legs and peeled the bedcover back. With David's assistance, Alice climbed onto the bed, confident of what to expect; the whole sensation was exquisite.

The next sensation for Alice was waking up in David's arms, and then, looking at her wristwatch and realising, it was eleven-thirty pm.

"My Mum," Alice exclaimed, "I must ring my Mum."

From the bedside table, David passed the extension of his landline phone saying "If you like you can stay here tonight, Alice."

Once again Alice was temporarily confused but decided that as much as she'd like to stay, she really should go home.

"Ok, Alice, you call your Mum and tell her I'm bringing you home in a Cab."

Chapter 9

The following morning Alice made sure she was up and dressed for work before her Mum and Elsa.

At the store's employee entrance, she arrived well before time and met her friend Penny, also waiting at the door.

"How are you, Alice?"

"Fine thanks Penny, couldn't be better! Meet you in the Canteen at first break for a coffee; I have fantastic news to tell you."

"What about?" Penny asked with curiosity.

"Tell you at coffee break." was Alice's brief and enthusiastic reply.

Time just flew by, and Alice was sitting with her cup of black coffee at one of the canteen's tables watching other staff enjoying a break.

Enthusiastically, Penny approached and sat down with Alice but before either could say anything, *The Bull*, her supervisor approached, pointed at Alice and said, "YOU, in my office, now and *I mean now*!"

Alice just stared at Penny and with trepidation arose from her seat and followed her supervisor across the floor of the large and busy warehouse to her tiny office situated in the corner of this extensive building.

Other workers stared. They were sure Alice was in trouble just by how the supervisor strode with Alice following in her wake, a distance behind.

There were two small seats and a tiny desk, not much bigger than the two chairs, oh and of course the proverbial filing cabinet.

Alice automatically sat down in the vacant seat when the supervisor shouted,

"And who asked you to sit down!"

Responsively Alice stood up.

On the desk was one buff folder with Alice's name on it.

"I hear you've been complaining about me to the Personnel Department!"

"What?" was Alice's simple response?

"About health and safety." *The Bull* replied without the least hesitation.

"Honestly Mam I don't know what you are talking about." Alice pleaded.

"Don't you. You little shit-stirrer; well let me tell you this, somebody has made a complaint about me and my reaction to your fucking back a few weeks ago."

"Well, it wasn't me!" Alice protested a second time.

"I don't care who it was but understand this, if I get criticised again or called to HR, you're OUT, and this time I mean it! Now get on with your fucking job you useless piece of shit."

Returning to the canteen, Penny had already finished her coffee break and left.

The day had started joyfully for Alice, but now it had developed into one of utter despair, even more so as she had absolutely no idea who had complained to HR.

Arriving home, Alice walked in and sat down at the kitchen table. Her fundamental question "Hi Mum, how are you?" Fooled no-one.

"What's the matter, Alice?"

"What do you mean?" I asked.

"Last night, you were exceptionally joyful, and now I detect a significant difference; Somethings wrong Alice! What is it?" Mum asked intuitively.

Another voice behind her said, "What's up, Sis?"

At this particular point, last night's memorable experience had vanished entirely from her mind and replaced with her traumatic experience at work.

Alice explained the circumstances.

"What if I lose my job?" she struggled to mutter as her eyes filled with tears that flowed down her pretty face, leaving visible streaks in her make up.

She felt a tight squeeze of her hand and that sympathetic little voice said.

"Hey, Sis, you are much better than that 'orrible woman; you could do her job; easily. Just don't let her bully you. Tell her that! You're not going to put up with it.

Tomorrow I'm coming to work with you………."

As I often did, I cuddled Elsa tightly and reminded her, what a special sister she was.

This loving cuddle was so very mutual.

Much later that evening when Elsa had departed to bed,

Mum Jennifer sat down beside Alice and commented on Elsa's earlier remarks.

"For once Elsa made a lot of sense, and it wasn't just emotional comments you'd typically expect from her. That woman is a brute and not fit to hold the position of Supervisor.

Go to her and say you won't put up with her threats anymore and also tell her she can forget about anybody complaining to Human Resources on your behalf; YOU will do it yourself. Bullies usually back down when confronted.

Right Alice, now tell me about something a lot happier; how did your evening go with David?" Mum questioned.

"It was fine, thank you, Mum, we had a great evening, and he's got a nice flat overlooking the Thames; incidentally do we own this house?"

"No Alice, we used to live in a place called Sindlesham, but when your Dad got work in Caversham, we moved here and rented this place. A few years later, your Dad met this woman and left us.

We were too poor to buy a property; it was expensive enough just renting this house, although nowadays I couldn't even think about renting a bed-sit around here. This dwelling belongs to the Council."

Alice's response was interrupted by a rap-a-tap, tap knock on the front door; It was late?

Before opening the front door, Alice shouted: "Who is it?"

"It's Penny." was the unexpected reply.

"Sorry it's so late Alice, but as I was leaving the store, I had an unexpected visit from my Foster-Father, Ted.

He explained he was in the area and decided to drop by and tell me in person that he and my Foster-Mum, Molly, was finally moving to Tiverton, Devon.

Anyway, I just wanted to make sure you are Ok after your confrontation with that horrible supervisor of ours, what did the *cow* say to you?"

Hesitating I said, "Just a minute, Penny, your Foster parents are moving to Devon, when?" I asked, perhaps more because Penny had now become a special friend and I was interested in her circumstances.

"This weekend," Penny replied. "He's fed up, struggling here in the Thames Valley, although I've known about it for some while; They have finally managed to get work down there.

They currently live in Bracknell and have been fostering children for years. He says Bracknell has grown out of all proportion since they first moved there; they've been Fostering for nearly fifty years.

I know I haven't talked about them much, but I am going to miss them.

Anyway, Alice, tell me about work and what happened this afternoon."

Mum interrupted, "Alice, at least invite your friend inside, as you knocked, we were talking about work and that dreadful Manageress or is it Supervisor; whatever she's called, anyway have a seat Penny."

Jennifer repeated what they had just discussed and of course, Elsa's outspoken recommendations. "Do you know who might have reported the Supervisor to the Personnel department?"

"No, but she is such a nasty piece of work; it could have been anybody," Penny responded from her own knowledgeable experience.

"Did you know Alice, a while ago, a Diabetic lad, just like Elsa, badly needed food and *The Bull* wouldn't let him eat anything until he had finished his shift. The poor lad had a bad Hypo, and the boy's parent's complained.

As a result of this complaint, *The Bull* sacked him!

He'd only been working a few weeks and therefore possessed no employment rights. What an absolute bitch she is Alice!

There are others at work, who complain about her but do absolutely nothing about it, so let's organise something. She can't do much when the whole shop floor complains to HR!"

"I know, Penny but it's not the sort of thing I like to get involved in; no matter what she's like." was Alice's considered response.

The three of them chatted the remainder of the night away, discussing various appealing ideas although none of them that practical or as violently amusing as Elsa's earlier suggestions. And certainly not realistic.

Penny accepted the invitation to stay the night but waited for Mum to go to bed before she told me what she believed was the real reason *the Bull* sacked the diabetic lad.

"The Lad told his Parent's about his Diabetic fit and how *the Bull* had been responsible for causing it, but I don't think he told them of his revengeful response shortly afterwards!"

"Penny, I don't understand?" I questioned with utter confusion.

"Well Alice, when he had recovered from his Hypo he took a packet of clingfilm from one of the supermarket's shelves and disappeared for a few moments.

As you know, *the Bull* had her own office with a personal lavatory. Later on, there was a scream, and she rushed from her toilet into her office and screamed again, although this time, it was most likely in anger as opposed to shock.

It turned out that while she was checking something in the store, the lad had crept into her office and then clingfilmed her urinal before lowering the seat!"

Trying to understand why he had done this, and why *the Bull* had screamed, I suddenly realised and burst into uncontrollable laughter.

Penny continued. "It wasn't long, minutes in fact, before the wisecracks started; somehow, it didn't take *the Bull* long to identify the culprit. Anyway, I believe that's the real reason she sacked the youngster.

I'm surprised you've never heard that story, anyway each year on the same date, oldtimers who have since left the business and some of the staff still here meet up for a drink and toast him.

I know it's crazy, but it is an excellent excuse for a fun night out and meeting up with old friends. I'll find out the date and let you know Alice."

Chapter 10

Approximately a month later the Regional Manager, with presumably an assistant, invited everyone to the canteen and made the announcement that nobody was expecting.

"The Board of Directors has asked me to officially notify everyone, that as of today and by mutual agreement, your Supervisor, Camila Abbot no longer works for our organisation.

Her position is now vacant, and as is the general practice, any staff members interested in applying for this vacancy must approach our Human Resources department."

He pointed towards the man standing beside him and continued. "In the meantime, Mr Alex Johnson will continue to manage this operation."

There was a period of utter silence before everyone raised a load and deafening cheer. It was a celebration of the utmost proportions for this big decision.

Mr Johnson was more casually dressed, than the Regional Manager in his suit, shirt and tie and brightly polished shoes. Surprisingly he stood there in a brown checked blazer, a crew neck jumper and beige coloured trousers.

Not that impressive, I thought, but then again perhaps his mode of dress was deliberately intended to demonstrate a more casual demeanour, certainly less oppressive than his previous counterpart.

I couldn't wait to get home and tell Mum, and of course, Elsa, whom I knew would share her delight at this most unexpected revelation.

When I walked in Mother and Elsa were in the kitchen peeling the veg. "Guess what happened at work today?" I asked.

"Somebody's whacked the Bull," Elsa replied, hopefully.

"No, better than that Elsa, she's left the business, although it's most likely she's finally been dismissed!"

Under such circumstances, I covered my ears as I knew what to expect from Elsa! Mum was pleased but far more dignified with her response.

During the following days, at work, nothing much was discussed at any length, by anybody, other than this particular dismissal.

There was, however, a few mysteries which would keep everyone entertained for some considerable while, at least until the replacement started.

Who was responsible for informing the Senior Management and why? Which members of the existing staff might apply for this management vacancy. Who might have the skill-set required; although we all had a rough idea, and of course, which of those employees possessed the relevant management qualities?

However, as much as we discussed this, Penny and I

both agreed that there wasn't a single staff member who stood out as an exception.

On more than one occasion, while sitting at the Canteen table, we talked about precisely who the new guvnor might be. Would it be another woman or a man and which one of our other staff members might take the reins?

Both Penny and Alice had similar views that the increase in wages didn't justify the increased responsibilities. For example, the hassle that went with it and almost certainly, the additional hours and late-night call-outs whenever there were emergencies of one kind or another.

"The pay's a bloody joke!" said Penny, closing the conversation most abruptly.

That evening Alice also discussed the situation at work with David; during one of their now frequent meetings.

Like Elsa and her innocent but enthusiastic approach to life, David also discussed the positives and why he thought Alice should think again about this opportunity.

"You're an intelligent girl, and despite what you see as drawbacks, you should persuade them you are the one to be offered, what is, after all, a senior position.

Then who knows how much further you could go; maybe to the executive levels in just a few years." David positively summarised.

"Don't dismiss it; consider it a little more Alice. And, remember your little Sister, is also a smart cookie, and she backs you all the way."

David made everything sound brilliant. And probably for the first time in my life, I was beginning to believe I was smart enough to become one of those people who had expensive holidays and drove around in big shiny cars.

The sort of individual that when they spoke to other people, everybody would say, yes sir, no sir or yes madam, no madam.

What is the expression; Rags to riches?

I cuddled up to David and kissed him on the cheek.

"It's about time they got rid of that bitch; she caused so much unhappiness for the staff, even hardworking staff. I don't know anyone who liked her!"

"Well David, whoever it was, has my heartfelt thanks and I guess everybody else's as well."

Although there was nobody else to hear, David whispered in my ear, "And, do you want to know who complained to HR about the Bull?"

"It was you, wasn't it?" I exclaimed, as now, I guessed it was pretty apparent.

David had been promoted to another store and was no longer under her authority. Also, the Head Office would have taken any complaint from David seriously.

Additionally, this would have reinforced any previous complaints received by HR!

"Coffee?" he said, a hypothetical question as he was already standing and walking towards the kitchen and the electric kettle!

Returning a few minutes later he returned with the coffees and tempting wafer biscuits and a bowl of brightly shining grapes, some black, some green, placed them on the table and switched on the TV.

"Let's see what's happening in the World? The news is coming up when this holiday programme finishes."

Alice crunched a wafer and looked across at the screen in the far corner of David's sitting room.

Wherever it was, the view was spectacular.

Children played enthusiastically on sloping pebbled streets outside their houses and parents were interreacting with their children.

David said the houses were of a traditional Spanish-colonial design.

They looked centuries old, although it wasn't apparent from the TV picture, whether they were imitations of the original structures and therefore built-in more recent years; whatever, they looked most appealing.

The inhabitants went about their work and children played in the streets, some kicking a coconut shell backwards and forwards.

The TV picture changed to a coastal view with sandy beaches and palm trees. People swimming, working small boats and some bringing their catch ashore.

I presumed it was two local inhabitants who were collecting coconuts from the trees. One is climbing the tree with apparent ease and the other man waiting below to catch them.

The odd few people lay in hammocks and snoozed as though they didn't have a care in the world. Most likely holidaymakers! Everything looked so enticing!

"I think that view, is somewhere in the Caribbean," said David and then as a subtitle appeared, he remarked. "Yes, it says it's San Andrés; looks stunning."

Again, David cuddled up to Alice and whispered, "We should go there, and I mean soon! Would you like that?"

"Oh David, that would be fantastic, but are you serious?"

"Of course I'm serious, how about sometime during the next couple of months? This weekend, we can enjoy ourselves looking at travel brochures and thinking about what we have to look forward to, maybe we could also take a break and visit the Cinema?"

"I think I'll give the pix a miss but thanks all the same David."

Alice could only think about the two of them spending at least a couple of weeks in possibly one of the most desirable holiday destinations on the planet.

David interrupted her thoughts and remarked, "Alice, think about enjoying a cold drink with ice clinking in our glasses as the warm water laps around our feet on a picturesque and palm-shaded beach somewhere."

Returning from her idyllic dream, Alice realised that although her Mum would understand precisely where she was sleeping tonight, she should as requested for safety reasons, always phone her.

The call was a short one although the only topic taking the majority of this brief call was not the Caribbean, but when Alice would next be spending some time at home, in her own bed!

"Trouble?" David asked, immediately the call ended.

"Mum is complaining that neither her nor Elsa see much of me these days. I suppose I'd better keep the peace and I told her I'd see them both tomorrow night."

A Dose of Insulin

"That's fine," David replied. "It's Thursday tomorrow, and at least we have planned the weekend together."

Arising early Alice was the first to shower and prepare for work; saying goodbye to David and repeating how much she was looking forward to the weekend.

She gently kissed him, wished him well and shut the front door behind her. A lightbulb had blown, and the stairway was dark and scary as she carefully held the rail and took each step one at a time.

Downstairs was a large storage cupboard. David had told Alice that vagrants used it for somewhere to sleep, and this added to her concern when walking the stairs alone, especially when it was dark.

The supermarket was deathly quiet and only three other staff present; nobody was doing anything although her immediate view told Alice the shelves needed restocking.

Additionally, there were tins of biscuits and washing powder stacked high beside each other, and as she knew, these entirely different products should be displayed separately.

The products partially covered the walkway and therefore, a potential *health and safety* issue.

A recently used phrase in this supermarket to describe anything that wasn't where it should be, whether it was dangerous or not!

Penny arrived, greeted Alice and asked what she was doing.

"Nothing," Alice said, "But I do think these products need moving, and there is also plenty of *shelving* that needs attention; the shop doors will soon be opening for our customer's. The other lazy bastards have done absolutely nothing!"

"Before I forget Penny, I've found out who complained to HR about *the Bull*; it was David!"

Penny acknowledged, although there was a look in her eyes that told me she wasn't surprised. My statement answered one of the questions we had discussed when *the Bull* left; surely, she would have been more interested than she seemed.

Without further ado, we rectified the problems on the supermarket's shop floor.

It was just in time as the temporary manager, Alex Johnson strode purposely along one of the aisles and opened the Shop's door for the customers, who were queuing outside.

Whatever was or wasn't happening in the store, everything seemed so much better and much more comfortable going than when *The Bull* had ruled the roost.

Chapter 11

Alice had enjoyed her time at David's but was nonetheless, extremely happy to be seeing her Mum and little sister after several days away.

Not surprisingly, it was Elsa who was first to open the front door; these days Mum couldn't compete with her young daughter's eyesight, hearing and just basic speed; not to mention inquisitiveness!

Elsa's arms stretched wide, and she screamed "Hi Sis what's 'appening?" and grabbed Alice around the waist; it wasn't so long ago Elsa would only have reached Alice's kneecaps.

"Well, at least let me sit down before you start your *grilling*."

I still hadn't reached the kitchen table when Elsa shouted again "Well, c'mon then, tell me!"

"What about?" I questioned but knowing I had great news and also enjoying the fact that I was playing games with Elsa.

"About anything, Sis."

I laughed as I could tell Elsa was frustrated by my delayed response.

"We're going to the Caribbean; David and me."

"What on holiday?" Elsa responded.

"No, *forever*!" I sarcastically stated. "Of course, we're going on holiday *my little drip*."

"Well, I don't know; you've spent so much time with him, it could've been forever!" Elsa seriously replied.

"Oh, Elsa I'm so sorry. Yes, on holiday for a couple of weeks and this weekend we're going to decide exactly which Caribbean Island and where. Fantastic, isn't it?"

"Yes, for some!" Elsa replied, perhaps with more than just a small amount of jealousy.

"And what about The Job, have you applied for it yet?"

"No and I'm not going to either; Penny and I discussed it and decided it would be too much trouble and the increase in pay would only be minimal."

Mum interrupted "In my early years it wasn't always about money but the opportunity to progress in your working life. Of course, after-tax, the disposable income wouldn't be much better than you are currently earning Alice, so I suppose it's not a consideration."

Picking up her thread of the conversation, Elsa asked: "Are you and David going to get married?"

"What?" Responded Alice. "Where did that come from?"

"Well, you are going on holiday, and you spend so much time together; you might as well get married?" Elsa naively replied.

Astounded at Elsa's question, Mum said. "Elsa that's absolutely none of your business."

The weekend duly arrived, and David and Alice dutifully

spent Saturday morning walking Reading's town centre and collecting holiday brochures from the various Travel Agents.

Whichever brochure, whichever holiday, they all looked fantastic with pictures of beautiful looking hotels, swimming pools, impressive sandy and crowd-free beaches with the background of clear blue skies. In these brochures, nothing was ever out of place.

The shops were busy, and it was the same in each one; immediately upon entry, David and Alice were approached and invited to take a seat and questioned about their holiday intentions by the shop's enthusiastic staff.

Weighed down with different brochures from all of the top holiday businesses, they considered resting and doing so at one of the various coffee shops, but despite this, they decided to struggle home.

David commented that although many of these travel stores had now merged and subsequently changed their names, several, are now owned by the same holding company.

They were pretty much the same businesses; just different levels of cost, sometimes for precisely the same room and the same hotel and resort.

Alice listened to David's comments, but in reality, she was only interested in the holiday and exactly where they would be going!

Back at David's flat, fortunately, somebody had fixed a new lightbulb on the stairway as the day was getting darker.

"Probably the chap living below us, as he seems to mend everything; a propper odd-job man!" David responded.

Struggling up the stairs to David's flat with the brochures and other shopping they had bought during the trip; David unlocked the flat door and as always, politely stood back for Alice to enter.

Placing the brochures on his coffee table, a couple of which were duplicates, although obtained in different shops, David suggested that Alice sort them out while he organised a drink and something to eat.

He was absent a while, but when he returned, it was clear why the delay.

Two plates, covered with crisp Iceberg lettuce, shiny red miniature tomatoes, green and black olives, spring onions, peppers, Palma ham, a selection of hard and soft cheeses, grapes and cracker biscuits looked most appetising. Suddenly I felt much hungrier.

David asked Alice to remove the Holiday brochures and placed the tray of salad on the coffee table.

And to finish it off, he walked back to the kitchen and returned with two glasses and a bottle of white Pinot Grigio wine, from the Shepherd Cellar, bought by David during a previous visit. It had cooled nicely in the fridge.

He unplugged the cork from the bottle of wine and filled the two lead crystal wine glasses almost to the brim.

They enjoyed the delicious food and drink before deciding to review the holiday brochures in relaxed comfort while finishing the remaining wine.

Deciding exactly where to go, there were a few factors to be considered; the specific town or village, the Hotel, the Hotel view, how close to the seafront, the distance from the airport.

And obviously whether or not transport between the airport and the hotel is included, in the overall holiday price. The brochure's write up, any website reviews and of course any associated costs.

"It's all a bit much, so how about we choose a few of the best and then consider those tomorrow; at least it will break the routine and give us more time to consider our various options," David suggested.

Looking at the many different and excellent holiday options, chatting about the most suitable destinations and enjoying the wine, the Saturday night soon merged into the early hours of Sunday morning. Realising this they finished their drinks, stacked the three brochures of choice separately and made their way to bed.

Enthusiastically, it was Alice who woke up first; it was only 7.20 am, early for a Sunday morning. Exceptionally early, she thought.

While waiting for the kettle to boil, she viewed one of the holiday brochures they had favoured.

Resulting from the general disturbance, it wasn't long before David joined her in the kitchen. "You go and sit down Alice; I'll organise some breakfast for us, and then we can finally make our holiday decision."

Despite only a few holiday brochures and pre-selected choices therein, it was 2.30 pm, before we made our final choice. The date of our holiday was a little later in the year than initially planned, as a result of cheaper pricing when taken outside of the school holiday period.

"Right, the Travel Agents remains open until four today, so let's go and book immediately. After all the effort, let's hope our choice is still available." David wishfully concluded.

The Sales Assistant invited them both to sit and called up the Holiday brochure destination on her PC.

A few minutes passed, and the girl complained about her PC and the problems she experienced whenever she urgently needed to use it.

"What's the problem?" David asked.

"Sorry to keep you but the holiday you want to book doesn't appear to be coming up on our database."

I was worried as the brochure details looked fantastic, and it was a real one-off holiday opportunity; something I could never have imagined. After all the time we had spent choosing this particular holiday, the last thing I wanted was a repeat exercise to select another holiday offer!

The woman struggled and turning to face us, she said. "I'm sorry, but if somebody in another of our shops sells a holiday, this happens. It's on a universal database!

Oh shit" she said before apologising for her language.

"Problem?" David asked again.

"Yes now the bloody screen has frozen; I can't believe my luck today." The assistant said with the sound of utter frustration in her voice.

"Here, let me have a look at it." David offered.

"Do you know anything about computers?" Hopefully, she asked David.

"Nothing at all but I've heard people say, when you have a problem, whatever it is, press control, alt, delete. Go on, give it a go!"

A smile appeared on the woman's face, and she shouted "Yes."

The system was now up and running but would our holiday choice still be there for the taking?

Eventually, and much to our great delight, the chosen hotel apartment was still available and on our preferred date.

But before the assistant asked for payment, she tried to persuade us to have 'A more exceptional holiday.' Also, to book a vehicle, as well as other holiday perks before she mentioned holiday insurance.

"Incidentally, do either of you like an alcoholic tiple?" She asked.

David said nothing audible to the salesgirl's question and just beamed a significant smile.

Specifically facing David, she said, "Well Sir, you'll be pleased to know the hotel you've chosen have an on-site distillery and make a well-known, established Rum.

Within reason, I believe you can drink as much Rum as you like and it doesn't cost a penny! Not for those staying at the hotel anyway."

Leaving the Agents, full of joy, David didn't stop talking about the free glasses of Rum and how interesting it will be to have a distillery on site.

"The woman even said we could watch the sugar cane juice as its distilled into Rum; how unusual is that Alice?"

David suggested we should go and tell your Mum Alice, and of course, Elsa, immediately.

Knowingly he said, Elsa, would want to know every detail of our holiday and its destination.

Mum and Elsa were pleased we had taken the trouble to visit them and explain the details.

In particular, Mum was interested to hear about our holiday.

"I've never been abroad; the farthest I've ever travelled is somewhere in the UK. Still, it may not have been as exotic as the Caribbean Islands, but at the time, it was exciting. I bet you're pleased about the Rum David!"

It was late in the evening, and Alice prepares her clothing for tomorrow and another day at work; looking forward to telling Penny about her holiday.

Penny was already present at the store and busily going about her routines.

"By the way, Penny, David and I have booked a holiday abroad – to the Caribbean!"

"The Caribbean Alice, wow, that's supposed to be brilliant! Bet it cost you a bomb!"

"Well, it wasn't cheap, but David paid for the holiday package. He told me I could pay for some of the trips while we were out there. He's so kind and generous Penny. Oh and the hotel we're staying at distils one of the Caribbean's famous rums."

Chapter 12

Penny was helping me with more substantial packages when Alex Johnson strode up and invited us to follow him to his office.

Walking behind him, Alice was too worried to speak to Penny as she wondered, *What now?*

The office hadn't changed at all since her last visit, although there was now an extra plastic and metal framed seat; Alex Johnson asked Alice and Penny to sit.

"I won't beat about the bush ladies, but I've had several applicants for the position I am temporarily holding and have noted that your two names aren't amongst them."

Initially, I asked myself whether we were in trouble for not applying.

Penny tried to say something, but he continued. "During recent weeks, you two girls have worked extremely hard and demonstrated initiative; so why haven't either of you applied for the job?"

Alice was concerned that Penny might be a little forthright with her answer and so she jumped in first.

"Mr Johnson, thank you for your most appreciated comments. At the moment, I have much going on in my personal life and don't believe I could take on the additional responsibility required for such an important position."

The discussion continued for a while with continued compliments for both women, as well as all the benefits the job would hold, although the salary didn't change, nor the possible emergency hours.

Later that evening, Alice repeated the entire conversation to David and how good it was to have someone believe in you, although she stated: "The job's not for me!"

"Well, what about me, I believe in you, or don't I come across that way?" David asked with concern.

"Anyway, that job's there because of my efforts with HR, and now you can't be bothered to apply for it!"

The general tenor of David's response was something she hadn't witnessed before.

"As I've said many times, just think about what you're giving up and the potential benefits you are discarding; it's stupid!"

A despondent Alice reacted immediately. "Are you calling me stupid?" she screamed.

"No, of course not but what if we settled down together, the joint income would be invaluable."

All of a sudden, Alice's annoyance subsided and after a while, taking the time to gather her thoughts, she asked: "What are you saying David; we could settle down together?"

"Well, under the circumstances, it's always going to be a possibility."

Alice's heart was moving ahead of her brain when she commented further "What, get married?"

The expression on David's face told the story, although he thought it necessary to explain. "Not marriage, but we spend nearly all our time together, we get on extremely well, and it just seems to make sense that we combine our assets while reducing the costs."

For the first time in this relationship, my anger levels began to grow. "Financially aware David, but what about us and the future; will it always be sharing *the buck* but just as boyfriend and girlfriend?"

Sensing the hostility in Alice's voice and her body language, David replied, "Well marriage is always a possibility, but it's also something we should discuss in a little more depth and under more relaxed circumstances; it's a big step in life Alice, although a future together, including marriage, isn't out of the question."

Alice was mindful to return home for the night, but she knew she wasn't really in the right mood and Mum would pick up on it as she usually did, and certainly Elsa.

Returning home would be more of a problem.

Alice found the evening's limited conversations with David difficult, as was retreating to the bedroom later that evening; the whole atmosphere was so uncomfortable.

It was very frustrating; Alice had nobody to talk to, although she knew Penny had a sympathetic ear, and she would, as always, meet her at work the next morning.

Penny was most understanding of Alice's tale of the previous evening's events but identified the positive points.

"From what you've told me he is attentive, kind, generous, and loves you lots. I mean he's not saying there is no future for you as man and wife.

Until now you have been so happy spending your time with him, so why not continue with life as it is and deal with events when and if they change; I mean what more could you ask? Just focus on your fantastic holiday to the Caribbean."

"Yes, Penny, in reality, I have absolutely no reason to distrust him."

"Good, so get on with it and think yourself so lucky you have such a gorgeous man in your life; I have nobody in mine," Penny concluded, while thinking about what she called, her 'dull existence'.

Penny's comments struck Alice's heart; here she was moaning about herself who already had a life most would be pleased with, and poor old Penny had virtually nothing, other than her menial job to discuss with others.

Spontaneously Alice said, knowing it wasn't quite the answer, "Why don't you apply for the Supervisor's job? I know you can do it and I'd always be there to support you whenever you need it?"

"But we've already discussed this Alice and the pay just isn't worth it," Penny said in desperation.

"Well everybody's telling me to think again, so perhaps you should Penny?" Alice responded.

"Ok but on one condition."

"What's that?" questioned Alice.

"That we both apply and if either one gets the job, then we both help each other when assistance is needed.

Also, we obtain Alex Johnson's agreement to this new condition as he's only recruiting for one individual."

"Mmm, I'd better discuss it with David first," Alice replied.

"What? Penny responded, after the way you told me he reacted last night? Make your own decisions and if you do get the promotion, think what a great surprise it would be for David and of course your Mum and Elsa! Not only that, but the odd perk did sound interesting."

"Ok, we'll catch Mr Johnson at some convenient time; mind you the job could have already gone. I know he's advertising in the Chronicle and other local papers."

Penny and Alice didn't have to wait for a suitable time as Mr Johnson approached them during their afternoon tea break.

"Have you Girl's thought any more about our discussion?"

"Yes." They replied in unison.

"Excellent. Mr Johnson said, then let's discuss it in my office."

Chapter 13

'AJ' as he was now known, expressed his delight that his two favourite members of staff were now interested in the position.

He spent most of the time repeating the opportunities and benefits to be enjoyed by the lucky candidate and then explained he would have to interview Penny and Alice separately.

Leaving his office, they discussed the implications in greater detail, and Penny stated, "Whatever the result Alice, we mustn't let it affect our friendship; as we agreed in our earlier conversation, we will be there to support each other."

"Without question." Alice agreed but at the same time, thinking how easy it could be to ruin close friendships!

"Alice, are you going to tell David you have reconsidered and are now applying for the promotion?"

"No, I don't think so, well not at the moment anyway as I'm staying at Mum's tonight and probably for a few more days until this upset between David and me cools down a little; anyway we'll see."

Mum was pleased Alice had changed her mind and

decided to apply for the Supervisor's job, although she had a concern when Alice explained that Penny had also decided to apply for the same position.

"Couldn't that cause a problem between you and your friend Penny, depending on one or other of you getting chosen?"

"We've already discussed this in-depth, and it will be ok." Alice confidently replied.

"So when are the interviews, Alice?"

"They're both tomorrow; mine in the morning at 10 o'clock and Penny's in the afternoon."

"Are you going to tell Elsa?" Mum asked.

"Probably not at the moment Mum, you know what she's like with her questions and advice!"

"You know she'll be disappointed," Mum said; stating the obvious.

"Yes but you know she'll also be disappointed if I don't get it; so I'll wait for the result, and if I don't get it, I won't have to say anything."

"Ok, it's your decision, Alice but good luck anyway. I wish I'd had this kind of opportunity at your age, instead of all the washing, cleaning, dusting and so on."

The next morning Alice dressed professionally and as smart as possible, although she always looked smart so there was no difference in her appearance.

She answered the many questions asked of her with aplomb, thanked Mr Johnson for the interview and left to meet up with Penny at their pre-arranged time in the works Canteen.

With great interest, Penny asked how Alice's interview went.

"I think it went reasonably well, but believe I messed my chances when I asked him about the salary and in return, what would he expected from me as Supervisor. He stated quite clearly that the salary levels were structured and graded by the Head Office, and there would be no increase offered."

"Thanks for the warning Alice; I'll strike those questions off my list!" Penny commented.

Penny's interview was a late one, and Alice had already left work when it finished.

As agreed Penny arrived at Alice's house just before she thought Jennifer would be dishing up the evening meal. Jennifer ushered them both into the sitting room alone, having remembered Alice's comments about not telling Elsa.

Penny's interview had also been a good one, but likewise, she also thought she'd asked a few negative questions or even given some unacceptable answers.

Jennifer invited Penny to stay for Dinner, although she was reminded by Alice to say nothing about their job interviews in front of Elsa.

"Ok Penny replied with a laugh, but whatever may the best girl win!"

The following day came and went without any decision about the job applications notified to either of the girls or indeed any other applicant.

It is now Friday morning, and Mr Johnson summons Penny to his office.

A Dose of Insulin

"Please sit down Penny; you were, or should I say, are an excellent employee and therefore an excellent candidate, but I must tell you, this time, you were unsuccessful."

"Well, thank you for explaining Mr Johnson," Penny said with a little disappointment.

Immediately Penny had left the office. Alice approached her and asked the result. "It's not me, so perhaps you are in with a better chance than you thought Alice."

Alice waited, and waited but no call to the office; no news is good news she thought.

During the day others were called but still no appointment to the role.

It was late on, the following day, Saturday, when Alice received her call. As far as she knew, every applicant had already been invited to Mr Johnson's office to hear their result, but no one selected.

Most likely she was top of the list or was it, somebody from outside the organisation. It could even be an employee from inside the organisation but from a different location?

Different thoughts went round and round in her head.

Sitting down at the desk, Alex Johnson sat with an unreadable expression before he smiled and told Alice she was indeed the chosen applicant.

"I'm so sorry for the lengthy delay Miss Edwards, but before I could notify applicants of the result, I had to refer my chosen few and the successful applicant to Head Office."

"Would you like to know why you were selected?"

With excitement, Alice relaxed in her chair and waited to hear the details for her achievement.

"There were several reasons; including the automatic

effort, you made to assist me without being asked when I first took over the reins. You and your friend, Penny, noticed that things needed doing and put them right.

You questioned the salary level and the responsibilities involved.

When I explained the reasons why there could be no increase in the salary offered, you accepted my answer without question and duly accepted the additional responsibilities. Your attitude was something I would have expected from any potential applicant.

Although I didn't ask the question, you explained things you would do to improve the store and its sales; that was most impressive. Oh, and you can tell your friend Penny that Head Office have agreed on the two of you assisting each other whenever there are unseen problems. This assistant's role will now be an official appointment."

Alice left the office with a broad smile on her face, and as one would expect, Penny was waiting.

Penny had correctly guessed the result and asked Alice whether she would be telling David that very evening.

"I'm still at Mum's, and honestly I'm still not sure I want to contact him. Certainly, Mum and Elsa should know before anyone else; can you imagine Elsa's surprise if not her reaction? I will have to stand clear of her arms, waving about in mad excitement.

Anyway, Penny, you will remember our agreement that whoever got the job, the other would assist if assistance was needed. Well apparently Head Office thought it a good idea, and it sounds as though you are 'officially' the Supermarket's number two! "

Despite her uncertainty and previous objections to applying for this job, Alice was pleased and believed that when she did inform David, it would add a few bonus points and strengthen their relationship.

Chapter 14

Alice wasn't quite sure how best to deliver the news, as so far, Elsa knew nothing about the interview.

Whatever she was going to make sure her little sister was the first to know, and obviously along with her Mum, Jennifer.

Alice opened her front door and Mum, and Elsa were both working in the kitchen; Elsa preparing the vegetables and Mum the meat, portions of chuck shoulder beef.

"It's stew for dinner tonight; obviously, you are going to join us again, Alice; how was work?"

"Ok, thanks; they announced the results of the interviews for the Supervisor's job today," I casually mentioned.

"How did you get on?" asked Mum hopefully.

"How did *she* get on? You weren't applying were you, Sis." Elsa said and believing Mum had got it wrong.

"Yes, Elsa, Mum's right. I eventually decided to apply, and guess what, I've got what they called the Supervisors' job. They've upgraded the role, and it's now called Supermarket Manager."

"Oh Sis, that's fantastic! I didn't think you were going to apply."

During the next few days, thoughts continually crossed Alice's mind about when she should contact David and notify him of her success; if at all.

Quite clearly, it was possible but not guaranteed; there was a future for them as an on-going partnership.

Of course, there was also the Caribbean holiday to think about, if indeed David still wanted to take Alice.

These questions continued to trouble Alice; whatever everyday life continued.

That evening Alice met with Penny for a drink and something to eat at The Hay Stack, in Theale, a little village on the outskirts of Reading. It was somewhere Alice had often visited during her lunch breaks when she had worked nearby.

"The food is good and the staff so pleasant and friendly, you can also eat and drink outside in the rear garden when the weather is good. When it's not so good, there's a traditional open fireplace inside." Alice had informed Penny.

Upon their arrival, the fire was burning, and the exposed brickwork and timbers just added to the overall atmosphere in the airy lounge.

They both looked at the individual food selections displayed on the large board hung on the wall.

But placing their order, they chose their meals from the counter menus on the bar, taking their drinks to a table near the fire while they awaited their food.

"You were right Alice it's a pleasant pub; so what's your latest news and what did your family think when you told them about your promotion?"

"They were ecstatic, and you can imagine Elsa's response; her excitement was that which I had initially anticipated. As I told you previously, she didn't know I'd applied."

"So, what about David; have you made up your mind about telling him?" Penny questioned with interest.

Alice explained her dilemma about David and the possibility of their future relationship. "He can make excuses, but it's too late for him to change what he's already said. He'd already done the damage when he said it, and now he can't alter that!

The possible holiday and just about everything else going on in my life is so complicated at this particular moment in time Penny. I said with great feeling.

Elsa is lucky; at the moment, she doesn't realise all the complications she is going to face as she grows older." Alice continued thoughtfully with an extremely wry smile on her face.

"Forget about Elsa; this is all about you and what you need to do and do it now!

Think about it. Your holiday is only months away; whether or not there is going to be a strong or even an on-going relationship between the two of you, you can't go on holiday together when you aren't even talking; it would be disastrous."

"Yes, I understand what you are saying Penny, but I'm the one who has to deal with it – and believe you me, it's not easy!" Alice responded. "Anyway, Penny, tell me about anything exciting in your life."

"Nothing and as you know, still no man." was Penny's terse reply.

They finished their meals, phoned a cab, thanked the landlord, and made their way home.

That night Alice lay in her bed and once again all her confusion and worries just spun around and around in her head.

Penny's well-meaning advice had served to confuse Alice even more.

Some days later, Alice and Penny were leaving their store together and standing by the kerb, was an immaculately dressed David.

I was taken by so much surprise, that at that particular moment I couldn't think of anything to say, not even Hello!

"Can we please talk Alice; just the two of us; there's a coffee shop just around the corner?" David requested.

The coffee shop wasn't any distance, and during the walk, obviously, David also found it embarrassing as, like me, he also found it difficult to say anything.

Inside, it wasn't that much better although David *broke the ice* when asking Alice to choose her drink, although he was already aware of her favourite coffee.

They found a seat at the back of the narrowly structured shop where it was a little less noisy, although this considerably heightened their level of embarrassment.

David, who had carried both cups of coffee, placed them on the table but slopped some of Alice's coffee in the saucer; naturally, he apologised.

Alice politely responded, "Don't worry, it happens."

David then continued "Thank you for agreeing to talk

to me; I didn't want to leave everything the way it is; I miss you so very much, Alice."

Without even thinking, Alice replied, "Me too."

"Good, I do believe it was all a total misunderstanding; it was just me, my big mouth and the stupid way I say things or express myself; I'm so sorry," David said apologetically.

"Yes, and I suppose I don't always think about exactly what is said and the actual message."

Alice couldn't believe it; after convincing herself, it was all David's fault, here she was mentally 'looking inwardly' and now accepting some of the responsibility for their disagreement. But then again, she considered, *it takes two to tango!*

The conversation continued harmoniously, and David bought up the matter regarding their not too distant holiday. "Do you still want to go?"

Alice was extremely pleased with the discussion about the holiday taking place, but in her mind, she still wasn't 100% clear.

There were other factors which come to bear before that of holidaying together; She didn't refuse but opened the mental door a fraction.

"Thank you, but I don't know; I'll have to think about it."

"Think about it?" David responded. "What do you mean think about it?"

"Well, what about us?" She anxiously asked, unsure of exactly what David's reply might be.

There was a pause before David replied. "Until I upset you, we were getting on fine and enjoying life. We were also looking forward to our time in San Andrés. Please don't let us throw all that away, Alice, can we try again?"

Feeling comfortable that David had genuinely considered everything and that he accepted part of the responsibility for their fallout, Alice agreed.

"Elsa will be pleased!" I said with happiness.

"Yes but before telling Elsa, haven't you got something to tell me?"

"About what, in particular?" Alice enquired.

"About work," David said.

"Oh, yes, that! I have been appointed as the Store Manager, replacing *the Bull*!" I replied casually.

"That's fantastic," David responded. "I did know you were the chosen applicant as news travels fast on our Company grapevine."

Our conversation was interrupted when a coffee house assistant asked whether we would like another drink before she cleared the empty cups from the table.

"Well, what now; do you want to come back to mine?" David asked.

"No, thank you; I'd better get home as Mum, and no doubt Elsa, will be wondering what's happened to me."

"You can call them on your mobile."

"Thank you, David, but no. Tonight I should return home." I said with frustration already having made my decision that home would be more relaxed, even with Elsa present.

"I understand, so when can we meet again, if only to discuss where our relationship goes from here; tomorrow evening at mine?" David replied with an equal level of exasperation.

Alice agreed 'Seven o'clock.' and made her way home thinking about Mum and Elsa's reaction and of course Penny's, at work the following day or possibly later that evening.

As the lock turned in the door, Mum approached saying "Oh Alice I'm so glad you are ok; you're later than normal, and I thought you might have had an accident."

"Oh, I'm sorry, Mum, I'm ok but why didn't you ring my mobile?" Alice asked.

"I did, but there was no answer; I also text you."

"I'm so sorry. The batteries probably run down. Anyway, I'm home now, and I have some news. It's most probable that David and I are back together."

Elsa, who had been sitting anxiously at the bottom of the stairs; also worried about my late arrival, burst into cheers that were loud enough for people to hear at the end of the street!

Both Elsa and Mum continued to question everything about my excellent news for what seemed like the whole evening; throughout dinner and right until Elsa finally retired to her bedroom; it was late!

Mum asked whether I'd like another drink; once again, there was that look on her face when she had something to say but wasn't sure how to approach the matter.

"What is it, mum, you want to say something?"

"Yes but please don't be upset with me, Alice."

"Oh Mum, just get on with it!"

"Your story about David waiting for you outside your shop, and the two of you rekindling your relationship.

You had already told me that the job was yours, and you Alice, were now appointed as the new Shop Manager.

Somehow David already knew; was this the reason he was there? I mean, would he have been waiting outside the store, if you hadn't got the job? Think about it, Alice."

This particular question hadn't even occurred to me, but perhaps her issue warranted a little more thought. It put me on edge!

"Well, Mum, just tell it how it is!" I said with annoyance.

To close this particular aspect of the conversation, I told her she was, as ever, being overprotective and whatever, I was meeting David tomorrow evening.

"Please don't bother about any dinner for me," I said as I returned to my room, checked my mobile, which had now fully re-charged and phoned Penny.

It was very late, but Penny was pleased to receive my call as she was desperate to hear the outcome of my meeting with David. When I explained Mum's reservations, she replied: "She's a typical Mum, I wouldn't worry; just get on with it."

"Penny I'm so sorry, but I'm meeting him tomorrow night so we will have to cancel the night out we planned."

"Don't worry about it Alice and when you have both settled down again, perhaps the three of us can meet up for a drink one night? I'm so pleased for you both. Anyway, this time, think about what he says before jumping in with both feet!" I could hear her giggles down the phone line.

Chapter 15

Tentatively, Alice entered David's sitting room. He ruffled the cushion, patted the sofa seat and invited Alice to sit.

Alice obliged and looking around the room, She noticed the walls had been repainted in white, obviously since she had last been at the flat.

"Do you like it?" David asked, "Without you, the whole room was just so dreary that I decided to brighten it up."

Alice didn't know whether to appreciate the comment or look for a bucket; it sounded a pleasant comment, and this was typical of David, but it also sounded a little bit cheesy.

"Anyway, you'll also note there is a bottle of your favourite wine, Pinot Grigio and two empty glasses sitting on the coffee table and waiting for us to explore them!

Shall I open the bottle?"

Indeed, David had thought of his approach and how to start the evening on the right foot.

Although the bottle had been already waiting on the table when Alice arrived, it was still cold, as white wine should be, so obviously another tick in the box.

The tatty carpet hadn't changed, but the sitting room

smelt fresh, most likely the smell of lavender. The furniture and window had been polished and cleaned.

"Right," David said, "Let's talk about San Andrés."

"Such as?" Alice replied although she thought her response was a little less than the reaction David would have expected. However realistically, her mind was already back in the tropics and imagining those lovely sands and warm blue seas.

"Such as what we need to prepare for; holiday insurance, clothing, footwear, sun lotion, mosquito repellent, medical checks and any injections we might require and so on!"

It was clear David was serious about the holiday as he had given this whole situation a great deal of thought.

The evening was most enjoyable dreaming about San Andrés and just what beheld them both on this Robinson Crusoe Island with its picturesque towns and cobbled streets. As well as the other satisfying topics they had discussed with excitement a few weeks earlier.

Surprisingly, David never mentioned the job and my promotion, and I also noticed he hadn't said anything about our future relationship.

He had taken everything for granted, but at the evening's close, he did ask if I had intended to stay the night.

I didn't have to consider, just that I needed to let my Mum know I wouldn't be returning that night.

After a hesitant start to the evening, it ended pleasantly; everything was back to normal, or so I hoped!

At work, the next troubleshooting role for Alex Johnson hadn't yet been decided and accordingly, there was a delay in my full-time appointment.

"Although you will have to wait a little longer, he said you should still adopt the role while I watch over you. It'll be excellent training." Johnson suggested.

Not that this worried me in any way as I was the Manager in waiting, and this idea would give me longer to prepare myself for perhaps what was to be a daunting role.

My new title and responsibilities didn't alter my friendship or attitude towards many of the staff who had initially been my peers.

Alex picked me up on this, explaining as a manager I couldn't afford to make friends with my staff; It would lead to them taking advantage rather than obeying the rules and regulations!

I spent the next few weeks spending time between home and David's, although mostly at his delightful Caversham Bridge location.

Between us, life was back to normal until I suspected something was seriously wrong!

I didn't know who to talk to, whether Mum and perhaps even Elsa but discounted them both and decided on Penny as the most favourable to discuss my worries.

Without explaining my particular concern to Penny, I told her it was something I didn't want to discuss on works premises. We agreed to meet that very evening, once again at 'The Hay Stack' in Theale.

Sitting at our favourite fireside table with my glass of wine and Penny a glass of the Hay Stack's classic beer, she said: "You ought to try some."

After the niceties, Penny got to the point and said: "OK, Alice, *Spill*, what's the problem?"

"Well, I'm late! Later than I've ever been and I think I might be pregnant." Alice stated with a worried expression on her face.

There was no response from Penny, facially or verbally, and after a few impatient seconds, Alice asked, "Well Penny, say something!"

Eventually responding, Penny said, "OMG, have you taken a home pregnancy test?"

"No, but I intend to buy one tomorrow from Boots."

"Ok but do it, and quickly! Have you told anyone else?"

"No, I've only told you."

"Have you said anything to David?" Penny continued.

"NO, ONLY YOU!" Alice shouted in frustration.

"Oh I'm so sorry Alice; test yourself and then let me know immediately."

Chapter 16

Taking the test, I prayed I wasn't pregnant. I waited a few seconds before looking.

Focussing on the tester the colouration indicated I was pregnant. My test was positive.

Alice stared at her mobile phone and then as promised, tapped in Penny's number.

"Hi Penny, well as I thought I'm pregnant!" was her brief statement.

"Well, you must inform David immediately."

"Yes Penny, I've thought this situation through and had already decided that if the test was positive, I really should notify David, the Father, before anyone else."

"Good, then do it now!"

"No, he's at work, and this needs to be a face to face conversation so I'll tell him tonight," Alice responded.

That evening David arrived home with a hearty looking smile on his face and a paper bag in his arms; from the strong odour, it was curry for our evening meal.

While David dished the Lamb Vindaloo, our favourite curry from the various tubs, onto heated plates, he said: "This is to celebrate Alice."

Celebrate; how does he know I'm pregnant? I questioned with amazement.

"Today, I had an unexpected one-to-one with my boss, and he's thrilled with my efforts and also the regional increase in sales. We're now the number one supermarket in the Thames Valley area."

I tried to interrupt and tell him we had something else to celebrate, or maybe not! But David continued with his story.

"Of, course it won't be long, and you will also be contributing to our local impact," David continued with enthusiasm.

My mind is filled, with my news and exactly how I would tell him.

"Oh, good." was my only reply.

"Good. Is that all you have to say?" He said with extreme exasperation.

"Needless to say, I'm pleased for you, David, but before we eat, I need to discuss something else with you."

"Ok then start discussing," David said, more with a sense of sarcasm than one of serious interest, as nothing could be more overwhelming than his fantastic news!

There was a lull in the conversation, while I continued to think about the best way of presenting my information; our information!

"Well come-on, what is it?" David asked, impatiently.

In response, I just blurted "I'm pregnant, David!"

There was another lull before David shouted just one word "WHAT!"

"I'm pregnant," I repeated.

"Are you sure; have you tested yourself?"

"Of course, I've tested myself; this morning, and it was a positive reading."

"Well, how the fuck did that happen?" was David's ridiculous and insensitive response.

"How the bloody hell, do you think it happened, David! You're not that fuckin thick."

"What about your Doctor; has your Doctor confirmed the pregnancy?" David asked.

To me, his question was quite clearly a question of desperation.

"What did your Mum say?" He continued.

"I haven't told her."

"What about Penny, I guess she knows!" David stated.

"I discussed my suspicions with her before I took the pregnancy test and Penny agreed I should tell you of the actual result before I told anybody else!"

"And what are you going to do now?" David questioned, in a most palpable manner.

"I'm going home to tell Mum; will you come with me?"

Another lull in the tense conversation and he replied: "No you go; I have things to think about."

"Such as what?" I asked him while reasoning; surely, nothing could be as important as my pregnancy and the prospect of a newborn baby.

David displayed absolutely no sign of excitement; he didn't even cuddle me. He was most objectionable.

Chapter 17

David's attitude dumbfounded me; he hadn't even offered to ring a Cab. But then again, it had been a shock to me, and perhaps he also needed time to come to terms with it all.

Mum commented, "I wasn't expecting you home tonight, Alice; is everything ok?"

"No Mum, can I have a coffee?"

"Of course you can, sweetheart; now sit down and tell me all about it. I guess David's upset you again."

"It's a little more than that Mum, in fact, a lot more!"

Taking a long and careful sip of my hot coffee, I looked up at Mum and just told her "Mum, I'm pregnant! At least I'm pretty certain I am."

I could see she was lost for words as she wouldn't have known whether I was pleased or upset and therefore, how exactly she should respond.

"So what do you think about it?" Was her diplomatic comment, before immediately continuing and asking, "And, what did David say?"

"He said a lot, but I'm not sure about what he feels. Still, he's thinking about it, and like me, I guess when he gets used to the idea of being a Father, he'll be pleased; I mean it's not every day you realise you have a baby on the way." Alice remarked.

"No, Alice, it's an extraordinary moment in anybody's life. And then you stop and think and ask yourself how you can afford to bring up a child, *or even two*!" She said humorously.

"It's the question nearly everyone asks themselves, but then we get on with it. And it's never regretted.

Still, let's get you an appointment at the Docs and confirm the pregnancy before we start thinking or planning anything else."

Elsa had realised I was home as I could hear her footsteps coming down the stairs. She opened the kitchen door, dressed in her pretty patterned pyjamas.

"Hi, Sis." She said, "What's happening then?"

"You'd better tell her," Mum said although it was more of a statement than a suggestion.

For once that confidence, Elsa always possessed appeared questionable. "Tell me what?" She asked with a puzzled expression on her face.

"Tell you I'm pregnant; at least I think I am. I still need to see the Doctor."

"Wow, Sis! That's great. If you are pregnant, you and David can finally get married."

I didn't respond verbally but just nodded my head, thinking I do hope David sees it that way!

Elsa continued with her many questions and utmost enthusiasm, although I genuinely didn't know how to respond as much would depend on David's ultimate reaction.

A Dose of Insulin

I rang the Doctor's early the next morning. I then had to explain why I needed to see my doctor before the receptionist would grant me an appointment; the earliest date she provided was in two days.

The appointment was accepted as there didn't seem another option.

I didn't know whether I should meet up with David after I'd seen my Doctor or perhaps beforehand and inform him I had made the appointment!

Over the next 48 hours or so, Elsa's enthusiasm continued unabated.

"I'm going to have a baby Nephew or Niece, and I will be an Aunty! What are you going to call it; have you chosen any names? If it's a girl, Ava's a nice one or even Amelia and if it's a boy, how about William or Billy. I can also feed the baby or change the nappies for you.

Oh, I'm so looking forward to it Sis. Whatever it is, I can buy some pretty clothes for the baby to wear."

A phone call from Penny interrupted Elsa's delight. "So how are you, Alice, have you heard from David."

"Nothing Penny; and judging by his outrageous reaction, I'm guessing it won't be any time soon!"

"Ok, Alice so how about you and me having a break in Bournemouth this weekend?

It'll be a change from whatever's happening around here. Also, it will help take your mind off your current situation, and even David and his lack of a positive response."

Yes, this was a most desirable thought and something a little out of the ordinary.

"A walk by the seafront, a few drinks and who knows

we might even meet up with a couple of hunks!" Penny said, followed by a hearty if not a hopeful chuckle.

"Sounds a great idea Penny but please don't forget, I have my Doctors appointment 10 am Friday."

"Oh yes, so how about I come to the Doctors with you, and we travel on down to Bournemouth from there? If it's ok for you, I'll organise the trains and the hotel."

Penny's idea didn't need much thought; anything, such as a trip to Bournemouth would help to dispel my anxieties.

"Right, sounds a plan! I'll let Mum know and see you here around nine on Friday morning; thanks for the thought Penny I think your idea sounds fantastic."

"So what was that all about Alice; it sounded like one of Penny's hair-brained schemes!" Mum asked.

"It was a great idea; we're going to spend the weekend in Bournemouth."

"Wow, can I come?" Elsa shouted with anticipation.

"I'm so sorry, Elsa, but it's going to be a big girl's weekend."

"Well, I am a big girl," Elsa replied hopefully.

"But not quite as big as you need to be," I said with sympathy.

I was thinking about how wonderful it would be when my little sister was old enough to come with me and the fun I knew we'd have; wherever it was!

Mum interrupted "But that sort of weekend won't be good if you are pregnant; you will have to think about the baby."

"Penny's coming to the Docs with me, and if the Doc does confirm I'm pregnant, then I'll think again, dependent on the Doc's overall advice. I mean even if I am pregnant, it's still only very early days.

It's not as though we're going mountaineering."

"Whatever, it's your body, Alice and what do I say if David calls for you while you're away?"

"Tell him the truth Mum; I'm in Bournemouth with Penny and sharing a relaxing and stress-free weekend! Oh, and you can also ask him whether he's finally thought about 'The things he needed to think about'; it's taken him a long time to do it." I said irritably.

Instantaneously I thought about my response to Mum's genuine concerns and apologised accordingly.

Chapter 18

It was only 8.30 in the morning, and Penny was knocking on our front door; "Where's your luggage?" I asked her.

"Luggage, I've got everything I need in my handbag and my little rucksack; we're only going for the weekend, not emigrating!" Penny replied.

"Anyway, I've booked the tickets, and we're on the 14.52 which arrives in Bournemouth around 16.30; they're off-peak returns and cost £30 quid each."

"Great and what about the Hotel. Is it a good 'un?" Alice asked.

"I managed to get us a double room for Friday night until 1000 Sunday morning in The Royal Beach hotel.

It's a little costly, but according to feedback, it's got an excellent reputation, and it's only a few paces from the beach.

Also, it's only a couple of bob more than some of the other local hotels that aren't rated as highly, so what the hell!"

"Well, I hope the room's a big 'un as I've got a bit of luggage," Alice mentioned casually.

With that, Alice turned around and then slowly wheeled a

family size suitcase into the hallway, immediately followed by her Mum, Jennifer wheeling a similar-sized suitcase with just as much difficulty.

Stopping at the front door, Mum stood erect and said "Right Alice, you haven't forgotten anything, have you? Oh and what about the other case upstairs; whatever don't worry, I'll get it all sorted while you're at the Docs."

Penny couldn't believe it and then in utter disbelief said: "What the bloody hell Alice, *three* cases, and we're only going for the weekend; two bloody days!"

Mum and I couldn't keep straight faces for a second longer and just burst into howls of laughter.

"Oh, *very* funny; what an absolute sucker I am!" Penny responded with a smile on her face.

Mum and I were still laughing, even more hysterically at Penny's reaction as we wheeled the two enormous and empty cases back into the store-cupboard under the stairs.

"Right, enough of your stupid humour, Alice, we'll be late for your Doctor's appointment! And talking about taking the piss, don't forget your urine sample." Penny said with composure although she was still smiling at our stupidity.

Penny and I arrived with time to spare for my 10 o'clock appointment, and it was nearly another hour or so before the receptionist called me to see my Doctor.

While waiting, we discussed our forthcoming trip and how much we were looking forward to the break away from home and the change to our usual routine. However, I was sad as I didn't have the opportunity to say goodbye to Elsa!

Even before I had entered the Doctor's surgery, I knew what the result was going to be.

Over recent years, I had heard examples of young women getting pregnant and how it completely changed their lives and the opportunities they could have had if only they had been careful; what idiots! And now I was in precisely the same position! Who was the idiot now, I questioned myself?

The Doctor asked me several questions, and then took my small bottle of urine, that fortunately, Penny had reminded me, not to forget.

"Have you already taken a pregnancy test?" The Female Doctor asked.

"Yes, and it was positive," I replied.

"Right, let's see what your urine tells us?"

There was a pause before she looked at me, directly in the eyes and said "Well, your hCG shows as positive, so accordingly it is almost certain you are pregnant. Is there anything else you'd like to ask me?" She questioned.

At this stage, I just wasn't sure about what else I should ask. The Doctor told me of all the help and assistance I would receive from the NHS and where I could get it. "Having a baby today is much easier than it was 50 years ago, Miss Edwards. If you have any worries whatsoever, come back and see me immediately."

I thanked her and left the surgery.

"It's what I expected Penny. Anyway, no delay longer than we anticipated, so we won't miss our train.

At least the Doc didn't say I shouldn't go to Bournemouth,

but then again I suppose I didn't mention our weekend away, in the first place."

Penny smiled but temporarily looked confused at my statement.

"Yes, so now you must try and concentrate on our weekend!" Penny said.

Chapter 19

On and off, Penny couldn't help but smile about me and Mum's antic with the additional suitcases.

As we approached our specific seats, previously booked by Penny, there was some commotion, or perhaps it was just fun and games as a group of four lads laughed and joked further down the carriage.

We sat down quietly as we didn't want to attract any unwanted attention; all we hoped for was to enjoy the 90-minute journey. In some ways, it brought back sweet memories of Mum and our trips to the seaside but this time, without buckets and spades!

However, we had only been seated for what seemed like minutes, when one of the lads approached and asked where we were going?

I didn't answer as I wanted to discuss a little more with Penny about my situation and in particular, David.

However, Penny did reply and told him it was Bournemouth.

He turned to his friends and shouted: "Hey chaps, they're going to Bournemouth as well!"

With this, all four of them were occupying our precious

space, introducing themselves and swapping names, although, at the time I was still upset and thinking about David's untenable response and couldn't remember any of them.

They told us what they could remember of Bournemouth and the best places to visit, especially for a pint or two!

As the conversation became jovial, Penny couldn't resist telling them all about my suitcase prank. "What, and you believed her!" One of the lads asked before they all started chuckling at Penny's complete and utter sense of gullibility. Overall they seemed like pleasant chaps.

Their company continued for the rest of the journey, and before we knew it, we have arrived at Bournemouth station.

As we lined up at the taxi rank, one of the lads who had spent a good bit of the journey time talking to Penny waved at her and said: "Hope to see you on the Beach Penny!"

"*See you on the Beach Penny?*" Frustrated, I said, I thought this weekend was just for you and me; "Have you agreed to meet up with him?"

"Well, I did say we might find a couple of Hunks," Penny said with a hopeful expression on her face.

She was referring back to her conversation when we initially discussed the idea of a weekend in Bournemouth.

"So, did you get his details?" I asked.

"Only his name; Christopher, although he told me he prefers to be called Chris."

"Well, whatever, good luck to you, Penny, you deserve a good time," I replied, remembering Penny's frustration of having no man friend to accompany her. I even felt guilty, having questioned her about meeting up with somebody else, instead of spending all of her time with me!

We climbed aboard our taxi as the driver loaded my small case and Penny's rucksack into the boot.

Penny provided the driver with our destination, The Royal Beach Hotel and left him to take us there without any mishaps.

Everything looked idyllic; the sandy beach, people enjoying themselves, young children with buckets, spades and ice creams in hand.

It reminded me so much of my youthful days with Mum and Elsa. I even considered the likelihood of meeting up with Graeme, although I probably wouldn't recognise him now, even if he were holidaying in Bournemouth.

Driving along the seafront, Penny screamed: "There's Chris."

The four mates were walking to their destination, and it seemed quite clear that the other three lads were laughing and almost certainly *taking the Mick* out of Chris.

More than likely because of his departing comment to Penny at the Station, of *seeing you on the beach Penny.*

The Royal Beach Hotel sounded most glamorous, but on arrival, it was part of a set of terraced buildings; probably bed and breakfast accommodations.

Mind you, the striking blue and gold sign, set midway up the building looked far more majestic than some of the nameplates hanging from a peg above and alongside other entrances.

Inside, the hotel was compact but clean and tidy. The

design was entirely different from specifically built hotels as opposed to converted Houses.

We booked in at reception, and a porter kindly offered to help us to the room with our luggage.

Our room was a double, with two separate beds, although it still wasn't that big.

"At least we've got a sea view," Penny remarked, attempting to limit any possible complaints.

The room smelt fresh, as did the bedding, a faint smell of lilac. The room seemed as high as it was wide and picture rails circulated the white room, with the odd picture of Bournemouth, its town centre, and the pier, hanging from them.

Two large and plain curtains hung in front of the panoramic window and from what I remember Mum telling me, they could have been *blackout* curtains, the type used during the second world war.

We were on the seafront and overlooking the roadway. Yes, at night, when the curtains were both pulled over the large window, they would block the light and provide all the privacy we needed.

Once our luggage had been stored away in the cupboard, there was sufficient room to walk around the beds without too much effort, so in reality, there wasn't anything, either of us could find to complain about, to the Management, or even ourselves.

Although Penny commented, with a humorous smile, "Go on, Alice, think about it, you can always find something to moan about!"

I unzipped my case and carefully hung some of my

clothes on hangers where I hoped creases caused, while crammed in my small case would drop out. I then laid my other items tidily in the drawers.

Thoughtfully, there was even a shoe rack attached at the bottom end of the wardrobe and two extra draws beneath this rack.

Penny commented that her minimal clothing would remain in her ruck-sack as thoughtfully there was an electric iron at the bottom of the built-in wardrobe if indeed she needed one.

It was just approaching early evening, and after the tiring day, we decided to stay in the hotel and enjoy a few drinks in the bar.

The bar was located by following the sign, which directed us to a larger room at the back of the Hotel. It overlooked a lawned rear garden.

There was no *real ale*; so for Penny, it was only a choice of keg beer, while naturally, I chose a glass of white wine.

Whatever, we relaxed in our comfy seats and spent the evening talking about my pregnancy and my likely future with David.

Oh, and of course, whether Penny would meet up again with Christopher.

It was late, and the bartender asked us whether we would like another drink before the bar finally closed. We later learnt that the bar didn't close until their guests had decided it closed; within reason, of course.

Climbing the stairs to our room, Penny tripped a few times, and I took her arm and helped her to the top. Quite clearly, despite Penny complaining about Keg beer and how weak it was, it was stronger than she had thought, at least considering the quantity she had drunk.

We changed into our nighties and climbed into the beds, Penny with difficulty and both of us looking forward to a good nights sleep.

Although I was to be most disappointed as Penny's snoring sounded more like an express train and for the whole night, this made sleep almost impossible for me.

Don't even think about complaining about keg beer again Penny, was my continued reasoning.

Understandably I was awake early, although I had only slept in fits and starts; we hadn't ordered breakfast, the night before.

I attempted to wake Penny.

There was no response other than her continued snoring as she lay curled up in what seemed like a hibernating position.

Penny's senseless state was due to alcohol!

I endeavoured to drag the bed covers from her, but automatically she clung on with all her might. Eventually, she gained consciousness, asking what the fuck I was doing and why.

"I'm still tired Alice, so I'm gonna miss breakfast." She turned over and with the bedcovers again adequately covering her body, the snoring automatically continued.

Chapter 20

I was hungry, so I left Penny in her bed and went downstairs to ask one of the kitchen staff whether I could have breakfast, although I hadn't ordered any the previous evening.

They weren't busy, and the girl kindly offered to serve me some of the egg and bacon they had cooked earlier. She also brought me a couple of slices of toast.

Sitting alongside the window, I noticed a blackbird also digging for its breakfast in the lawned area of the picturesque garden. Alongside the lawn were many different flowers budding as well as beautiful shrubs and trees highlighted by the morning's sun rays.

Finishing my breakfast, the blackbird was still digging for his!

I thought it a shame that Penny had missed breakfast and this captivating view.

Upstairs I could still hear her snores before I even opened the door!

I sat on the chair and watched people either walking or playing on the beach, but after another hour I became annoyed, and in a loud voice I shouted; "For god's sake

Penny, what's the point of paying for a weekend somewhere like this and then snoring most of it away in bed!

Penny stirred and gradually rolled over and asked what the time was.

"Time you got up; it's nearly eleven!" I said in annoyance.

"What, 11 pm?" She joked.

I didn't find her remark in the least bit funny and said nothing in reply!

Penny dressed and told me she needed some fresh air, so we decided on a stroll along the beach.

A bracing wind hit us when we stepped outside the front door, and most of the people I had watched from our hotel window enjoying themselves on the beach had left; either because of the windy weather or maybe for something to eat in Bournemouth's multitude of cafes.

We must have been strolling for at least an hour when Penny said she felt dehydrated.

"Oh what a surprise Penny," I said with amusement. "How about we find somewhere to have a drink."

Just the thought of that and Penny told me she was almost sick on the spot!

"No Penny, I mean a cup of tea or coffee and perhaps something for lunch!"

Without trouble, we found an establishment that served our purpose and was reasonably priced.

I had eaten a late breakfast, so I only chose a sandwich and a cup of coffee. Penny selected a bottle of water!

Back at the Royal Beach Hotel, there was a familiar noise coming from the bar area; it was Chris and his friends.

"So you did give Chris your details!" I said

"Must have," Penny innocently replied.

"Hi Penny, come and have a drink with us," Chris shouted.

I was now past the point when my body told me I needed sleep, so I made my apologies and told Penny to go and enjoy herself.

Flopping on the bed, I must have fallen asleep instantaneously although it didn't last as long as I'd hoped.

Penny burst into the room saying "Hey Alice; I've got a date tonight with Chris and the other chaps have also asked whether you would like to join them!"

"No thanks Penny, it's not for me, but you go ahead and enjoy yourself."

My response wasn't so much about not wanting to have a drink with this lively crew but more out of frustration with Penny as my weekend away with Penny was once again disappearing and disappearing fast!

Selfishly, I was beginning to think that maybe, just maybe, I'd have been better staying at home and having a laugh and a joke with Elsa!

For what must have been the whole afternoon, Penny talked about Chris and tried on her few pieces of jewellery and clothing although she had decided, much to my amusement, that she hadn't brought enough to choose from and none of what she had, suited her for a date.

Eventually, she settled on a patterned skirt and the same crew neck jumper she had worn earlier.

"Cmon Alice, get yourself ready, after all, meeting up with these guys will be more fun than spending it by yourself, whatever you decide to do tonight!"

During the last hour or so, I had thought in depth about Penny and her intentions and remembered her saying beforehand that she was hoping to meet a hunky guy.

I should be annoyed with myself feeling the way I did.

"Yes, you're right Penny, let's go!"

Chris and his friends were already waiting for us in the bar when we came downstairs.

Once again, the boys all introduced themselves, and we ordered our drinks, although no food as I wasn't too sure how long I would remain in their company. Penny chose a lemonade!

One of Chris's friends, Brandon, asked me how I was enjoying my time in Bournemouth, although there was little I could say as we had only been here for a day and all of it spent in the Hotel or on the beach. All my other memories were those from my childhood days and therefore, inappropriate.

However, rather than abruptly ending the conversation, I replied: "It's a pleasant location to spend a weekend and brings back memories with my Mum and little sister."

"It's a great place; we all come here quite regularly," Brandon replied.

"How regularly?" I asked.

Laughing, Chris interrupted "Quite regularly, Brandon? This time, is only our second visit, you bloody dimwit."

Brandon also laughed and continued his discussion with me.

"I remember you told us on the train that you two Ladies are also from the Reading area? We all live there and are old school mates from our time at Prospect school in Tilehurst, and since leaving, we have kept in touch."

Pointing at his other friends, Brandon said: "You know Chris, he's the one who's been emotionally slaughtered by your mate." He noted with amusement.

"The other one is Bob; we kept in touch with him because he was kicked-out of Prospect school and then took up bank robbery as a profession; that is until he got caught."

I was amazed that anyone could be so forthright, especially sitting right next to the relevant individual.

"Don't believe any shit he tells you, fucking idiot." was Bobs, immediate, and less than courteous response. "I'm a truck driver."

Bob must have been shorter than me and lightly framed; and I found it extremely difficult to imagine him driving a lorry, even a small one.

Genuinely interested, I wanted to know more about what he did and the difficulties he encountered, but he seemed reluctant to talk about himself.

Whatever, I was drawn towards Brandon, possibly because of his manner and weird humour. As a point of general discussion, I mentioned to his party of friends, that he was a witty individual.

The fourth member of Brandon's crowd was a chap called Paul.

He wasn't going to be left out of this fun and looking in the direction of Brandon and me while drinking, in one gulp, what seemed an impossible quantity of beer from his glass; he said: "If wit was shit, e'd be constipated!"

It only took me a matter of seconds to cotton on, and I

smiled but only briefly as I didn't want to offend Brandon, and I also thought the remark a little unsavoury.

"And what do you do for a job Paul," I asked, thinking the change of subject would calm any potential upset between him and Brandon.

"I'm on the Social. Get more from 'em than I would in wages, so why bover workin.

Makes sense dunnit, know what I mean, girl!"

The conversation between Brandon and I continued, and then as I had anticipated, he asked whether I was dating?

It could have been out of genuine interest, nothing more than that but rather than explain the specific details of my current relationship with David, I just confirmed I had a partner.

Despite this, Brandon and I seemed to have natural empathy and our evening finished much better than I had anticipated beforehand when Penny first suggested the meeting between us all.

In some ways, I was disappointed that mentally I wasn't in a position to take this friendship any further.

Back in our bedroom, Penny continued talking until the early morning hours, about her time with Chris and how they would be meeting up again when they both returned to Reading. "Small world isn't it." She concluded.

Despite everything, I was delighted for Penny; at last, she had met a guy who she seemed happy to be with and quite clearly enjoyed his company. He was a lot more reserved than his friend Brandon.

Whatever, I just prayed she wouldn't again, snore the

night away as we had to arise early, to clear our room in readiness for our departure and journey home to Caversham.

The train journey back to Reading appeared equally efficient as had the trip to Bournemouth a few days earlier.

Was Penny's time with Chris a weekend romance, or would he keep his promise to meet up with her?

Chapter 21

There were no delays, and I arrived at my Caversham home much earlier than anticipated.

Mum was keen to hear about my weekend; likewise, I was curious to know whether or not David had called.

"Yes, David did call but let me tell you first that Elsa had another serious Hypo; she accidentally overdosed again, although this time I bought her round and didn't need to call the medics. However, it was frightening." Mum said nervously before continuing. "Neither Elsa nor I had any logical idea what might have caused it. I did, explain to her, once again just how dangerous insulin and the control of it could be."

I was concerned for Elsa but so pleased she had recovered, and I wanted to know more about David's call.

"There's not much to tell; he just wants you to call him on your return."

Settling in, I made the phone call.

"Hello, it's me; you wanted me to phone you."

"Yes, thank you, are you ok?"

"Yes, I'm fine; thanks, David."

"Has your Doctor confirmed your pregnancy?"

"You mean *our* pregnancy David; well, yes she has!"

"Ok, can we meet up at mine tomorrow night, say 8 pm?" David sounded almost business-like rather than a boyfriend or ex-boyfriend, that is!

During the next 24 hours, I was most apprehensive but arrived, not knowing what to expect.

The traditional black coffee was placed beside me, where I sat, but David remained standing.

"So you spent the weekend in Bournemouth with Penny. And what did you both get up to?"

"Just walked the beach and generally relaxed. I replied. Are you going to sit down?" I asked, as his general demeanour was irritating me.

"No, I'm ok thanks. So you have you seen your Doctor?"

"Yes, and as I've already told you, she's confirmed my pregnancy."

He didn't mention the word pregnancy again but continued "During the past week, I've been thinking thoroughly about our situation.

Do you realise this will almost certainly mess up your job opportunity, and because of my involvement with the child, it could create problems with my job as well? Not only that, but it could also make our holiday more complicated. We might even have to cancel it."

"So exactly what are you saying, David?" I naively asked.

There was the usual pause before he bluntly said: "You could get rid of it! At this time, I'm not ready to be a Dad, and a child could ruin my life."

I just stared into his lifeless eyes and told him "I can't do that."

"Are you sure, Alice?"

"Of course I'm sure David, I wouldn't even consider it!"

"Then we're finished, Alice. And don't even think about asking me for maintenance." David said in what had recently become that frosty manner of his.

Tears flowed down my cheeks, and yet his only response was one without emotion or feeling. "Go on, Alice, get out of my life!"

Mum's comfort was what I needed, but then again, I also needed solitude.

I remembered the lads from Bournemouth and comments about their school at Prospect School. It wasn't far away, so I took a casual stroll to the park nearby.

The walk did little to relieve my mental anguish. The people I passed either said hello or nodded their heads, mostly with a smile. To them, everything seemed fine.

With exceptional pride, a Mum pushed her light coloured pram towards me.

Moving to the roadside to let her pass, I turned and looked at the tiny occupant.

The child attempted to sit and smiled in my direction.

I wanted to say something to the child's mother, but couldn't. I could feel the tears welling in my eyes.

It was with great relief that I entered Prospect Park.

Except for two men, jogging in the far distance and a woman walking a tiny dog, the park seemed empty.

The air smelt sweet and fresh from the recently cut grass.

I walked for a while, across the grass and along the pathways before sitting on a wooden bench beneath a tree.

Above me, the birds; Blackbirds, Thrushes and other small birds, I couldn't identify, flitted backwards and forwards between the branches; they seemed to have no such worries.

The amount of time I spent in the Park was immaterial; it was pleasant and peaceful.

While walking home, I made my decision; I was going to keep my child.

Chapter 22

Mum and Elsa were both at home and Mum asked me to tell her what David had said.

I bluntly explained that David had told me to have an abortion or we are finished.

Elsa screamed "The Bastard; you're not going to Sis! Are you?"

"No," I responded, "You, my little treasure is going to help me bring it up!"

Elsa's reaction was apparent, while Mum's thoughtful reply was a little more contemplative.

"I'm pleased you have made that decision Alice but have you thought about the many consequences? Especially about your job and what the future will hold for you."

"Yes, and I know what I want to do." I briefly stated.

The following day I notified Alex Johnson of my situation and the choice I had taken.

He was sympathetic in every possible respect but informed me that he would have to refer the matter to Head Office.

It was a short referral as I am called back to his office that very afternoon.

"I'm sorry to tell you, Alice, but because of your circumstances, Head Office has explained they must withdraw their offer of the Manager's position.

They need somebody to take immediate responsibility, and pregnant women are never allowed to apply because of health and safety reasons; at least that's what Head Office said."

It was what I had expected, although I considered Mum's words and how my life would now change dramatically. "Are you saying I must resign Mr Johnson?"

"Not at all, Alice. You can continue the shop-floor role, although obviously at some time you will have to take leave, although the job will be held open for you."

I understood what he was saying and why, but considering everything that had happened in recent weeks, I couldn't cope with the routine of my staff role; especially as I should have been the Manager.

Without any pressure from me, Mr Johnson accepted my resignation.

That evening, I waited for Elsa to retire to bed and explained to Mum the day's outcome.

"Your choice was a most considered one, Alice, but as I said last night, you cannot expect to continue your life as it is and with all the opportunities it generally presents. However, I think perhaps you should have given it a little more time and thought before handing in your notice.

While I wouldn't ever suggest you settle down with David – the heartless beast, a stable relationship with somebody else will be difficult while you are carrying another's child, and possibly even more so when your child is born."

I knew that Mum's words were those of sympathy and understanding as she had also suffered the turmoil's of bringing up Elsa and me, without a man in her life.

That night I slept heavily.

The following morning I walked directly to my Doctors. I sat and waited for an emergency appointment.

I notified the doctor, I wanted a termination. She consulted her records and said "It's close, but you are within the period required. You will need to spend between 24 and 48 hours at a medical clinic, and I will immediately organise this for you. For your information, you will have a scan, and then you will be provided with the relevant pills."

At home, I explained to Mum that I would be absent from home for two days and the reason why. I asked her not to say anything at this stage to Elsa.

The night before my appointment, I lied to Elsa and told her I was spending some time with Penny, obviously with Penny's knowledge and agreement.

I had hated not telling Elsa the truth but considered I had no other option knowing what her response would have been. My abortion wasn't the sort of thing I wanted to argue!

Considering the forthcoming event, it absorbed me. The finality of what I was going to do!

While I waited in the clinic, I continually questioned myself whether or not I was doing the right thing. It was my child, and I remembered how distraught I was with

David's response, and now I was questioning myself about my decision.

Overnight in the clinic, all kinds of images were apparent to me; as was the decision I had reluctantly made.

After this mentally stressful event, Penny collected me from the Clinic and escorted me home in a Cab. I was unable to talk to my friend about this whole experience; the thought of having a baby with the man I loved, David's unbelievable response, and the terrible decision I had just taken.

It was so upsetting, at this particular moment, I couldn't bring myself to discuss it with anybody.

It made me realise what other women must feel like following an abortion. It was a most distressing situation.

Traumatised was an understatement.

Fortunately, Elsa was still at School, but Mum thanked Penny for her continual support and sat me down in our sitting room where she guessed I'd be a little more comfortable than seated, as we usually did, in the kitchen.

During the next few days, I suffered extreme nausea and vomiting, and it was evident to Elsa that something was wrong, although, at this stage, she probably had no idea exactly what.

My mental attitude and depression didn't help, so I agreed with Mum that I would tell Elsa sooner rather than later; In fact, I would inform her that very evening.

I couldn't eat anything but let Elsa finish her dinner before we all sat down in the sitting room.

"My dear sweet Elsa, I have to tell you the reason I've not been well; I'm not going to have a baby."

Elsa was sensible enough to know the reason why and just replied: "Ok Sis."

Just that one brief reply told me everything I needed to know about her response. I couldn't help but feel guilty about my decision and how it would also affect my kind and adorable sister, although it was apparent she was most upset by my sudden and unexpected statement.

However, during the next few weeks, it was also clear to Elsa just how this whole situation with David and subsequently, the pregnancy and the termination had emotionally reduced me to an absolute mental wreck.

Sitting down with me in our sitting room, while Mum was out shopping, Elsa took my hand and said, "Sis, I do understand how you must be feeling.

The decisions you've had to make and the fact that you made those decisions without any support from that bastard David. A real asshole if you ask me; how could anybody be so bloody despicable?"

"Is there anything you can do about it?" She asked.

"Such as what?" I enquired.

"I don't know, but it should be something nasty." Elsa angrily stated. "I thought he loved you, Sis. I know what I'd do if it were me, he'd shit on."

"You don't like him, do you, Elsa?" I said. An obvious statement but at least it lightened the mood a little.

She laughed and then her little chuckle disappeared when she seriously said: "He needs to suffer, as you are. and hopefully a lot worse than you!"

Her statement, while sympathising with me, her big

sister, was most frightening, and despite his comments, I hoped David would never meet up with her in a dark alley!

"Well, thank you, my little Angel; but I suppose, what he's said and done can't be undone and you, like me, should try to put this particular experience behind us. Whatever, we have to get on with our lives," I stated magnanimously, but knowing this was far from the anger and upset I was feeling.

Elsa made absolutely no comment; she wanted to penalise him for failing me to the extent he had, and the misery he had caused.

However, Elsa hadn't finished with her advice, "Do you know what I'd do, Alice?"

"No thank you Elsa, and I'm certain David wouldn't want to hear your solution either!" For the time being, this particular conversation ended.

Chapter 23

Penny phoned with the news I'd hoped for, Chris had made his promised contact with her.

"He's taking me out tonight, although at the moment I don't know where and even what we're going to be doing; it's a surprise!"

"I'm so pleased for you, Penny and whatever he has planned, enjoy yourself." I genuinely replied, although there was little more to say or even think about after our trip to Bournemouth.

Penny talked on for a while before she suggested we meet up for a drink in a few days and try somewhere a little closer than our favourite Pub in Theale.

This Pub was pleasant, but it didn't possess the atmosphere or indeed the hospitality we enjoyed at the Hay Stack.

Whatever, we were there to update each other on our lives since returning from Bournemouth a while earlier and of course an update on Chris.

"Yep," Penny replied, "We've organised another date, and I'm growing closer to him each time we meet.

Chris is a pleasant chap, but until now, I never realised

just how exceptionally desirable I was!" Penny said with a broad laugh.

"Yesterday we went shopping; actually, It was me who went shopping - for shoes. Chris just tagged along and carried my bags.

I saw a beautiful pair of suede calf-length boots, but they were far too expensive for me, and, as you know, my cash is severely limited after our weekend away, so I placed them back on the shelf. I was seeking something cheap or cut-price but still a decent style.

Chris must have seen the look of disappointment on my face because he picked up the shoes, carried them to the counter and paid; such a kind and generous person."

"Well if he ever gets bored Penny, you can tell him to take me shopping!" I said with a giggle. "Anyway, what's happening at work?" I asked with frustration and perhaps a lot of jealousy.

"Not a lot, AJ's still there, and everyone is saying he might become permanent; shame you let it go!" Penny replied.

"Why didn't you follow it up, Penny. After all, AJ said you were up there with me when we originally applied for the role?"

"I did think about applying, but it was odd; when you left, things seemed to change. I can't put my finger on it, even AJ's attitude became different."

"What do you mean, different?" I asked as I was puzzled at precisely what she meant.

"It's hard to explain Alice; maybe he believed he had better opportunities awaiting him, and now, AJ was trapped where he was. Could even be he had a soft spot for you, Alice!" Penny laughed.

"Whatever it was, his attitude towards me completely changed.

Then again, it was possibly my fault as I kept telling him when he was doing something wrong!"

"OMG Penny, how often did you do that?" I asked.

"How often, Alice, you ask me how often? AJ's a bloke, so it was every day!" Penny replied with a chuckle, although I knew she wasn't serious.

"So, Penny, tell me more about Chris and you."

"There isn't much more to tell, honestly, oh that is apart from Brandon, he keeps asking about you and how you are? He's extremely interested."

"Yes, maybe he is Penny, he's a nice guy, but after David, I'm just not in the right state of mind to enter another relationship. The misery it caused could've put me off men for life." I was joking, but there was an element of truth about how I felt.

We chatted the evening away, and I was so pleased that Penny had finally met, what she believed was an exceptional guy. I wasn't jealous of her.

Whatever the future might hold, I just hoped that her relationship with Chris would be a good one. Hopefully, even her less than amicable moments with him, wouldn't be anywhere near the same as my distressing history.

As a passing comment, Penny said: "Alice, you're not wearing the *Friendship ring* I bought you a few years ago for your 18th Birthday; you always wear it, have you lost it?"

"No, my jewellery box is still at David's; I'll have to collect it sometime."

"I wouldn't trust him, Alice, you never know what he might do; out of spite he just might sling any belongings of yours in the rubbish!"

My mobile started ringing, and Penny mischievously commented: "Bet its Brandon."

It was Elsa.

"What's up my little Drip?"

"It's Mum, and she's not well. Please come home immediately, Alice!"

Elsa and her tone of voice emphasised that urgency even more.

For a while now, I realised I had to prepare for such calls, but when they happen, it wasn't going to be easy to manage.

"It'll be much quicker to walk than wait for a taxi," Penny stated. "I'll come with you!"

I rushed home in a panic, accompanied by Penny, although I didn't have any idea of what exactly was wrong or just how bad Mum was.

It was late, but instead of her bed, Mum was lying on the settee and breathing heavily; Elsa was correct; Mum didn't look right.

"Are you ok, Mum?" I asked.

"No, I feel fragile Alice and think I need a doctor; urgently."

This request was unusual for Mum to make as she always believed she was wasting the Doctor's valuable time and rarely called them to her home. She knew how poorly she was.

I dialled the Out of hours number, and frustratingly the recoded voice told me I would receive an answer as soon as possible. I looked at my Mum again and anxiously, asked myself exactly what the surgery meant by *We will answer your call as soon as possible?*

Fortunately, the response was quicker than expected, less than ten minutes, although the Doctor initially told me it would be approximately an hour before he could attend.

As you will understand, with Mum breathing heavily and complaining just how weak she felt, an hour would have seemed like an eternity.

Elsa informed me she had offered Mum a drink, but she felt too ill to consume anything at all.

Sitting on the settee, and surrounded by cushions, she wore a dressing-gown over her other clothing, but it made little difference as she trembled from the intense cold. The sitting room felt warm, but I checked the radiators anyway. Elsa must have switched them full-on as the one I touched was burning hot!

I stroked Mum's numb hands and asked Elsa to collect a duvet from the bedroom as despite the heat her whole body was freezing.

Penny asked whether there was anything she could do to help, but all I could think of was to make Elsa and me a coffee and perhaps a hot drink would warm Mum a little.

Elsa promptly returned with the Duvet and helped me cover Mum's chilled body.

"Thank you," Mum muttered.

The Doctor arrived, announcing himself as Dr McArthur.

Firstly he took Mum's temperature and then checked her blood pressure.

He informed us that it didn't appear to be anything seriously wrong with her heart, my initial concern, but to be safe, Dr McArthur wanted her thoroughly checked at the St Olives Hospital.

Initially, I hoped his diagnosis was a good one, and whatever it was, her illness wasn't too serious.

That is until I heard him phoning for the ambulance service.

Elsa also heard his call and burst uncontrollably into tears.

"It's ok young lady, don't worry; it's just me being precautionary." Dr McArthur said, easing our concerns.

The ambulance men carefully laid Mum onto the ambulance, trolley stretcher and carefully wheeled her outside to the ambulance. It was late, and I was pleased that fortunately, there were no onlookers.

For years afterwards, I thought of this occasion and always how kind and caring these people are.

Despite the seriousness and the reason for their call out, they managed to put the patient and those around them at ease. And then assist the convalescent as necessary. It just seemed a natural response.

There was only enough room for one of us to accompany Mum in the ambulance so Penny said she would follow on with Elsa.

Laying down in the ambulance, Mum was asked by one of the Medics how she felt, and she replied 'Much better, thank you.' Although I guessed this was because she was in medical hands and not necessarily because bodily, she felt better in herself. I was still deeply concerned.

Stopping at the Hospital's Ambulance Bay, the ambulance trolley was lowered to the ground and wheeled into the Hospital reception area where they were expecting Mum's arrival.

Followed by the Nurse and me, two hospital porters wheeled her into a cubicle where she would await a Doctor.

Under these circumstances, everything in this area of the Hospital seemed to be one of great concern. With urgency, people are being pushed on the trolleys by hospital staff. Serious-faced receptionists all add to the feeling of pending doom. It didn't feel any better while we waited in the curtained cubicle.

There was no delay in the Doctor's arrival at which point he carried out what appeared to be the same tests Dr McArthur had checked at home.

"Well Madam, there is nothing immediately apparent, but for safety reasons, we will be keeping you overnight to monitor you. The Porters will take you to Hemsworth Ward where you will rest until officially discharged."

His courteous manner and melodic voice relaxed Mum from what must have been a most frightening experience.

Not too much later, Penny arrived with Elsa, who still had tears in her now blood-shot eyes.

"How's Mum?" she anxiously asked.

"Better but they're going to keep her in the hospital tonight, just to make sure she's ok," I said, hoping this would put Elsa's mind at rest.

"I've been informed by a nurse that I can stay the night, in the seat beside Mum's bed," but when I explained to Elsa, there wasn't enough room for her to stay as well; her tears started again.

Penny comforted Elsa, "It's Ok you don't have to go home; you can wait with me in the Casualty reception area. At least they have seats there, and I'll stay with you. It won't be for long as it will soon be morning.".

Although the Doctors hadn't seemed too concerned, it was still a tough and worrying night for all of us. Especially as Mum was informed, another Doctor's check would happen before her eventual discharge.

Were they still unsure about Mum's condition after all? Dressed in a hospital apron, Mum looked far from good. Everything seemed a worry.

In the ward, nurses regularly visited, to check Mum was alright and whether there was anything she needed.

The following morning at 10 am, Mum asked one of the nurses when a Doctor would be seeing her.

"It's a Specialist, Mrs Edwards, and he will be here as soon as he's completed his rounds."

"A Specialist? I asked the Nurse. What type of Specialist?"

This particular comment made everything sound much worse than it had done previously. A Specialist; a Specialist is required when something is seriously wrong, or so I believed!

"A Cardiac Specialist, after all, this is the Hemsworth, a Cardiac ward." The nurse replied.

A Dose of Insulin

Now my worry was Elsa, and what I should tell her, or better still, not tell her.

Mum's condition didn't seem to change. I stroked her hands which were nice and warm and told her I would go and see how Elsa and Penny had dealt with their night in the casualty reception. I also wanted to update Penny on the situation.

Elsa seemed reasonably ok, after what she told me, was a sleepless night.

It had been so noisy and bustling in casualty with many people coming in and out, although as one would expect, her first question had been about Mum.

To avoid telling her the real situation, I just explained Mum was still waiting to see a doctor and suggested that we all find the canteen and have something to eat. I was undoubtedly starving and guessed we all were, as none of us had eaten anything since yesterday.

I wasn't sure of how long we had been away from the ward, but I was feeling replenished, although still most anxious about Mum's condition and with Penny and Elsa, made my way back to her Ward.

Partially draped curtains had earlier been around her bed for privacy, but now they surrounded all of it. Instantaneously my heart flipped a beat. Nurses were rushing in and out of her bay, and every one of them had a look of concern on their face.

I feared the worst and stopped one of the nurses. She put my mind at rest, telling me the Specialist, Mr Robertson, would soon be examining her. They were busily preparing for his visit, and I would be able to see her in a few minutes.

The examination finished and Mum, hearing a discussion I was having with a nurse, called me to her side.

Mum asked the specialist, "Would you like to tell my daughter what you have just told me? I hope she understands the medical jargon better than I do."

He placed a piece of used tissue in the receptacle and turned to face me with a comforting smile said "Well, to put it as simply as I can, I believe your Mother has what we call, CHD, Coronary Heart Disease.

It's caused by a fatty build-up, on the walls of the arteries around the heart, the coronary arteries. It makes them narrower and restricts the blood flow to the heart muscles. The process is called atherosclerosis; a mouthful isn't it!

However, it is treatable and from what Mrs Edwards has told me, a few lifestyle changes such as what she eats; a low-fat vegetarian diet would certainly help as would her stress management.

Now, young lady, you keep an eye on her and makes sure she takes her aspirin and the other medication I've prescribed and also does what she's told. He stated with a grin. You can now take your Mother home."

It was such a relief for me, although considering the Specialists comment about stress management I was worried about my historical relationship with David and whether this had caused her any problems.

Chapter 24

I arose early and thinking about David, negatively, you understand, I decided to collect my jewellery. I rang his mobile phone; in fact, I rang several times. He didn't even bother to answer. The creep!

Stepping from the taxi, I asked the driver to wait while I collected something.

At the top of the stone steps were a group of people, three, in fact, a woman and two men, entering the house.

As I climbed the steps, one of the men asked me if he could help.

"No thanks, I've come to see David Wilson."

"Mr Wilson." He said, "Well if you do find him, please let me know where he is as he owes me two months' rent. Not only that, but before Mr Wilson left, he must've intentionally destroyed my carpet as it's now in tatters; these two people are his replacements for the flat!"

Thinking about that tattered old carpet, I wanted to laugh. The carpet was already in tatters when David moved in! Although realising David had left without even paying his rent told me what an absolute bastard David is! Perhaps another tale for Elsa to chew on, I considered.

Then again considering the past 24 hours, there was no way I could mention it to her, just in case poor Mum found out about it and in her dubious condition, it made her even worse.

With the Landlord's permission, I searched the flat for my jewellery. The flat was empty, no kitchen utensils, no furniture and as expected, the jewellery box nowhere to be seen!

The landlord looked at me directly as I started laughing; there were strips of carpet, each one cut approximately six inches wide. The carpet wasn't so much in tatters; it was shredded!

Penny answered her phone and wasn't surprised in the least to hear my tale of despair. She quickly changed the topic to tell me that AJ had left and there was a new manager in place.

"What you?" I asked.

"Unfortunately not; it's another stranger, a chap called Jos something or other. Anyway, there's a story behind all this; do you remember me telling you AJ's attitude had changed after you left?

Well, rumour has it that he'd been expecting a big promotion elsewhere and for the time being that was put to one side as after you left the business, he was trapped here as temporary manager.

The pay he received for the job here was apparently, much less than he would have received at what should have been his new role. Whatever he still managed to buy a beautiful house on the banks of the River Thames."

"Lucky him," I replied.

"As you know Alice, he was always in the store earlier than the other staff and was still here late at night when all had left for home. As the store manager, it was his responsibility to ensure the cash receipts were ready for collection by the Cash transit van each evening when it arrived to collect the day's takings.

AJ hadn't been expecting it, but an internal audit team turned up for a couple of days, and during those two days, the takings were recorded much higher than they were during previous weeks."

"OMG Penny, don't tell me he was stealing cash from the Company!"

"Wait a minute Alice. When the Auditors first confronted him, he told them he had already expected something was wrong and was investigating several employees who he suspected of being involved.

He also had a plausible explanation for the purchase of his new home.

He named the members of staff he suspected.

As you will understand, these staff members had no idea of these cash shortfalls and were amazed when the questioning started and then shocked when they realised they were suspects!

This investigation continued for a while, and I guess it was during this period that his whole approach changed, towards me and everybody else!"

"Please, Penny, tell me what happened?"

"Well, it soon became apparent that AJ was the guilty party, much to the relief of the innocent parties and from what I understand he is on a charge and awaiting trial."

"Would you believe it Penny, he seemed such a decent man!"

"Yes but I feel sorry for his wife and kids; their Thames side home's up for sale, presumably repossessed by the supermarket and his wife has left him and taken the children with her.

Anyway, the new boss appointed, Joss, was one of those internal auditors.

Oh well, what about you Alice, have you found another job yet?" Penny asked although I was still intrigued by her story.

"No, I haven't even started looking, but I suppose I must start soon. Money is tight, not just for me but the family and under the circumstances, I don't want Mum to start worrying about something else." I stated with concern.

"And how are you feeling in yourself, Alice?" Penny inquired.

"If I'm, to be honest Penny, with everything that's happened recently, I'm in a state of absolute and utter despair. I'm still spending a lot of my time just sitting in my bedroom and crying."

"Oh, bless you!" Penny earnestly replied. "Maybe we ought to have another weekend in Bournemouth." She concluded with a little hilarity, obviously trying to ease my pains.

I couldn't understand why, but her suggestion of another trip to Bournemouth made me think of the Caribbean holiday and how much I had been looking forward to it, and this made my depression even worse.

Penny was a great friend, but at this moment in time, the

only person I wanted to give me a cuddle and a kind word was my dear little sister.

The following morning I got my wish; as usual, Elsa knocked on my bedroom door.

"So how're things Sis?" she inquired.

Although I had previously decided not to tell her, my sorrows flooded out.

"The horrible slob had gone; he's moved out of his flat and not a word to me, I should've expected it!"

"He was a piece of trash, Sis, and believe me. You are better off without him."

As I had with Penny, I also told Elsa of my current desperation.

Giving me that soothing cuddle of hers, she said: "Look Sis I can't tell you I understand how you feel as I haven't suffered like you, but please, please talk to me if your desperation gets worse."

I thanked her, returned her cuddle and kissed her on the head. She was a few years younger than me but an understanding adult in every other way.

It was essential I found another job, but knowing how important it was, mentally, I didn't think I would be able to cope, whatever type of occupation it was. I knew I wouldn't be able to concentrate, and of course, I was always in tears.

Nobody would want to employ an emotional wreck like me!

Mum was recuperating upstairs, in her bedroom, and I thought, I must check how she is and whether she would like some tea and toast or whatever her choice.

At least thinking about or spending time caring for

Mum, my anxieties are, temporarily dismissed from my mind.

Mum did look much better after her worrying experience and time at St. Owen's Hospital. She was comfortably snoozing, although my entry woke her from her dreams.

"Oh, good afternoon, Alice, how are you."

"I'm good thanks, Mum, but it's not about me; it's about how you feel that matters. And, have you taken your medication?" I asked as though I was a hospital matron!

"I'm alright thank you Alice; would you please open the window for me as it feels a little stuffy in here."

Our white window frames were of an early seventies design, and now tricky to open at one attempt. The flow of fresh air was pleasant, certainly for Mum.

"Thank you, Alice. A cup of tea would also be nice."

After Mum's early struggles, she had now reached an age when she should have been enjoying life, but considering the changes Mum now needed to make to her lifestyle, I knew she wasn't enjoying it at all.

Elsa had also considered Mum's woes, as well as mine, although I didn't realise what she had in mind when joining us both in the bedroom.

"I know we don't have any savings, but I could get a part-time job, and I'll soon be old enough for a full time one. I can save enough and take you both on holiday somewhere nice."

The little treasure, she did care for us so much, such thoughts were always in her head, and indeed her heart.

It was such occasions as these which kept me on the straight and narrow path; while, at times, life was so mentally bad for me, and I just wanted all my worries to end.

In reality, there was Mum and Elsa, my guardian angel, to consider.

Whatever, I continued to suffer my horrendous depression for what seemed like months.

One storm swept evening; Elsa arrived home with a smile on her face.

"And what mischief have you been up to?" I suspiciously asked.

"Oh Sis, as though I'd get up to any mischief; anyway, I've got a job, a part-time one."

"Wow, go on then; tell me about it?" I asked with great interest.

"Well, as you know I was going to Shepherd's Supermarket for a few of our basic needs. There was this old man, who seemed to be struggling with his wheelchair on a Zebra-crossing; he had no gloves, and his hands were frozen. Also, he had difficulty turning the large wheels on his wheelchair.

Anyway, I pushed him back to his Care-home, in Church Street, not far from Shepherd's. The nurses or whatever they call them, thanked me and I guess, jokingly, one asked 'Do you want a job, we need people like you?'

I think they were surprised when I said yes and more so when they realised I was serious and not joking in return; they took me to see the woman in charge. She's called Mrs Warwick, and she was very friendly.

She asked me a few questions, and when I explained

about You and Me looking after Mum," she said: "Ok, we'll give you a try!"

"So what will you be doing at the Care-home?" I asked with interest.

"I will be wheeling the book trolley to their rooms and sometimes making them drinks. Also just chatting and keeping them company; to start with it will be three times a week, and if Mum says ok some weekends as well."

"Incidentally how much are they paying you?" I enquired.

"I know I should have asked Sis, but I didn't; I was just pleased to be offered such a pleasant job."

"That is fantastic news, Elsa, now go upstairs and tell Mum; she'll be happy for you, especially after such a kind effort helping the old man!"

Mum was happy with Elsa's news and had absolutely no objection to her working the hours, even at weekends.

Our excitement had barely diminished when there was a knock on our front door, and it was Penny. "So how's Jennifer after her unexpected trip to the Royal Berks?" She asked.

"Seemingly Ok," I replied.

Mysteriously, both Penny's arms were behind her back. "What are you doing?" I asked her. Suddenly she produced a large box of chocolates, and a beautify spray of flowers.

"These are for your Mum, and the box of Chocolates are for everyone to share. Anyway, how are you all."

"Well thanks, Penny, please take the Flowers upstairs to my Mum, and then I'll tell you all about my lovely sister, but thank you so much for your exceptionally kind thoughts Penny; It's typically you."

"Elsa eh? That sounds interesting, Alice, and I also have something to tell you."

Penny was pleased to hear my news about Elsa, and now I wanted to listen to whatever it was that Penny had to tell me.

Whatever Penny's news, it had to be amusing as she kept smiling at Elsa and me.

Chapter 25

After her release, the Hospital had supplied Mum with a wheelchair, and she now felt fit enough for me to take her out somewhere in the fresh air.

I wrapped her in a warm blanket and took another one, just in case she needed it.

Just from looking at her joyous face, I could tell she didn't care where we went, she was pleased to be away from her bedroom and out in the open air.

I'd heard of an exciting location called 'View Island' a nature reserve converted from an old derelict boatyard near Caversham Lock and thought it would be just what Mum would appreciate.

It didn't take me long, pushing her to the Island; it was beautiful, and there was a path that looped around the edge. I stopped by a secluded seat which overlooked the River, and Mum commented on the beautiful panorama, the pleasant and natural view of the trees and undergrowth on 'the Island' and also the sight of Caversham Bridge.

In the undergrowth were many old tree stumps, which somebody had artistically carved into the shape of faces. "The faces are so realistic Alice," Mum said, "and the

A Dose of Insulin

artists or carpenters; whatever they call themselves are so clever."

She talked about the waterfowl on the river and those that flew onto the island near us, and fluttered backwards and forwards from the river, obviously hoping we had food for them.

People walked past with their dogs, some walking sedately by their sides and others dragging their owners along behind them. A couple of the dog owners even stopped and pleasantly chatted to us about the weather, a British tradition, the different benefits of the Island and anything else that came to mind.

A pair of Magpies rested in a tree nearby; "Morning Mr Magpie, how's your wife and kids?" Mum said, explaining the expression was supposed to bring good luck; not that it had ever brought her any!

She then asked whether I would take her to the far end of the Island as there was something she would like to see.

Gently I pushed her to a bend in the pathway with a panoramic view of the River, the barges and boats, and of course, it's waterfront buildings.

She knowledgeably informed me that today, unlike the past, most were pleasure craft as opposed to working barges she used to watch years before, unloading their wares onto the Wharf.

"They were busy days, and the Dockers worked long hours and extremely hard either unloading by hand or using the cranes. A friend of mine married one of them, so I knew of the work they did, in all weathers and the long hours they worked.

They started their work very early before most people had even thought about getting up and then finishing late in the evening. And I don't think my friend's Man, ever had a day off work with illness. These days the kids seem to moan about the most straightforward tasks and even just getting out of bed." She said with a sarcastic smile on her face.

"See those red brick buildings, well that's where the Wharf used to be, and years ago my school chums and I used to go swimming near there, that is until Wally Peacock ruined it all; we all decided his Christian name was certainly most apt.

There was a massive oil slick which leaked from the old boatyard, and he decided to test his theory that he could float much easier on oil than water.

None of us could understand why he thought that, but he tried out his theory and swallowed a load of oily water when he sank and ended in hospital. Our parents subsequently banned us all from swimming in the Thames.

Look over there on the other side of the Bridge; that's a Riverside Park off Richfield Avenue, and I often sat there with some of the boys while they were fishing. They were such wonderful days."

It suddenly occurred to me that this was the same stretch of the Thames I viewed from David's flat, and I couldn't prevent my grief and rejection from returning with a vengeance.

At home, Mum told Elsa of her enjoyable outing and how it had brought back memories from years past, also just how grateful she was to me for taking the time to make sure she enjoyed herself.

It was clear that Elsa also appreciated the description of our day out and just how pleasant it had been for Mum. But the look on her face told me, she realised I'd also have been thinking about David and his flat.

That night, as I tucked Mum up in bed, checking she was comfortable and she had plenty of water on her bedside table, she took my hands in hers and said.

"Thank you for today Alice, you and Elsa are such special children, and I love you both so very much."

Downstairs Elsa, had made us both a night-time coffee. We sat at the Kitchen table, and I told her of Mum's comment. "Bless Her." She said. "Mum enjoyed herself, and you must take her out again soon. Let's make it a day when I can also come along; I'd like that."

"There are quite a few interesting options to choose from Elsa, Forbury Gardens, where they have a food market in the grounds of the old Abbey or if the weather's bad, Reading Museum. There would be plenty to interest her, and it would be inside, undercover." I suggested.

"And there are also pleasant riverside pubs; if it's a warm and pleasant day, we could eat and drink outside and watch the world travel past; I know Mum would like that, she loves watching the different boats," Elsa added.

"Yes and that idea wouldn't need a lot of planning and organisation, although you'd have to have lemonade as you're not quite old enough to have a proper drink!" I said with laughter.

Elsa noted my humour and commented accordingly that the day out, had been good for me as well as Mum.

"You seem a little more relaxed, and for the first time, for ages, Alice, you are thinking about something other than David.

And talking about Me and a trip with Mum to a riverside pub, Elsa commented, I'm so looking forward to my 18th Birthday and celebrating with a glass of wine, alongside the two most influential people in my life.

Incidentally, before I forget to tell you, a friend from the Care-home and I have joined a local badminton club."

"That will be nice for you; something different to keep you occupied. Right, Elsa, now I'm off to bed."

For a while I sat on my bed thinking of Mum and her on-going welfare and then of Elsa's comments; maybe I was turning the corner, although in many respects I didn't feel like I was. Perhaps I could at least start to seek a job opportunity of some kind.

Mum seemed a lot better, and I was sure, that between Elsa and me, we could manage any support she needed.

I bought a copy of the Chronicle and looked through the job section. None of the vacancies suited me.

Naturally, I did question myself whether or not it was a case of me still not feeling confident enough about almost anything after all.

That evening, I mentioned my attempted job search to Elsa.

"Well Sis, one of my friends at the Care-home is leaving for another job."

"What and you have a vacancy?" I rudely interrupted.

"No, but they've opened a new Boots shop nearby, and she's gone to work there; they are still looking for staff. If you like, on my way to work tomorrow I could show you where it is."

I checked with Mum that she would be ok and agreed to accompany Elsa the following morning.

"That's great Sis, said Elsa and please don't think I'm unpleasant when I say, you shouldn't mention to them, your recent bout of depression."

I fully understood Elsa's reasoning and thanked her accordingly.

"Now you tell me about your job Elsa and how it's going."

"It's excellent, and I enjoy talking to the patients, although I've been told not to call them Patients but Residents. They so enjoy their little chats, and Mrs Warwick has said I should think about signing on full time whenever it's possible."

My mobile phone rang, interrupting our conversation and it was Penny.

"Hi, Alice, how are you today?"

I told her about yesterday's outing with Mum and my discussion with Elsa about work.

"Fantastic, she said. Well, I've got something to tell you; Chris and I are going back to Bournemouth for a few days and we both wondered whether you might like to join us?"

"Oh, is that what you were going to tell me the other evening but we got so tied up in Elsa's news that you never mentioned it?"

Thanking her I explained that I needed to be close to Mum, so at this moment in time, it was a non-starter!

"Sounds like you and Chris are getting on," I said, also remembering that at one time, David and I even got on well!

"Fantastically well, Alice; he never complains about me going out shopping, and he helps me with, what most men call women's work," Was her satisfied reply.

"I have something else to tell you, he's asked me to move in with him; either that or we both find a place to live together."

"That's interesting. I said cautiously and where will you be looking?"

"Not too sure, as you know, it's so costly around Reading; still we'll see." She replied.

"Oh well, good luck Penny; have a great time in Bournemouth and tell me all about it when you get back home."

Chapter 26

The next morning I dressed smartly and accompanied Elsa to the newly established Boots store. Inside it was busy. I found a member of staff and explained I was seeking a job.

"Have you brought your Curriculum Vitae, your 'CV'?"

I didn't have a 'CV' and told her I would return with it tomorrow.

"Well, here's a business card and I would suggest before coming back to the shop, you send your 'CV' to the email address, printed on the back of this card and somebody will then reply with an appointment date."

Leaving the shop with a feeling of the utmost anxiety, I rushed home, explained the situation to Mum and asked whether I could use her PC.

I didn't have a PC and always used my mobile phone when I needed to contact friends.

Sitting down at the Kitchen table and having made myself and Mum a cup of tea, I realised I had no idea of a 'CV's' configuration, nor what I should write down. Penny would either be at work or preparing for her weekend away, so I didn't want to bother her.

I wasn't even going to think about asking Mum as I felt she currently had enough to deal with, so it would have to be Elsa, although her experience of writing such a document was limited; probably non-existent.

Apart from that, I wasn't too sure about how Mum's PC operated although I experimented a little and eventually got the hang of basic operations.

I decided to search the web and find anything about writing a CV. Some of the information appeared complicated, but I eventually found an article that listed most things in bullet points. Writing the 'CV' was much easier than I expected, especially for me, as I could take things slowly, a single bullet point at a time.

Of course, I'd only ever had the one job, and even then there wasn't much to tell, other than stacking shelves and helping customers. I could hardly say I was appointed as the Supermarket manager but resigned immediately after that!

The website article suggested that specific details of a person's experience would be much better for an applicant than a document that read more like a book.

That, of course, was great for me as I didn't have to overthink about what to say, only those actual responsibilities I had been given at the time.

I was still writing the document when Elsa arrived home. She checked what I had completed so far and said it looked Ok; although she did recommend a few changes at the same time acknowledging, as I'd guessed, she had no experience of writing such things.

Looking at the Boots business card, she then helped me to attach and send my 'CV' by email.

A Dose of Insulin

"You must keep checking Mum's PC as you never know when they might reply, although it certainly won't be tonight and also unlikely it will be first thing tomorrow.

I'd probably start looking from tomorrow lunchtime; I know it's Saturday, but Boots is open all weekend, so who knows when they might reply. Whatever, good luck Sis."

Elsa went upstairs to check on Mum, and I accompanied her. She appeared in a stable condition and then I explained about my 'CV' and I would be looking for a reply sometime from Saturday lunchtime.

"Oh, my goodness Saturday lunchtime, it's tomorrow - I have an appointment at St Olives hospital tomorrow morning at 10!" She exclaimed.

Instantaneously, Elsa and I shouted, "What tomorrow; why didn't you tell us?"

"I thought you knew I had an appointment, Alice, and if you'd forgotten I was going to get a Cab; I just didn't want to bother either of you."

"Oh bless you, Mum; Saturday morning?" I queried.

"Yes, I don't know why, but St Olives is now open on Saturdays," Mum replied.

"Well, I'm ordering a cab for tomorrow morning, and ordering it now," I said to Mum.

"And I'm coming with you both," Elsa stated.

"But aren't you working tomorrow, Elsa?" I queried.

"Yes, and I am going to phone them on the landline and explain I won't be in!"

Although it was a Saturday morning the Hospital was busy; we wheeled Mum to the Hemsworth Ward, booking her in at the Reception desk.

As usual, we waited well past Mum's appointment time of 10 am. Elsa kept telling Mum, what she should do and what she shouldn't, although one of her recommendations or should I say orders, was correct.

"When he asks you how you are Mum; tell him the truth. Do not tell him you feel better than you do!"

The tannoy announced Mum's name 'Mrs Edwards, room number eight.' A hospital porter wheeled her to the applicable room, Elsa only a footstep behind.

I didn't know what was happening, but it must have been a thorough examination as it was approximately an hour before the Porter wheeled her back to us in the wards reception area.

"You ok Mum?" was Elsa's first question.

"Yes, but I didn't see Mr Robertson. He was such a nice man. I just saw a normal doctor."

"And what did he say?" I asked.

"He said there was some improvement and also thought that our day out at the Island did me a lot of good; he's been there and said it was a superb location, especially for wheelchair users.

Anyway, I've still got to be careful with my diet and stop drinking full cream milk as it's got a lot of fat in it. Nevertheless, he's written everything down, so I don't forget. I've also got to try and lose some weight."

Mum wasn't what I would call overweight, just the additional burden that some people gain as they get older, but nothing substantial.

"Excellent, now let's get you home, Mum," I said Joyfully.

A Dose of Insulin

Elsa and I eased Mum onto her settee, and hopefully, I checked her PC, but as expected, there was no reply regarding my job application, and most likely, there would be none until next week, at the earliest.

"Right, Mum, you have a rest, and I'll make you a nice cup of tea." I made her tea, a little stronger than usual, as there was less milk and asked her to show me the examination details written down by the hospital Doctor.

Somewhat reluctantly, Mum handed them to me.

"Mum! He's said to reduce using or eating fatty products – such as chips! You're always eating them."

"I didn't mention that Alice; you both know how much I like chips. Life's not worth living without chips." She said with an understanding laugh.

"Please Mum; don't even joke about things like that," Elsa commented.

"And butter, you must cut that out completely; In future, it's low-fat margarine," I stated.

Overall, I felt most sympathetic.

"And where's my tea?" Elsa interrupted.

"On the table, you've only got to put some of your normal fatty milk into the mug!" I said with a laugh while looking at Mum and the expression of utter resignation on her face. Immediately I felt terrible for commenting about Elsa and her milk.

It was Wednesday when I received my reply from Boots, asking me to contact them to organise a suitable interview date.

Phoning Boots they were fully-booked on Thursday, and a 9.30 interview time, was arranged for the Friday morning.

I suddenly realised I hadn't contacted Penny to ask how her weekend in Bournemouth had gone. She hadn't contacted me either, and I began to feel concerned for her.

She eventually responded to my call after about a dozen rings and answered somewhat embarrassingly.

"What's the matter, Penny; you've been back from Bournemouth a few days now, and I haven't heard from you – is everything ok?"

"Oh, I'm so sorry, Alice, but something happened in Bournemouth, and I wasn't sure how to tell you because of your historical situation with David."

Puzzled, I asked, "What the hell are you talking about Penny?"

Penny had sensed what she was about to say and guessed that under the circumstances, maybe she shouldn't. She continued anyway.

"Chris has asked me to Marry him, and we're getting engaged."

I wanted to offer my congratulations, but I couldn't bring myself to say it; there was just silence. Penny was the first to break it.

"I knew I shouldn't have said anything, Alice, at least not at the moment!"

Penny and Chris, getting engaged, although happy news, this was just another upset for me, although I realised that Penny had done absolutely nothing wrong.

After all, she wasn't responsible for my unfortunate relationship with David, but it didn't alter how I felt about their decision. It just brought back sad memories for me as their happiness was the kind I should have encountered with David.

There was nothing more I could say before our phone call ended, knowing that once they were married, it was unlikely our conversations and contact would be anywhere near as frequent as they were now. In reality, our friendship would never be the same again.

A few hours later, Elsa arrived home, and I told her about my job interview at Boots.

"Well done Sis and it's not long to go; bet you'll get it!"

I then proceeded to tell her about my phone conversation with Penny and how distressed I was.

Elsa didn't reply immediately, but when she did, she said "Look, Sis, you're upsetting yourself much more than you need to.

Think about you and David; what if you had eventually married him, your own life would then have involved Penny much less than it does now. That's just the way it is! However, you have a real friendship, and they last forever!"

Elsa was right although I didn't want to accept it!

"Just a thought Elsa but when do you next have a day off work?" I asked.

"Next Wednesday, why?"

"I was thinking; we could take Mum out for a few hours,"

"Brilliant Sis, do you have anywhere in mind?" Elsa asked enthusiastically.

"Not at the moment but we can think about it or better still, have a chat with Mum a little closer to the day and find out where she'd like to go."

I had set my alarm for 5.30 am Friday, well in time to prepare for my 9.30 interview.

So the usual difficulty, what should I wear, should I be suited and booted or maybe smart casual; then I thought I'm applying for shop assistants role, not a management position.

Still, as always I liked to appear my very best. Therefore, I took my black suit from the wardrobe, a plain white blouse and my shiny black 'boots', if you'll excuse my unintentional pun, or maybe my black shoes would be more suitable.

I looked in the wardrobe mirror, and I have dressed appropriately, and then just as I was about to leave, I noticed with alarm, a large stain on my suit trousers.

I attempted to find the stain, and if possible, quickly remove it, if that was possible. I looked but couldn't find the mark. I removed my suit trousers for closer inspection. Fortunately, my trousers looked elegant, and there was no stain; it was a dirty mark on my wardrobe mirror. I sighed with relief.

Having time to spare, I read my 'CV' again, to familiarise myself with exactly what I had written.

I checked Mum was ok, and left the house in plenty of time, ensuring I wasn't late for the interview.

The interviewer thanked me for attending and asked the basic interview questions and a few more questions, arising from the details I had recorded in my 'CV'.

During that latter stage of my interview, the manager asked about my role at the supermarket and why I had left. This part was undoubtedly more thorough, and I answered as best I could.

My interview finished within about twenty minutes, and I asked whether there would be a round of subsequent Shortlist interviews.

"No, not for this particular position; in fact, there are several such vacancies, and there have been many more applicants than we expected. Everyone will be notified of the result in writing, hopefully within the next few days."

I had managed my interview much better than I thought possible and hoped signs of my recent depression hadn't been apparent and thereby ruined my chances.

Chapter 27

Discussing where Elsa and I would take Mum this coming Wednesday, we watched the long term TV weather forecast. Mum said Wednesday didn't look as though it would be pleasant.

Sunday looked to be so much better, and as Elsa was also available to accompany us that day, Sunday and our Thames-side pub outing was the unanimous choice.

There were a couple of other possibilities, but none of us was sure of the most appropriate decision, as we needed somewhere where they would accommodate Mum's wheelchair. Also, we needed someplace where it wouldn't be too crowded, noisy and perhaps even a little stressful for her.

Mum had enjoyed her trip to the Island, so she asked me whether I minded another visit.

"Wherever you'd like Mum; it's your choice."

I also suggested a pub, right on the edge of Caversham Bridge, which also served daytime meals. It was only a short walk from *View Island,* and we would combine the Island visit with something to eat in a nearby pub.

Chatting to Elsa that night, I mentioned that our choice

of a lunchtime meal was literally only a short distance from David's old flat and yet I had suggested the location without even thinking about it, or indeed David.

"Fantastic," she replied. "That tells me, you are finally recovering from the stress and trauma David created for you; you've discarded some of it and are now looking at the time to come. That's brilliant Sis.

In future, you don't date anybody until I've vetted them. All the bad ones' will find themselves on Caversham Bridge with a rope tied to their ankles and a concrete block on the other end." She chuckled aloud.

Once again. I could so easily picture Elsa, doing precisely that!

Sunday morning, we were all up, washed and dressed by 8 o'clock; breakfast was a reasonably quick event.

Pushing Mum to the Island, the weather, as forecast, was clement and much was happening around us to occupy her attention. As we reached the entrance, Mum suddenly asked us to stop.

With concern, Elsa asked, "Are you ok, Mum?".

"Yes thank you Elsa; I just want to try and walk along the path to my favourite spot on the corner over there." She pointed to the area we had both sat during our visit a few days ago when she had discussed with me, the memories of her early years.

We both helped Mum to her feet, and I held her by the arm as Elsa pushed her wheelchair.

For the first few yards, Mum walked slowly but with caution. "This is great," she said.

Still holding her arm, I then had to ask her to slow

down as her walking speed had increased a little, and either of us might have fallen.

Sitting on the Island's corner bench, the views looked as beautiful as they had previously.

Mum repeated the stories of her youth and her many memories to Elsa; the morning had flown past, and we insisted she sit in the wheelchair as we made our way to the riverside lunch destination.

Although the Dining room is crowded, with many people already eating, there was more than sufficient space around our reserved table for us all to sit comfortably and indeed Mum.

"Drink's ladies?" The waiter asked.

"I'll have a glass of white wine," said Mum.

"Wine! Like chips, alcohol was also on your Doctors list of prohibited items." I remarked.

Mum laughed, "Don't exaggerate Alice, his list didn't mention wine, and I know a glass will complete my lovely day, and I promise, it's only going to be one glass."

"You're right Mum, his list didn't mention wine but it quite clearly mentioned the word Alcohol!"

"Oh, that's just the difference between two words, Alice!" Mum replied with a smile on her face.

Whatever, neither Elsa nor me were going to deny her this little pleasure and accordingly ordered her drink.

We all worked our way down the menu, and fortunately, there were choices suitable for Mum, an exceptional selection of salad based meals.

As usual, Mum gratefully thanked Elsa and me for her outing although the thought that came to my mind was how well she had managed to walk around the Island and how this would have benefited her once again, both mentally and physically.

During the next few days, I also began to think about my upsetting conversation with Penny, about her and Chris. I hadn't spoken to her since that occasion and felt guilty about it; after all, she'd done nothing wrong.

I call her mobile phone, but there was no answer; I phoned a few more times but still no answer; I must have said something to upset her! Fortunately, ten minutes later, Penny called me back and explained why initially she couldn't answer my calls. She then asked how I was.

Everything seemed reasonable, and our conversation continued most naturally, although I was reluctant to tell her about my job application to Boots until I received the letter informing me whether or not I had been successful.

However, Penny told me she now disliked working at the Supermarket and had decided to look elsewhere.

She wasn't sure where to look or even the type of job she wanted.

Therefore, I changed my mind and, told her of my Boots application and how I was hopeful of being chosen as there were quite a few opportunities available.

"Penny, you could also apply to Boots. At the moment I'm waiting for a letter informing me of my result; I should receive their letter during the next few days."

Our conversation continued for quite some time, and thankfully it told me our special friendship would stay the way it had always been; as Elsa had said previously, *real friendship's last forever*! Looking back, I had to accept that our conversation and my eventual fallout, was unrealistic anyway!

After our phone call ended, I heard Mum's faint call from her room and rushed to her bedside.

She didn't look too good but said she was feeling alright and just wanted a glass of water as she felt thirsty and her water jug was empty.

Although she was resting in her bed, it did occur to me that perhaps her second trip to the Island had been a little too much for her. Whatever, I fetched her water jug partially filled and more manageable, and also a small glass of fresh orange juice.

"Alice, do you remember when my next check-up is due?"

"No, I'm not sure, Mum; are you sure you're ok?"

"Of course I am, now stop worrying about me Alice, and look after yourself. Mum replied. I'm only worried that I don't miss my next appointment."

"Alright, but you must tell me when you don't feel well," I stated.

"Of course I will, now for goodness sake Alice, stop worrying about me."

During the next few, days, I regularly checked her condition although there didn't appear to be any deterioration in her wellbeing and needless, to say I was most grateful.

There was a flap of the letterbox, and I rushed to the door to collect the mail; there was an official-looking envelope with my name on it and a Boots Chemist watermark printed on the top side of the envelope; I opened the letter with high expectation.

Reading the beginning of the first complimentary paragraph from Boots, I was pleased and assured of my successful application, that is until I reached one particular word, *but*!

Emotionally, I ripped the letter into pieces and threw them into the bin.

Penny was on her lunch break when I phoned her, explaining my Boots application had been unsuccessful.

"I'm not surprised, Alice. I took your advice, but Boots told me they had filled all the job vacancies."

That evening, Elsa's first question was; "Have you heard from Boots?"

"Yes, and it wasn't good news, anyway forget about me, I've got concerns about Mum, she hasn't seemed too good today, although as always she's making light of it."

Chapter 28

We discussed Mum and her condition for some while and exactly what Elsa and I needed to do about it. Elsa then looked me in the eyes and said, "I don't want you to think I'm treating Mum's condition as trivial Alice, but I have a few worries of my own. You know that sometimes I have accidentally overdosed on my insulin, well now, I'm recording everything I eat and drink in a book, also the amount of insulin I've taken."

"That's a great idea Elsa, and I guess it's working for you as I haven't noticed you suffering from Hypo's recently," I stated with pleasure.

"No, but now when I regularly check my blood sugar levels, they're continually high. For precaution's sake, each night I check my blood sugar, and even if it's at the level it should be, I still eat a little more to ensure my sugars are higher than they should be.

This supplementary food is so I don't suffer a Hypo when I'm sleeping as a result of the long reacting insulin which continues to work throughout the night, as that could be disastrous for me; imagine it, Sis, I'm unlikely to wake

A Dose of Insulin

up, and if nobody's around to wake me and help, it could be fatal.

I know that sounds a bit over the top, but it could happen, and that's why I eat extra at night; hence my increased blood sugar levels.

Anyway, this isn't acceptable either, as it demonstrates that my Diabetic control is actually out of control." Elsa said, apparently with a fair amount of agitation.

"As you know Alice I take two different types of insulin, and I think the long-lasting insulin might be causing my nighttime issues, anyway I did think about not using it, but apparently, this could have a detrimental effect on my kidneys, so I continue to take it."

"Shouldn't you be discussing this with the Doctors during your Diabetic check-ups? Why are you having these problems, Elsa?" I asked.

"I've no idea, Alice. This latest problem leaves me feeling lethargic, and at times I find myself falling asleep when I should be working; I'm worried about losing my job!"

"I wouldn't wait for your next Diabetic check-up; I'd make an immediate appointment to see our local Doc."

"Sis, I know I should, but whatever I do, seems to be wrong; too much insulin can leave me unconscious and too little makes me feel sluggish and sleepy. Whatever, I won't need sleeping tablets!" Elsa said with one of her enigmatic smiles.

I was left wondering just how serious everything was and realised I had both Mother and Elsa's health to worry me. But then again, as you would expect, I loved them both so dearly that I wasn't complaining.

In reality, I was there to assist them whenever they needed it. Mentally and physically!

The following morning I heard Mum calling Elsa and me from her bedroom. Obviously, she was feeling well enough to talk and talk quite loudly.

Climbing the stairs to her bedroom, I explained Elsa had left for work.

"Oh, sorry Alice I didn't realise how late it was anyway would you be kind enough to make me a cuppa and put some of those crumpets under the grill – that is if we have any left. Incidentally, I have something I want to say to you."

"What's that, Mum?"

"I'll tell you in a minute, Alice."

"Well, tell me now, Mum; don't leave me in suspense!"

"No Alice, if you don't mind, I'll tell you when you've made my tea and crumpets."

We had run out of crumpets, so I made Mum a couple of slices of brown toast with margarine spread lightly on top.

Carrying the toast and tea upstairs, I wondered what Mum had to tell me.

"Here's your tea and toast so now you can tell me what's so important?

"I don't know how to say this, but I've been thinking."

"Thinking Mum, and I thought you were going to have a rest," I said with a laugh. "Anyway, Mum, what about?"

"Alice, David isn't right for you; he never was."

I was amazed as Mum rarely criticised Elsa and me for decisions we'd made or had been going to make, no matter how stupid they were. 'We live and learn by our mistakes,' she was always telling us.

"Why not?" I asked with uncertainty.

"It's difficult to explain Alice, but from the beginning, I had my suspicions about him. It might have been the cheesy language he used when telling you how much he loved you or possibly because initially he promised you so much and nothing came of it.

Now and again I thought he might be interested in somebody else. He changed the smell of his aftershave and also his sudden changes of appearance when he was working. I thought it was likely to be somebody at work but then again nearly every evening, he was with you."

"I don't think he was interested in anyone else, Mum, but you are a smart and contemplative person."

"I'm not clever; these were things I regularly experienced when married to your slob of a Dad! Or maybe it's just a Mother's intuition; perhaps that protective feeling you have for your offspring. Whatever it was, I never believed he was the right man for you, Alice.

Especially that time he surprised you when he was waiting for you outside the Supermarket. You thought it was love. I thought it was because you had got the Manager's job and the money and perks to go with it! It was always about David, never both of you!

Would he have been waiting for you if somebody else had got the job?"

Looking back on my relationship with David, maybe Mum had this particular level of perception. Whatever I didn't believe she wasn't wrong!

Chapter 29

Also wondering how Penny was, I decided to give her a call.

"Hiya Penny, its Alice, how the devil are you? Have you and Chris managed to find a place to live together."

"Yep it's a flat, not far from here and hopefully, we will be moving in there, in two weeks when the existing occupants leave."

"Whereabouts?" I asked.

"Tilehurst, near where Chris and his mates used to live, and it's not far away, so you can come over when we've settled in."

"I hope you checked the carpet before you signed up," I said, smiling to myself and thinking of David.

"And what about your Job Penny, have you found somewhere else to work?"

"Nope, I'm still there. She frustratingly replied. I had to put it on the *back-burner* while we looked for somewhere to live as that's taken so much of our free time."

As we ended our conversation, I could hear a shuffling noise from Mum's bedroom; climbing the stairs and there she was attempting to change her sheets and bedcovers.

A Dose of Insulin

At the time, I said nothing and helped her to place the freshly aired covers on her bed. It was afterwards when the task was complete that I suggested. "Next time Mum, please let me know, and I will help you."

Without any warning, Mum started breathing heavily, and without any comment from me, she sat on her bed.

"On Mum, for goodness sake, you shouldn't do things like this, it's far too much for you."

"Yes, alright Alice, incidentally have you remembered Elsa's 18th Birthday, its next Saturday." She said.

I guessed she asked deliberately, to avert my attention from her needs. I hadn't forgotten this critical date, and during one of our conversations, I had already asked Elsa whether she had anything planned.

"Nothing special, she replied. I was thinking of inviting a few friends here for a drink, but I'm not sure Mum would cope with all the fuss. Anyway, I'd rather stick to my original plan of celebrating somewhere with just you and Mum."

"Oh, that's so nice of you Elsa, but you really should invite a few friends as well," I said believing that despite her honourable intentions, it might be a little boring for her as it would be her special day and with just Mum and Me it would be no different from usual.

"Well I could ask Tim, he's a friend that I play doubles with at the Badminton club; a nice guy and perhaps Gabriella, a pleasant Spanish girl from the Care-home. We call her Gabby. And you could also invite Penny and her boyfriend." Elsa suggested.

"Tim? You kept that one quiet Elsa; you haven't mentioned him before." I questioned with interest.

"No, he's just a friend. Nothing more, although time will tell." She continued with a beaming smile on her face.

"C'mon Elsa, tell me more."

"Honestly, there isn't more to tell." She said, closing further conversation about her 18th Birthday.

Friday night arrived, and I still wasn't sure about Elsa's intentions the following day.

"Elsa, so what's happening tomorrow?" I asked.

"Well, Gabby and Tim will be meeting me at our Thames-side pub. Is that location ok for you and Mum? Oh, and have you asked Penny?" Replied Elsa.

"It's ok for me, but I'm still waiting for Penny's phone call; I've left her a message, so hopefully she'll be calling me back, although your celebration is tomorrow; I'll send another text telling her where it is. What time are you planning?"

"Around 7 pm," Elsa replied.

Fortunately, I had already bought Elsa's card and present; the 18th Birthday card incorporated a sterling silver heart pendant, engraved, *Always my Sister. Forever my Friend.*

The present also included a Sterling Silver bracelet with an adjustable cord, a matching pair.

I was in the process of sending a text to Penny when my mobile theme tune, *You really got me*, by the Kinks, a sixties group, interrupted me. It was from Penny.

"Hiya Alice, sorry I messed your earlier call but what's happening?"

"Elsa's 18th Birthday; She's having a casual celebration tomorrow evening, starting at seven and has asked me to invite you and Chris, if you can make it."

"I'd love to, but Chris is out at the moment, so I'll ask him when he gets back; whatever, we've nothing planned tomorrow, well not that I know of and if he can't make it, tell Elsa I definitely won't miss it. Where's it going to be?"

Penny knew of the location and then asked me when I intended to visit her and Chris at their new flat, for a drink and a bite to eat.

"Sorry, Penny, but I was waiting for you to decide a suitable time and date and call me," I said with embarrassment.

"Oh, it was just a misunderstanding, Alice, anyway, I'll chat with Chris, sort out a suitable date and let you know tomorrow when we meet up for Elsa's get together."

"Anyway, how's it going with you and Chris?" I asked with interest.

"Great she replied, in fact, with our Landlords permission, he's just built a beautiful shower room, big enough for us both to shower at the same time!" Penny said with a laugh. "It's only taken him and a mate, a couple of days; that's why he's out at the moment, trying to find something he needs to complete the work."

"Sounds like fun Penny," I said, imagining them scrubbing each other's backs.

Penny laughed and then said, "I bet Elsa's looking forward to her big day tomorrow."

"Yep, she certainly is, and I think she might have met a chap she likes, I think Elsa's being secretive about it but his name's Tim, and he'll also be there tomorrow night so we'll have to watch their body language." I giggled.

Chapter 30

The morning arrived, and Elsa was the first one of us to arise. Mum had also decided to make her way downstairs, and the three of us sat in the sitting room.

Mum and I, wished Elsa many happy returns of the day and passed her our Birthday cards and presents.

Mum hadn't known what to buy her for this particular day, her 18th, and on Mum's behalf, I had purchased a Pandora love knot ring, something Elsa could wear for life and also remember her lovely Mum.

Elsa opened her cards and presents and was genuinely delighted with everything.

"Thank you both so much; they're brilliant presents. All I need now is a Safe to lock it all in." She commented with her usual humour.

Later that afternoon, we all prepared our clothing, ready for the evening out.

For once Elsa made no comical remarks about my smart dress code although I did notice that she had dressed like an absolute goddess, in a long black dress, pink blouse and pink cardigan and finished it all off with the jewellery we had bought her. She looked stunning.

It was only a short walk to the Pub, but she looked impeccable, so I dialled for a cab. Also, I didn't want Mum to overdo it and possibly have to leave the celebration earlier than she had intended.

The chosen few were already waiting for us, holding an 18th birthday banner between them and cheering Elsa as we entered the Pub.

I was extremely pleased that both Penny and Chris had managed to attend, although I was more interested in meeting Tim. Elsa's, *He's just a friend.*

Penny and Chris greeted me and the three of us went over and talked to Tim and Gabby. To introduce ourselves you will understand!

Mum was resting at the table; everyone sat down so she wouldn't feel excluded. Then two bottles of champagne were ordered.

Chris asked us all to stand, except for Mum, whom he suggested should stay seated. He raised a toast to Elsa.

The atmosphere was most friendly, that is for the first 30 minutes or so when Tim cried aloud "Oh no!"

A young girl, probably about Elsa's age, although much bigger strode purposefully towards our table.

Facing Tim, she said, "So this is the fucking scab!" Turned to Elsa and grabbed hold of her hair and continued her foul-mouthed rant "You ditched me for this piece of shit. And then facing Elsa, I'm warning you to keep your fucking hands off him!"

Chris then grabbed her arm, and with a struggle, removed her hand from the grip she held on Elsa's hair.

"Look this is a special day, and you're ruining it for us all, now sod off!"

The girl lashed out with her feet and violently kicked the chair where Mum was sitting.

Mum attempted to hold on but didn't have the strength and toppled to the floor.

Gabby, immediately put her glass down and assisted Mum to her feet, and as best she could.made sure she was ok. Elsa's friend continued to talk to Mum, keeping her occupied and attempting to take her mind off the disturbing event.

Although visibly shaken, fortunately, she didn't appear to be physically injured; this violent disturbance had unnerved her considerably.

A member of staff took hold of the woman, who still screamed verbal abuse at Tim and Elsa and even ignored the bartender's threats.

He threatened to call the Police, as he physically bundled her outside.

Whatever Mum, as she always did, refused to accept anything at all was wrong with her!

Several broken champagne glasses are swept up and carefully removed from the table and the surrounding floor space, the table wiped over, and order eventually restored.

Penny whispered in my ear "We don't need to watch anybody's body language. I think that little episode told us all we need to know!"

Tim apologised to all, explaining that the woman, was his ex-girlfriend; he had recently finished with as the result of similar instances whenever they were out, and he spoke to, or even looked at another woman.

I agreed and realised that at the very first opportunity, I must talk to Elsa honestly about her friendship with Tim, if only for her safety. That woman was an absolute imbecile and could, without doubt, be somewhat dangerous.

Eventually, the evening continued in a manner more harmonious, although I thought Elsa's special day had been, irreversibly ruined.

Elsa eventually managed to thank the Spanish workmate, Gabby caring for Mum. Her command of the English language was exceptional, although she explained this was because she was born in Britain! Whatever she was a delightful young woman and spent the remainder of her evening, making sure Mum was ok after the unexpected upset.

Penny lightened my mood by telling me about her time with Chris, their flat, their newly built shower room and how much her life had improved since meeting him.

I'm sure I missed a few details, although that wasn't important.

"Oh, before I forget Chris and I would like to see you at our place this coming Saturday, say anytime from 3 pm if that's ok with you Alice. Anything, in particular, you'd like for dinner?" Penny asked.

"No, thanks," I replied.

"Ok, put the time and date in your diary, now!" Penny said with a sense of authority.

I checked again that Mum was Ok and then Elsa. "How's your head, Elsa? Your hair's a little dishevelled, but at least that vile woman didn't hit you with anything; like a handy Champagne bottle," I said laughing, although, in reality, it wasn't a laughing matter.

"I'm ok, thanks Sis, but I'm so pleased she didn't manage to get hold of the lovely jewellery you and Mum bought me."

During the short taxi journey home, I apologised to Elsa for her upsetting evening.

"Why are you apologising? It wasn't your fault Sis, anyway it turned out great, and fortunately, you're ok Mum!" She said as she looked at Mum and sympathetically stroked her hand.

"Turned out great!" I questioned Elsa with absolute amazement. "What do you mean great?"

"Not now, I'll tell you when we get home, Alice."

Immediately we stepped inside; I asked: "Ok Elsa, so what exactly was great!"

"Well Tim said to me that although we aren't going out together, his Ex, obviously thought we were, so we might as well do it!"

"Do what exactly?" I asked.

"Date each other. As I had already told you Tim was just a friend!" She replied.

Mum took the words out of my mouth saying "But Elsa, what about that idiotic woman; what if she finds out?"

"Don't worry about her Mum, believe you me, if she tries anything like that again; I'm prepared!"

It was the sort of reaction I would have expected from Elsa when anybody upset her, but like Mum, I too was concerned; for Tim's ex that is!

Chapter 31

Considering everything that had happened recently, the next few days were reasonably quiet, and now and then Elsa would discuss the time she'd spent with Tim, although one night she was extremely flustered.

"Tim and I met up for lunch and Fiona Brotherton, his Ex turned up and started on me again."

"How did she know you'd be there?" I asked with suspicion.

"That's exactly, what I asked Tim, and he said it's where he and Fiona used to meet for lunch."

"I'd suggest you find somewhere a little safer; somewhere Fiona's not been before," I recommended.

As I approached Penny's front door, it was just past 3 pm, and I could already smell a gorgeous aroma drifting from the flat; obviously, Penny was cooking something exceptionally pleasing for Dinner.

"Something smells good Penny," I said.

"It's a Vietnamese recipe I found in a magazine and thought I'd give it a go; just hope you like it, Alice."

"Sure I will, Penny. Oh hi Chris," I said as he came into

the kitchen. "Let's have a look at your shower; I didn't know you were a handyman."

The result looked most professional, and the showerhead was enormous a welcome treat on a cold day; he'd even thought of installing a hinged plastic seat for a more relaxing shower.

"That's Bournemouth, isn't it?" I asked when seeing a framed photograph of a Pier, hanging in the small hallway alongside the shower room.

Penny replied, "Yes, that's Bournemouth Pier, Chris had one of his photos enlarged and then framed; he said it was to remind us both of where we first met."

"That's so romantic Penny," I commented.

Penny then showed me around the flat before sitting me down at the table and opening a bottle of my favourite wine.

"So how's Elsa getting on after that unbelievable upset on her Birthday?" Penny asked.

"Well that's a story I have to tell you Penny; after that particular evening, quite genuinely she wasn't dating Tim, but she is now. We also know his Ex is called Fiona, and the bitch is still following them both."

"OMG, Chris replied. She needs sorting; the fucking head case!"

"Anyway Alice, have you seen any tasty men you might consider dating?" Penny asked.

"Nope, our roles have now reversed Penny, you have this gorgeous man beside you, and it's me looking for somebody decent. At least I now feel a little more confident, of at least meeting up with some guy for a drink."

"That's brilliant Alice; now Chris, are you going to tell her or am I?"

"Tell me what?" I asked, not having the remotest idea.

"Chris and I are getting engaged, and the date for our engagement party is going to be in three months; on the Saturday of that particular weekend.

You and your Mum will be receiving an official invite shortly and of course Elsa and Tim, that is, if Elsa is still dating him at the time."

"By the way, did you see a new Ford car downstairs, well that's Chris's, and he's going to drive you home tonight," Penny said proudly.

"That's great, thanks, but you are renting an expensive flat in Reading, and now you buy a new car! Exactly what does he do for living, rob banks?"

"Ha, bloody ha, you know he's an accountant Alice."

"Well, that's close enough," I said with a laugh but of course, without intended insult.

"No, we don't own the car Alice, it's a company car."

As the evening moved on, I realised what a pleasant guy, Chris was; everything Penny had told me about him, how delightful, how caring, how thoughtful, it was all true.

How lucky she was and how fortunate the two of them had kept in touch.

Monday night, I was shocked when Elsa arrived home, later than usual.

She had a black eye, and her face was severely scratched, and obviously, her mouth and nose had been bleeding as there were bloodstains on her blouse and a damaged top lip.

"What the bloody hell happened to you?" I asked.

"The Badminton Club; it was that fucking woman again. After Tim and I had finished playing, I had a shower in the ladies shower room.

I turned around to pick up my towel from the hanger and saw Fiona, his Ex and some of her cronies entering the room. They beat the crap outa me!" Elsa said in absolute exasperation.

"Didn't the staff do anything to stop them?" I asked with concern.

"No, the bitch and her friends finished what they had started, while other Club members just looked on, and then they left. However, after the event, the other people did help me and made sure I was ok."

"Didn't you call the Police?"

"Cmon Sis, you know we don't do things like that, it's unheard of; we sort our own problems!"

Without thinking, I mentioned to Elsa, that previously she had said *Next time I'll be ready for her!*

With feeling Elsa replied "Shit Sis, there was a gang of them, what did you expect me to do?

Whatever, I'm not going to put my life on hold for that slut; honestly, that was the last time that shit-bag is going to get away with it. And this time I do mean it!"

"Well I'm just pleased you're not injured any worse than you are Elsa; now go and clean yourself up, you don't want Mum to see you looking like that, do you?"

Chapter 32

As promised, we received our invitations to Penny and Chris's engagement party. I explained to Elsa that as she could see, her invite was also to Tim, but clarified that if she was no longer seeing him, she could bring somebody else along.

"Why shouldn't I be with Tim she said, we're getting on so well, and he's a fab sorta guy!"

"It was just Penny's thoughtful comment Elsa; you know, just in case" I explained.

During the next few weeks, mentally Mum was fine, and to a degree, she was now actively spending more time downstairs instead of laying in her bed.

Fortunately, it appeared her health was improving.

When she told me, she fancied a walk around Reading Market place as not only would the stroll do her good, but she missed her shopping days. Especially since Elsa and I had taken over the chore, I was even happier for her.

I didn't want to keep her from this outing, any longer than I had to, so the following day was agreed. There were a couple of markets in this region of Reading, but we decided on Chow Friday Street food market, situated on Market Place.

The Market was busy, with people bustling backwards and forwards, a great selection of fruit stalls and one or two people hawking things like watches and jewellery from inside large suitcases.

Mum asked me to stop at a particular stall as she said it looked good as the different fruits were so well presented in their different colours. There was even a selection of exotic fruits.

She asked what I'd like, but before I could answer, immediately, she ordered half a pound of red cherries, a large brightly coloured Galia Melon and three large bunches of Banana.

"Bananas are good for you!" She said, handing over the cash from her purse and asking me to hold the carrier bag.

Strolling around the market place, I noticed one of the suitcase guys, not with fruit but with women's wares, and something I found of particular interest. I waited until Mum's attention was distracted and bought one of the products and secretly slipped it into the pocket of my fake Levi jeans.

We'd travelled to the Market by Cab and had been walking around for what must have been at least a couple of hours. I marvelled at Mum's incredible ability to walk as much as she had.

"Would you like to find somewhere to sit down and have a cup of coffee?" I asked her.

"No thank you, Alice, I think I've had enough, so let's

call the Cab and have a coffee at home; it'll also be much cheaper." She said with a smile.

When ordering the Cab I was told it would be with us in 10 minutes, checking my watch it should have arrived by approximately ten to three, but it was now a quarter past three!

Mum, bless her, was now looking most uneasy and I was starting to panic when the Cab finally arrived. The driver was one of Mum's favourite drivers as he would always chat amiably no matter how stressful his day might have been.

"Sorry I'm late, he said, but I was driving from a drop off near the Madejski Stadium, and the traffic was horrendous."

Mum understood his plausible explanation and commenced to tell him about her Market visit.

She chatted away with the driver, who she later told me was called Jack.

He said to Mum that despite the traffic jams and customer's who complained about such circumstances, his job was most satisfying because of charming customers like Mum!

"After all, there's not much point in blaming the driver as we can't do much about traffic jams!" Jack stated with frustration.

Jack continued to tell us how, mostly, he could choose his working hours, and he did enjoy his vocation so very much.

His comment, once again, started me thinking about my livelihood and currently my total lack of work.

I interrupted their conversation and told Mum, I knew I

wasn't contributing financially to the household costs, but I might try the market place.

"They always look so busy, and you never know, somebody just might be hiring."

"It'll be hard work young lady as usually they only hire people to help them put up their stalls and take them down again; at least that's what I remember when I worked the market kiosks.

It's always early, unrealistic start times, and you don't get paid much for your time and effort."

Thanking our driver, and despite his comments, I didn't dismiss the idea out of hand. After all, whatever the pay, it would be much more than my current income; absolute zero! And I also felt guilty that it was only my dear sister Elsa, bringing in the cash.

As with Mum's previous trip outdoors, she had made a great effort, although it was apparent her energy had been somewhat depleted, especially as she asked me to help her upstairs to her bedroom; something she rarely did. She didn't want a coffee, after all, just a well-earned nap.

Chapter 33

Later that evening, Elsa returned home, and this time with Gabby, who wanted to say hello to Mum; Gabby stayed for an hour before leaving for home. I then happily explained our day's events, "Well Mum and I had another great time at the Market Place, you know Chow Friday Market and she's bought loadsa fruit and a year's supply of Bananas!" I joked.

Elsa was pleased and asked whether we had bought anything of interest; apart from the complete fruit stall.

"Yes, something exciting," I replied, "But I'll tell you about it when Mum's returned to bed."

"Mmmm, now you've got me intrigued?" Elsa said with excitement.

Mum left us to ourselves, going back to her bedroom much earlier than usual.

While we were in town, Mum had worn herself out. Even her late afternoon nap hadn't helped her recover from her exhaustion.

"Right Sis, now tell me what's so very interesting that you couldn't tell me in front of Mum?"

I removed the article from my Jean's pocket where it had

remained since I bought it, and let it drop onto the kitchen table, which it did with a resounding thud!

Mystified, Elsa said, "What the hell's that?"

"Well, apparently it's called a Monkey Fist; at least that's what the salesman told me. It's a key chain with a large steel ball wrapped inside of a leather pouch and used for self-defence.

I was thinking of that damn woman and of course her thuggish mates. Tim's ex, what's her name? Fiona. I asked. Well, this is for you Elsa!"

"It's brilliant Alice; it will fit in my handbag so that I can carry it around with me, just in case I might need it; thanks again." Said Elsa.

Chapter 34

A couple of days passed, and Mum had finally recovered from her active day at the market although she was still asleep in her bedroom when Elsa arrived home just after midday; today had been early working hours. "Had another tough day?" I asked her.

"Yep." She hesitantly replied.

"Because I've been watching over Mum and keeping her company, we've prepared nothing for Dinner; however, there are a few microwave meals in the fridge."

"Thanks but I'm not that hungry, I'll have a sandwich a little later," Elsa replied.

She then switched the Television on and selected Meridian news, which she watched in silence, as she asked me not to interrupt the programme.

Strange I thought as Elsa's usually's most vibrant and since arriving home she'd said almost nothing. She also had the TV on full blast as well as one of the local radio stations, Heart. She was listening to both simultaneously.

How unusual, what was it she wanted to hear about; yes, it was something on the news. "What are you listening for?" I asked her.

"Nothing important; I just want to hear what's happening locally."

"What about?" I asked again.

When Elsa wasn't in the front room or the kitchen, she was doing something in her bedroom; wherever she was, she deliberately kept her distance and avoided answering any more of my questions. The situation was undoubtedly role reversal.

Unusual for Elsa as she is the queen of questions and answers.

It was nearly 5 pm when I had my answer; a loud knock on the front door and unusually Elsa didn't rush to answer it.

I opened the front door, and there were two police officers, a man and women.

"Elsa Edwards?" the Male Sergeant questioned.

"No, she's indoors," I replied suspiciously.

"May we please come in?"

I led them into our sitting room where Elsa was sitting on the settee, obviously expecting the visit but for what reason I had absolutely no idea.

"Elsa Edwards?" he asked.

Elsa acknowledged.

"We would like you to accompany us to Reading Police Station."

The less I knew, the greater my worry increased. What had Elsa done; was she involved in something illegal?

Without asking either of the Police Officers why, she agreed to accompany them, walked outside and climbed

A Dose of Insulin

into the rear of the vehicle beside the female officer. Elsa knew why she was going to the Police Station!

With extreme puzzlement and considerable worry, I explained to Elsa that I would check Mum was ok and then follow on.

Mum awoke from the disturbance and asked me what was happening.

I was stressed, and the last thing I wanted to do was make Mum worse. Before I said anything to her, I had to know what this was all about.

"Elsa's had to return to work as there's some problem or other. Nothing to worry about Mum." I said, knowing that sooner or later, I would have to tell her the truth.

I couldn't leave Mum by herself, so before leaving for the Police Station, I phoned Penny.

Penny was surprised. "Police Station? What the hell's she done?"

"No Idea Penny but I'll let you know when I find out."

"Do you want me to come to the Police Station with you, Alice?"

"It's very kind of you Penny, but although I have no idea what this is about, I feel Elsa would be happier if it were only me around."

"I understand Alice, Hell, what about your Mum?"

"That's the other reason I'm calling you Penny; I've told her Elsa's had to return to work. Until I know what's happening with Elsa, I don't want to alarm Mum.

Anyway, I don't know how serious this is and when Elsa and I will be home. Would you be kind enough to pop round and make sure she's ok while I'm at the Police Station; poor Mum, this is the sort of stress she could do without!"

"No matter what Alice, I'll be there in a few minutes."

Mum was resting in her bed and true to her word, Penny arrived.

"How are you, Mrs Edwards?"

"I'm fine, thank you, Penny, but I'm not sure about Elsa there seems to be a problem of some sort."

"So I understand; I had agreed to meet up with Alice, but now she's going to help Elsa with something at her work. Alice said she doesn't need my help, but I'm going to wait here just in case she does!"

"Oh that's so kind of you, Penny; anyway we can have a nice chat while she's gone."

Although I'd lived in the Reading area all of my life, I'd never had a reason to visit the Police Station; it was a most formidable building.

Inside I approached the counter and told them I was Elsa Edwards older sister Alice.

He checked a logbook and told me she was currently in the process of being questioned. I was requested to sit down and wait.

Without another thought, I realised it would be tough to sit down and wait when I had no idea what this was all about.

"Please tell me what's happening?" I asked with increased concern.

"Sorry, Maam but I'm the desk officer for the day and don't have such details to hand; if you'd be kind enough to sit quietly, I'm sure it won't be long before you know."

People walked in and out of the building although, apart from those dressed in Police uniform, it wasn't clear whether they were Police Station officials, Solicitors, Defendants or perhaps like me, relatives or friends of the accused.

After I had been waiting for about an hour, a woman stopped at the desk in front of me and asked for her belongings.

"My names Fiona Brotherton," the woman said.

Immediately I recognised the name and now had a good idea why Elsa was here; it was Tim's Ex.

I also recognised her from Elsa's 18th Birthday party when she created uproar; she had unkempt blonde hair that was certainly dyed. Her jeans jacket was torn and ragged, and she looked an absolute mess.

She was requested to sign a receipt for her property and possibly something else.

As she walked away from the counter, she glanced in my direction with a look of hatred, possibly even recalling me from the day of Elsa's 18th birthday celebration.

I was of a mind to follow her and ask about Elsa and what was happening, although I decided against it, as I didn't want to end up in a cell alongside Elsa!

Had Elsa been charged with something; if so, what? While considering any number of options, I dozed off to sleep.

A gentle prod in the side awoke me.

"Wake up Sis."

To my relief, it was Elsa.

"Oh Elsa, what's happening?" I asked.

"I'll explain when we get outside," Elsa replied seemingly with a great deal of relief.

"Ok now tell me what this is all about?" I questioned with impatient interest.

"Well, I was walking down Archway Road, on my way home from an early shift at work, when that bitch, Brotherton attacked me from behind; she'd been following me.

She pulled me to the ground by my hair and then started kicking me.

Somehow I managed to get up and fortunately I was still hanging onto my handbag and pulled out the *Monkey bar* you bought me.

Without hesitation, I hit her with it a few times, and I hit her hard; you should have seen the alarm on her face! It was a great feeling, finally getting my own back!"

"OMG. I said And how did the Police become involved?"

"A crowd had gathered around us and somebody, possibly a shopkeeper, broke up our scuffle and told us he'd called them.

I thought, oh Shit, walked a good few yards before dumping the *Monkey bar* in a roadside Skip and dashed home.

That's why I was listening to the news, in case there was anything about our scuffle.

The Police must have arrived after I'd left and I guess Brotherton had given them my address, although I've no idea how she knew it.

Anyway, at the Police Station, we were questioned separately. I explained how she had been harassing me recently; gave them details of where and when and the various witnesses, like at the restaurant and the Badminton club.

I didn't know the names of these witnesses, but they must have checked with the owners or staff of these places to verify what I'd told them was correct. And yes, I explained what had happened outside the shop in Archway Road when she attacked me from behind and confirmed I was only attempting to protect myself."

I wanted to interrupt, but I could tell there was much more Elsa wanted to say.

"She told them I'd hit her with something heavy and hard and when the Police questioned me about it, I just said it was my fists and feet. They hadn't found the *Monkey bar*, or so I had hoped.

Anyway, to cut a long story short, Brotherton said she'd drop any charges against me if I decided to do the same for her. She knew I had a list of complaints against her.

With that, I was cautioned and warned against causing any more such disturbances in public places, and I guess Brotherton would also have received a similar warning."

"You're so lucky Elsa; now if you don't mind, I'm going to call Penny and let her know you're ok."

Chapter 35

At home, Penny gave Elsa and I a cuddle. We chatted briefly about Elsa and then Mum, who she said had been ok and reasonably talkative until she nodded off to sleep.

Upstairs, Mum appeared to be fast asleep. Tugging her arm, she thankfully responded and confirmed she was feeling ok. She asked me what was happening at the Care home, and I was again economical with the truth saying everything was now ok.

It wasn't long before Tim arrived, although Elsa was surprised as she hadn't called him!

Knowing Tim and Penny were downstairs, I apologised for disturbing Mum and recommended she try to get back to sleep.

Downstairs, Elsa, Tim and Penny were talking about the days' events. I made hot drinks for everyone and a cup of tea for Mum, which I took back upstairs, just in case she was still awake and wanted something to drink.

I could hear a loud argument developing.

It was Tim and Penny, Downstair again, I asked them, "What's the problem?"

Penny was the first to reply, "Elsa told us what had

happened and how that fucking bully, Brotherton had attacked her again and how she defended herself, with the thing you'd bought her so she could protect herself; lucky that you did!

Anyway, Tim called her stupid for reacting the way she did and then it started!" Penny reported.

Tim intervened, "I was trying to explain to Elsa that she could have been charged, at least for possessing an offensive weapon!

She would have been much better to have run off; escape is always the best option in these situations."

"What? Until she finds me again and beat's the living crap out of me as she and her friends did after we played badminton? Are you joking Tim?"

"Well then, you must be more strategically aware Elsa, keep an eye on who's around you and what's happening."

At this point, Penny butted into their conversation, "So what you're saying Tim, is that Elsa's continually attacked by this sodding lunatic, she defends herself, and she's the one in the wrong!"

"Mind your fucking business Penny, this has sweet bugger all, to do with you!" Tim shouted in reply.

Penny was about to say something, which I guessed, would not have been in Tim's best interest, when Elsa interrupted them both.

"Stop everyone. I get it, Tim, it is all my fault, I'm the one to blame, and there's no support whatsoever for me.

Ok, you and me, we're finished. That's it, and I do mean finished now get out!"

Tim attempted to reply but was stopped dead in his tracks when Elsa continued again.

"Being you're current girlfriend is just too much trouble and on several occasions, it had put me in the sort of danger I've never experienced before I met you. That's it, now go!"

Mum had heard the commotion and struggled downstairs, "What's going on?" She asked with concern.

"Nothing Mum, I answered, as I said earlier it's just something about Elsa's work,"

With that, Mum held her chest, groaned and sat on the bottom step.

"I need to sit down." She said.

I retrieved the mobile from my pocket and Mum said she was ok and not to call the Doctor.

"Mum something's wrong so please don't complain, but I'm calling Doctor McArthur." Penny and I helped Mum from the bottom step of the stairs and assisted her to the settee where I knew she'd be far more comfortable.

By the time McArthur arrived, Mum seemed much more relaxed and was breathing normally.

He asked us all to leave the room and give him some privacy with Mum.

Walking into the Kitchen, some ten minutes later, he explained he had carried out a few relevant tests, and she was, much to our enormous relief, ok!

He also provided additional advice on how to care for her. Once again, he discussed the essential matter of avoiding unnecessary stress.

"I'm so pleased your Mum's ok Alice; she must have heard us arguing and it upset her," Penny suggested.

A Dose of Insulin

Looking at Elsa, who now appeared even more traumatised, I asked her how she was.

"I'm ok thanks, Sis, right now, you think about Mum, not me and make sure she is ok! At least Tim's gone so there shouldn't be any repeat." Elsa said.

I thanked Penny gratefully for her much appreciated intervention, and then Elsa and I assisted Mum back to her bedroom.

Penny had left when we returned downstairs, and our conversation about the overall event was interrupted by a knock on the front door.

It was Jack, Mums favourite cab driver.

Puzzled I asked, "Has Mum ordered a cab?"

"No, he replied, it's you I've come to see Alice."

Puzzled, I invited him inside and asked how I could help.

"Recently I remember you were talking about seeking a job in the Market, well our firm's looking for another switchboard operator, you know, to take punter's calls and communicate with the drivers, and I thought of you.

The money's not great, but it's certainly a lot more than you'd earn in the Market place."

"Thank you kindly," I said with genuine gratitude. "What do I have to do now?"

"Come down and see the boss as soon as you can, at the moment I don't think anybody else has applied; he'll give you some headphones and a microphone and try you out, and if all's ok, it's likely the job's yours.

As you know, we get some real mutton heads for

passengers, but I know you'll manage them without too much trouble." He finished with confidence.

"Can I come down tomorrow?" I asked.

"That's fine. I'll tell the boss, about 10 am as he's always at work by then; is that ok Alice?"

After Jack's departure, Elsa entered the Kitchen, where I was making myself another drink.

"That sounded great Sis." She exclaimed.

"Possibly, but you must've been listening in the background, you nosey little git!"

"Well, you know nothing gets past me," Elsa said with her usual giggle.

"Yep, tell me about it! Anyway, I know you said you were ok after the bust-up with Tim, but how are you feeling, and I mean honestly?"

"I know, as always you have my best interests at heart, but I'm pretty upset and don't want to talk about it; well certainly not at the moment Sis," Elsa responded.

I could see the upset and emotion in her eyes so backed off from discussing the event any further.

My opportunity at the Cab company now took precedence over anything else, apart from Mum's wellbeing that is.

Fortunately, in preparation, I didn't have to think about much other than whether I could manage a switchboard; it couldn't be that difficult!

Checking the business card Jack had given me, I opened our A-Z of Reading streets. Jack was correct; the walk was a short one, between five and ten minutes.

I was up earlier than I needed and ready in plenty of time to meet up with the owner of the Cab company, Cabs4U.

A Dose of Insulin

It was warm, and the sun was shining brightly; a perfect day, I considered, just what could go wrong this time.

The Cab office is outside a line of shops in Milestone way, and there were two cars, an estate and another large vehicle like the one Jack often used, lined up outside with the Companies name emblazoned clearly on the side of the respective cars.

"Mr Roberts?" I asked. "No, he's out the back making himself a drink, can I ask who wants him?"

"Its, Alice Edwards."

A man appeared from the back room. "You're the young lady Jack recommended for the switchboard job," he stated, "I'm Mr Roberts, but everyone just calls me Steve."

He was a kindly looking man, not much taller than me but dressed smartly in his casual clothing. He was bald and spoke with a soothing voice; not really what I had in mind, although I suppose I didn't know what to expect, only that Jack had said he was a great boss.

Steve asked a few questions, such as whether or not I knew the different types of vehicles and which might be suitable for invalids or larger families. I answered honestly and said I had absolutely no idea.

He took me to the windowless backroom, small but tidy, apart from what appeared to be a few patches of plaster which had crumbled from the wall, and sat me opposite him at a table with two sets of microphones.

A single bulb hung from the light socket, and without a light shade, the room appeared somewhat *Spartan*. Just fortunate I didn't suffer from claustrophobia.

"Right, he said I'm going to be the *punter*, it's an

expression we use for all of our customers, and you are going to be the switchboard operator."

For what seemed like ages he asked me various questions and I replied as accurately as I could.

Mr Roberts, finally put down his microphone and said "Miss Edwards, may I call you Alice? I put you under a lot of deliberate pressure and often rudeness, and despite not knowing about different types of vehicles and their possible uses, you remained calm. I detected you listened to my questions and thought about the answer before replying; well done.

We have quite a few cabs and ten drivers, although they're not all working at the same time; anyway, you will get to know about our different Cabs, and which punters they're best suited to, we call it *learning on the job*. And it's not a big deal anyway!"

"What, the job's mine?" I replied with gratitude.

"It certainly is; you're exactly the type of operator we need in this particular role, a polite and composed individual with a remarkable degree of common sense and self-control.

Anyway, before you sign on the dotted line, let me now tell you about your conditions of employment."

Chapter 36

I knew Penny still hadn't found another job, so I called her using my mobile and arranged to meet her for lunch.

Her available time was short, so I quickly got to the point and told her of my new job working *the switch,* at Cabs4U.

"The owner's a nice kinda guy," I told her.

She was thrilled for me, and when I asked her about her attempts at finding another job, she replied, "At the moment, I'm not looking, and as I'm now feeling a little happier about everything, I'll probably stick it out a little longer unless of course, something better comes along.

Anyway, what about Elsa and her Diabetes and the high sugar levels; what did her Doc say?"

"Oh, Penny thank you for reminding me about that, she hasn't told me anything, so I'll ask her about it when she gets home tonight."

"Good, now you haven't forgotten about my engagement party as well, have you; It's this weekend?"

"OMG Penny with everything that's happened recently, I had forgotten about it; well not forgotten your engagement party you understand as it's in my diary. I haven't looked at it these last few days," I answered pathetically.

"Whatever." Penny replied, "I hope you won't be annoyed with me for not telling you earlier, but I didn't know myself until Chris told me last night.

You will remember Brandon, Chris's mate who you met in Bournemouth, well he's coming to our party and you know how much he likes you."

I thought for a moment before answering. "Yes, it's not a problem Penny, he was a nice man, or should I say is a nice man, but as you will remember, at the time I just wasn't into relationships."

"That's great, oh and before I forget Alice, Chris has received a promotion to Chief Accountant; his Salary has increased nicely, and he's getting a bigger company car."

"Fantastic Penny, for once everything is going well for both of us; makes a change, eh?"

Penny hurriedly excused herself as she only had seconds to go, and her lunch break ended.

Before returning home, I bought a bunch of Bananas as Mum had eaten every one of those she had recently purchased at the market although I guessed Elsa had helped her out a little.

Mum was grateful.

I put them in the fruit bowl and placed it on the small sitting room table next to where she usually rested.

A little later, I was preparing our evening meal when Elsa arrived home and remembering Penny's comment about Elsa's diabetes. I asked: "Have you made an appointment to see the Diabetic doctor?"

"Yes," she replied, "I've already seen him."

"And what did he say?"

"Quite a lot but to cut the story short, he's completely changed my insulin regime, and as soon as the chemists have dealt with my prescription, I'll now be taking quicker-reacting insulin during the day with each meal. And each morning, I will inject insulin that works for 24 hours, removing excess sugars.

Hopefully, this will reduce what they call my HbA1c blood sugar level."

"Oh that's brilliant Elsa, make sure that with all the doses of extra insulin injections that you keep everything under control and don't have even worse Hypos than you sometimes do!"

"Oh, and by the way," I reminded her, "Don't forget Penny and Chris's engagement party this Saturday."

Friday morning my clock alarm woke me, it was 5.30 am, and I washed and dressed, ready for my first day working at Cabs4U.

As I left home, I checked the time on my watch, and it was 6.30, sufficient time to reach their office by 7 am. Upon arrival, it was 6.38, an eight-minute walk.

Jack was working on the switchboard.

"Watchya girl, he said pleasantly, you're an early riser. I told Steve you were somebody worth considering and I'm so pleased he took you on. Anyway, he now owes me a pint for putting the two of you in touch and saving on the firm's advertising costs!

By the way, how's your loverly Mum?"

"She's ok thanks, but I think I also owe you a couple of pints for getting me this job."

"You don't need to thank me, and I always knew you'd be a suitable applicant and immediately available to fill this vital role. If you weren't here, me or one of the other drivers would have to fill the gap until Steve arrived each morning.

And that's what I'm doing here today; I'm not waiting for a *punter,* but Steve's asked me to sit down with you and if necessary help with any initial issues until he arrives."

The first few hours were busy, and with Jack's guidance, everything went exceptionally well. It was now 10 am, and Steve arrived and asked Jack how I had managed. Jack told him I'd coped admirably and with very little help from him.

"That's brilliant Alice, the problematic parts of the day are leading up to and including the rush hours." Steve advised; "Well-done Girl!"

"Incidentally, our driver's all have a weird sense of humour, so don't believe them. Especially if any of them tells you, you're only employed to make me copious cups of tea and to iron my shirt's – I've already heard one of them talking about telling the new switchboard operator that story on their arrival."

"Yes, and it wasn't me!" said Jack with a laugh.

"I hope you don't mind, but amongst the staff, traditionally it's Christian names we're called by, not our surnames."

Steve had explained to me previously that at the moment, there were two other *switch* staff, Helen and Jayne, although they sometimes doubled up as cabbies whenever practical. They were officially licensed to drive a cab.

The hours of work is set in place for us all, upon agreement between each other, they were flexible hours but sometimes, long ones.

If one individual is employed to work part, or even all of another's work shift, they are the one who will receive the applicable hourly rate. He couldn't afford to pay overtime, so understandably it was all paid at the single rate.

I had no complaints and thought the flexibility and agreeable attitude amongst the staff were so much more accommodating than in more substantial, corporate enterprises such as the Supermarket.

It was also brilliant that when an immediate but genuine emergency unfolded and subjected to Steve's permission, any of the staff would chip in and help.

Today, I was working a 12-hour shift, but when they managed to employ another operator, we would all be able to work eight-hour shifts.

Steve was right, during the day I got to know some of the drivers and their sense of humour; the wisecracks continued throughout my shift, but it was all great fun, and before I knew it, it was 7 pm.

I could now understand why Jack had previously told me he enjoyed his job so much.

And me? I was looking forward to my next shift which was what the lads called the *vampire shift*.

In this instance from 7 pm on Sunday to 7 am Monday. This shift was the day after Penny and Chris's engagement party!

Chapter 37

Fortunately, Penny had already told me, depending on what time their party finished, probably sometime early Sunday morning, I could stay and recover at her flat and kip on the sofa.

Whatever I'd now have to be cautious about exactly what and just how much I drank. I certainly didn't want to phone in sick or even be late; also I'm sure operating *the switch* in a less than a sober state, wouldn't be acceptable to anybody.

During my worktime breaks, I had phoned Mum a couple of times to make sure she was ok, and fortunately, she was, so I had no worries before arriving home.

Elsa had arrived before me, and both she, and Mum were keen to hear about my first days work at Cabs4U.

It was good to note that Elsa was already peeling the vegetables in preparation for the family's dinner as it saved me the task.

I told them of my great day, especially commentating on the Cabbies sense of humour and the mickey-taking continuing throughout the day.

"Although it can be long hours, it sounds great fun, Sis," Elsa remarked.

A Dose of Insulin

Taking me to one side, Elsa told me "I know you phoned Mum a few time, as did I, and she said everything was ok, but when I got home, she didn't look right. At times she struggled to move around the sitting room, although she continued to tell me she was Ok.

Unfortunately, we can't impose on Penny each time we're uncertain about Mum and her health. I do think that whatever she tells us we must keep a closer watch."

"I understand Elsa but what about now, do you think we should call Doctor McArthur?" I asked.

"No, Alice, when I suggested that to her, she refused the idea and looked most stressed; considering what the Doc had said last time, I didn't want to make her worse!"

"Yes, Elsa; you were certainly correct when you said we should keep a closer watch and simple things like making sure all the light bulbs are working, the TV is switched onto her favourite channels. Also, ensuring before we leave the house that Mum's mobile phone has been re-charged," I said.

Wracking my brain about what else we could do to make her day an easier one, I thought about food. "Oh, and make sure we've left her sufficient sandwiches and cooked lunches that she only has to heat up. At least she'll have a good selection of food to choose from."

"Great idea Sis, and of course we mustn't forget her bowl of Bananas!" Elsa suggested. "Also, how about us both making sure before we go to bed that she has her favourite clothes laid out and ready for her when she wakes."

Elsa and I both agreed that we'd thought of what we could to make things easier for her; none the less, I knew whatever we did wouldn't entirely eradicate our worries.

Chapter 38

It was Saturday morning, and I phoned Penny to ask whether they needed any help with their party preparations. According to Penny, everything was ready; the food was all prepared, and the bottles of champagne were cooling nicely in their large upright fridge-freezer, and all they now needed was their guests.

I had already selected the clothing I would wear, my purple Lipsy Lace Maxi Dress and my white Merino woollen cardigan. Footwear was again my Pigalle Follies printed leather pumps which still looked brand new.

As always, I wanted my appearance to look the very best. Then I thought of Brandon and ensured my facial makeup was one of perfection.

Before calling a Cab, I checked on Elsa's readiness; she was sitting on the setee and making the funny breathing noise she made when her blood sugar levels were deficient. She wasn't in a good state and certainly not fit for the party.

I fetched a tin of coke from the fridge and the honey jar from the kitchen; with great difficulty, I managed to spoon-feed her the honey.

A Dose of Insulin

Mother called weakly from her bedroom, asking whether everything was all right.

"Yes Mum, Elsa's having a hypo, but she's now recovering ok." I exaggerated.

Gradually she started to regain her composure, and I then opened the tin of coke which I knew possessed a large quantity of glucose.

Elsa started talking in riddles, but the honey and glucose drink did their job, and eventually, Elsa was talking sensibly again.

Mum's lectures had paid off!

"Sorry, Sis but I think it was my new insulin regime that caused my hypo; I'm getting used to it but trying to keep my blood sugar at a perfect level, it can be such a critical balance between perfection and hypos. Anyway, thank you so much for your help."

Elsa repeated her thanks several times; bless her!

This insulin was serious stuff! "Do you want me to help you get ready for Penny's party?" I asked.

"To be honest, Alice, I'm not of a mind to go after my break-up with Tim; I know you'll understand. Also, I can stay here and look after Mum and keep her company. Please give my apologies to Penny and Chris, and you enjoy yourself; what's his name? Brandon."

I phoned a Cab, obviously Cabs4U and within ten minutes it arrived, Helen wasn't on *the Switch* that night and was earning extra money driving as a Cabbie.

She opened the door for me and remarked how brilliant I looked; "You're going to knock 'em dead with that outfit!" She complimented me. "Anyway, please confirm your destination, Madam." She said as though I was a typical cab fare.

During our short journey, Helen asked how much I liked the job on *the Switch*.

"Well, I've only worked the one day and don't work again until tomorrow so it's difficult to make a positive comment at the moment but my first day was great and the boss, Steve seems a nice guy," I replied.

"Yes he's brilliant, and everybody likes him; he can, however, be very firm if you step outside the line, but then again he's a very fair and a most considerate individual."

We arrived at Penny's flats, and Helen asked whether I needed picking up later that night? I explained I would be staying the night at Penny's but would require collecting in the morning. "I'll phone the firm when I'm ready to leave, but thanks for asking anyway."

Approaching Penny's front door, I thought I'd be one of the first to arrive. However there was a loud commotion of music and people talking; somebody heard me ring the front doorbell, and it was answered by a person I didn't recognise, who then explained he was Penny's downstairs neighbour.

Chris spotted my entry, excused himself from the woman he was talking to and walked over. Welcoming me, he took me around the flat, introducing me to others. "I know it's crowded he said, but more friends turned up than we originally expected."

There must have been at least 20 guests, possibly more, which doesn't sound a lot in a Parish Hall, but this was a flat and not an unusually large one.

A Dose of Insulin

The guests occupy each room, the sitting room, their bedroom, the kitchen. Even the toilet had three people chatting with their drinks in hand and one of them, a lady, sitting on the seat!

Casually I looked around the room for Brandon but couldn't see him anywhere; perhaps he'd decided not to attend for whatever reason he might have had.

Still, I could ask Penny or Chris later when everything had calmed down a little; if indeed it calmed down at all.

My thought now was to get a drink, if only to refresh me as the atmosphere created by so many guests was hot and sticky; even with the windows fully open.

Somebody brushed past my back, and I moved slightly forward. Again there was a similar experience, but this time it was a definite prod. A voice apologised.

"Sorry Alice, but aren't you talking to me?"

Gradually I completed a slow 180-degree turn, and there was Brandon.

"Oh, Brandon, I didn't think you had turned up, but it's nice to see you again."

"And you Alice, you're looking stunning as indeed you always do, well, I mean when I saw you those few times in Bournemouth. Whatever, it's also great to see you once again, and Bournemouth was a long time ago. Anyway, how are you these days?"

I tried to reply, but the noise made it difficult for Brandon to hear me properly, so he suggested we step outside the front door where it would be easier to talk to each other.

Before moving, he remarked, "Hey, you haven't got a drink. Let me get you one."

"Ok thanks, I'll have a small glass of white wine; I need to take it easy as I'm working tomorrow."

"Ok he said, but I also need another beer as my can's now empty!"

I waited for him outside the front door where the air was so much fresher, and after a few minutes, he arrived struggling with three cans of lager, two in one hand and one in his pocket; my glass of wine in his other hand.

Unbelievably he said, "I've also got one of Chris's cushions for you to sit on as we don't want that wonderful dress to get dirty." He released the cushion from under his arm and with his foot moved it from the landing, onto the top step of the flats stairway.

"Anyway, you say your working tomorrow, so what do you do for a living?"

We chatted for what seemed ages; about the time in Bournemouth, how Chris and Penny had met up and were still together and now holding an engagement party.

I asked Brandon whether his other friends were here at the party?

"Which friends?" He enquired.

"The ones with Chris and you in Bournemouth."

"Oh, you mean Bob, the truck driver and Paul. Bob's a sad story; did he tell you at the time that he was married and he and his wife had a newly born daughter, a pretty little thing.

Well, she had a nasty disease, and their doctor told them it would be better for the little girl, I've forgotten her name, to live by the coast where the fresh air would be much better for her. They had moved to Kent, and that's where

A Dose of Insulin

he was living when you met him; he'd come with us, for the weekend to Bournemouth as it made a nice change for him.

Shortly after that we gradually lost touch, no birthday cards, no Christmas card; Chris reckoned it was more than likely something tragic. You know what it's like in those circumstances; you don't want to talk to anybody."

I knew precisely what Brandon meant, remembering how I'd felt after my abortion!

"Whether Bob and his wife are still together, I don't know." Brandon continued.

"So what about the other one, Paul, the chap who liked the Dole!"

"Well, Paul's an entirely different story. A rough diamond who eventually saw the light and joined a Cruise Ship, not sure if he ever told me what he did, but while working, Paul had a free berth and as much food as he could eat.

When I last saw him, somewhile ago now, he had to admit working on the Cruise ship was much better than existing on the Social, even though, he said there wasn't much difference in the available spending money.

He would be travelling all over the world and said his last trip was to the Caribbean Islands; a beautiful place, picturesque and warm."

"Yes," I agreed, remembering the travel catalogue pictures and the television programs before I came back down to earth, also recognising the agony and frustrations of the time.

Our general discussions continued for so long he had finished his three cans of lager.

And then the question I had expected at some time or

another, "And what about you these days? Is there now another man in your life?"

I told him there wasn't and didn't mention my previous experience with David as even now I didn't want to discuss it.

Anyway, I was pretty confident he would have heard it all from Penny and Chris. Indeed, when he told them, he was interested in meeting up with me again after our trip to Bournemouth.

It was only a short while since the Bournemouth outing, but I did wonder if I looked any different; Brandon appeared to look the same, although I couldn't remember him in great detail. Except for his ability to chat with women and drink alcohol with that consummate ease of his.

He was a little taller than me, and certainly not overweight; In fact, he looked quite trim.

I also noticed how much he smoked, and frequently, he would take another fag from his packet of cigarettes. While his smoking was none of my business, I did worry about how awful my clothes would smell.

Penny and Chris didn't smoke, and therefore nobody was smoking cigarettes inside the flat.

I suggested to Brandon that we return and he jokingly said "What Bournemouth?"

"No you idiot, inside the flat as I'm sure there are many people we haven't yet spoken to,"

"So, you're fed up with me already." He said with a laugh.

It was apparent Brandon wanted to chat outside of the flats general commotion, and as I was reasonably warm, I suggested we walk downstairs and into the car park where obviously the air was much fresher.

As we walked down the many twisting steps, he kindly supported the hem of my maxi dress, remarking that he never believed he would eventually become a *maid of honour*. After all, it was only an engagement party!

In the flat's car park it was a bright moonlit evening, and the sound of nearby traffic had almost disappeared; I guess as it was now quite late and most people were resting at home and probably watching the late film or something similar.

Brandon pointed out a bench on the edge of the slabbed pathway, placed the cushion, which somehow he had once again carried downstairs under his arm, while also holding my skirt tails. He put the cushion on the wooden bench and invited me to sit.

As in Bournemouth, most of our conversation had been about me, and what I was doing and I was somewhat intrigued about Brandon so asked him about his life and background.

"Well Alice, I was born at a very early age." He said while keeping a straight face.

"Bloody idiot," I replied.

"Seriously though, I have lived all my life in Reading, and as I think you know, I went to school in Tilehurst and Chris, and I was classmates at Prospect School.

When I first started work, I was a Navi on the local building sites and following that I worked a few years in different aggregate companies, selling such things as sand and gravel.

Then I worked in an Estate Agents for a short while, and now I'm self-employed as a tiler. In fact; I did the tiling in Chris's new shower room."

The brief story of his life, was interesting, although Brandon appeared reluctant to tell me anything about his love life, so I asked him outright.

"Do you have any children?" I asked tentatively.

There was a pause before he replied. "No children but I was married although she was a few years older than me and I was young and stupid. It didn't last long, and eventually, we got divorced."

"Are you involved with anybody at the moment?" I cautiously asked him.

"Only you." He replied with a grin.

Gradually people were laughing and talking aloud as they left the block of flats; obviously from the party.

Looking up at the Moon, while we had sat outside, it had shifted from one side of the car park and was now disappearing beyond the dark horizon at the other end. Brandon and I had been sitting outside so much longer than we realised.

Thankfully Brandon had finished the last of his cigarettes.

The moon disappeared and It was even darker; whenever the wind blew in the trees, everything sounded creepy although I realised Brandon was there if I needed protection.

"It's been an interesting chat, Brandon, but I do think we must go and talk to Penny and Chris," I said.

"Before we go, Alice, can I ask you something?"

"Of course you can," I replied expectantly.

With a grin, he said, "If you or any of your friends need any tiling done, would you please put them in touch with me, Chris has my contact details." He grinned.

But without missing the opportunity entirely, he continued "And of course, can I see you again, Alice?"

As we walked back towards the light of the Flats entrance and without me answering his question, he withdrew a couple of business cards from his pocket; *Brandon's TCT* and in the smaller type beneath the abbreviation *top-class tiling*. Handing me one, he then asked me for my contact details.

I thought how well, his friend Chris's relationship had progressed with Penny and how Brandon, at this moment in time, possessed a similar nature to Chris; I wrote my contact details on the other card and handed it back to him.

Upstairs, Penny and Chris were busily tidying their flat, so Brandon and I commenced with the washing up.

It was mostly drinking glasses, as Penny and Chris, had bought a large number of paper plates, plastic knives, forks and spoons for the food, and these were already being cleared, by them, in a large black plastic waste bag.

Afterwards, Penny made us all a cup of coffee, although Brandon asked whether they had any cans of beer left as he'd only had a couple of drinks all night.

"Are you sure it's only a couple of drinks Brandon if so it makes a change. Maybe you've been up to something else!" She said with a big smile on her face.

It was now approaching 5 am, and I was feeling in desperate need of some sleep, especially remembering I had a twelve-hour shift ahead of me, starting that evening at 7 pm.

I phoned Cabs4U and asked for Helen, but she had finished; it was Jack on the early morning shift, and he would be picking me up within a few minutes.

Saying goodbye to Penny and Chris, Brandon offered to walk me downstairs, another beer-can in hand, while I waited for Jack to arrive in his cab.

We had just stepped outside when there were sounds of a vehicle pulling into the car park; it was Jack.

Brandon kissed me with a peck on the cheek, saying he would be contacting me soon and went to open the back seat of the Cab.

I thanked him but explained this was a Cabs4U vehicle and Jack was a friend, so I'd be sitting next to him in the front seat.

Brandon blew me a kiss as he waved me off.

"So, I guess you had a great night, Alice; the bloke seemed keen," Jack commented.

"Yes, he's one of the guys me and my friend met up with, in Bournemouth and I guess we'll meet up again sometime. Anyway, I'm absolutely *cream crackered* and desperately need my bed."

"You're taking the *vampire shift* tonight, aren't you? Oh well, Alice, all the very best."

"Thanks, Jack, I was hoping to get some sleep at Penny's, but their party continued for ages."

"So your lack of sleep was nothing to do with the chap from Bournemouth?" Jack said with a smile.

Chapter 39

I climbed into my bed, and the bright sunlight shone through my window frame, so I pulled the curtains and curled up under my cosy quilt cover. Although I was exhausted, sleep was difficult as I couldn't help but think of Brandon and just when he might call.

A knock on my bedroom door awoke me; it was Elsa.

"Hey Sis, it's five-thirty, and you said you have to be at work by 7.30 pm. I didn't want you to oversleep, anyway can I come in."

I didn't have a chance to reply and in walked Elsa. "So how'd it go last night?"

Not wanting a series of Elsa's questions while I was preparing for work, I was a little economical with the truth and didn't mention Brandon at all.

Arriving at work, I was still tired, but I believed capable of completing my work.

The fresh smell of the office was a relief after the alcoholic odour from Penny and Chris's flat.

This time, the driver sitting on the tattered couch was Jayne.

"Good to see you Alice and I'm pleased you have come

back and not decided to chuck it all in after your initial trial, especially as Steve would have asked either Helen or Me to work *the Switch* overnight.

Anyway, are you looking forward to our Company do this Friday night?"

"Company do, what do?" I asked inquisitively.

"Hasn't Steve mentioned it? Every year he pays for a night out when all the staff and their partners are invited and thanked for their efforts during the preceding year.

This year it's being held at a local Hotel. Although you're a recent employee, I'm sure you'll still be welcome; anyway I'll check with Steve for you." Jayne offered most kindly.

The Switchboard bell rang, and I answered the call; it was Robin another of our drivers.

"Hi, it's me, Robin, that fucking women's done it again; I've got to her house on time, and once again she's changed her fucking mind – she doesn't want the cab after all. Anyway just to let you know I'm on my way back and should be with you in about ten, fifteen minutes."

I hadn't met Robin yet but explained to Jayne that he hadn't sounded a *happy bunny*.

"Oh, I bet it's that snotty-nosed bitch from Caversham Heights again; the one who told us she'd been left her posh house, some years ago by a wealthy Uncle who adored her. We think he was the only one who ever did.

When this woman first met her husband, she was already pregnant; they'd only been married a year when he subsequently divorced her, and she hasn't seen him or her son for about ten years.

We initially thought she only booked cabs, so she had

somebody to talk to and tell our driver's her latest news and often all her old news as well. Then, when they arrive, if she'd forgotten what her latest news was, she cancels the Cab; At least that's our opinion for all her cancellations.

Steve's such a nice guy that he's put up with it for years, saying she's an old woman and needs sympathy, but now, even he's thinking of blacklisting her."

Overall my overnight shift at Cabs4U went exceptionally well, and I was hoping that I would get a call from Brandon; if I got a call, that is, maybe even in time for him to accompany me to the works dinner on Friday night!

At home, Elsa had left for work, but when I climbed the stairs to my bedroom, I was pleased to note the little Angel had made my bed for me. I was exhausted, so it was a most welcome sight; Although it was early days, I did ask myself whether I'd ever get used to these 12-hour shifts.

Hearing Mum's soothing snooze in the background, I decided not to disturb her and climbed under my lovely warm duvet.

The duvet with beautiful pictures of the Thames and Caversham Bridge, which Mum had kindly bought for me a while ago on one of our market trips; in some ways, Mum sleeping was a welcome relief.

The more I worked my different shifts, the more I enjoyed working with the various members of staff and even some of the customers!

The continuous joviality was something I'd never witnessed at the Supermarket, and here nobody ever complained about us laughing and joking.

Talking to Penny that night, I told her how much I was

enjoying my work and also mentioned that I hadn't heard anything from Brandon.

"Hey Alice, it was less than twenty-four hours ago when you last spoke to him," Penny remarked astoundingly.

"Yes well, I hope he calls me before Friday as I'm off to a local hotel as it's the evening of our Companies annual party. I was hoping he'd come along as my partner; everything's paid for, even our hotel rooms. It sounds fantastic!

That way, the staff can have a good drink or two and stay the night. Yes, and then we don't have to worry about getting home."

"That's great, but what about those who have to work on Saturday?" Penny asked.

"Steve hires some old-timers for the day; people he trusts and who have worked for him previously."

"Oh, you are so lucky to have found this job, Alice. And the boss sounds a real good 'un!" Penny acknowledged.

Chapter 40

Before I know it, Friday night is here, but no call from Brandon. I couldn't deny it upset me!

Everyone has gathered in the bar for pre-dinner champagne and a toast welcoming us all to the Cabs4U annual celebration.

There is about forty of us, including partners; casually, everybody is introducing their partners to each other.

Steve raised a glass. "I know everybody says it BUT, our business does continue to operate because of you guys and only because of you and your professional commitment throughout the year, so please accept my heartfelt gratitude."

Everyone clinked their champagne glasses accordingly, and in return, the staff members cheered Steve, our lovely Boss.

"Right let's eat!" Said Steve. Everyone cheered again and then shuffled in an orderly queue towards the dining room.

There were several tables, and the seating places labelled with our name tags, neatly written in old English writing and placed on the table in front of us. Alongside were pretty glass jars holding neatly presented paper napkins with the companies logo; Cars4U, printed on them.

Next to our Menu cards, there is a selection of wines, Red, White and Rosé. One by one, the wine bottles are opened before anybody thinks about ordering food.

The chatter is noisy, and gradually, it quietens as we start to select our starters and main courses.

As the waiters take our orders, we are all told they would bring a selection of desserts after we have finished our main courses. Indeed, I wasn't going to overeat and hoped I'd save sufficient space for a sweet, or maybe two!

I wanted to be sitting next to Helen or Jayne, but they were both on different tables, Helen with her husband and Jayne, her long-established boyfriend.

Sitting either side of me is Robin and Brian, I'd spoken to Brian a few times on *the switch* but never seen him, face to face.

Brian had worked for Steve for several years, but with blue eyes, short auburn hair and a slight frame he looked most juvenile, in fact even younger looking than Elsa.

Now and again, he would comment on something but didn't seem to enjoy the general conversation circulating our table. He appeared on the shy side, which I found strange for a Cab driver as they certainly require an assortment of social skills, especially chit chat with fare-paying customers. Whatever, despite this, he was a charming man.

Robin asked me why I didn't have a partner present, and I exaggerated a little, saying his name was Brandon, and he was working tonight on a particular job that needed completing urgently.

A Dose of Insulin

Then again, I didn't feel too awkward about my lack of a partner as neither Robin nor Brian had a partner present?

As we were finishing our Dinners, there was a couple of loud bangs on the top table, and Steve called us all to order. A member of the hotel staff handed Steve an enormous but skinny package wrapped in brown paper.

The millimetre thin package measured approximately 36 by 18 inches. Everyone was mystified and waited with extreme silence for Steve to explain what this large envelope was all about.

Steve stood up, package in hand and a quiet voice, explained.

"This is something I have introduced this year, and as you will recall earlier this evening, I said that the continued success of Cabs4U was as a result of the effort and commitment provided by the staff.

It is, therefore, my intention to make this award to the person I consider to be, the Employee of the year, indeed the one who has contributed most to this business since it's formation.

This individual has been with me from the start, is always conscientious and thinks about the success of this business and is often spoken of most highly by customers and our staff alike.

The relevant person will be paid to take a long weekend, for two somewhere in Europe and will receive adequate funding to enjoy themselves, with Cabs4U's heartiest thanks."

It was another extremely kind gesture from Steve, an exceptional award and I'm sure everyone, like me, was longing to know what was inside this mysterious package and indeed the name of the winner.

Steve began to peel off the brown paper to reveal a giant-sized copy of a cheque marked *Bank of Cabs4U*. On the cash line instead of money it stated *A weekend for two anywhere in Europe*. Apart from its enormous size, everything about it looked like a real cheque.

Steve continued "And the winner is............. Jack Harrison." Jacks full name is written clearly on the cheque recipients pay line.

Most surprised, Jack stood up from his seat to receive the replica cheque and the holiday abroad. Everyone cheered him. Steve shook his hand and whispered a few words in his ear.

I remembered Jack's comment to Mum and me, about how much he enjoyed his job but never realised he was one of the first to work for Steve, many years previously.

He certainly deserved the award, and I was looking forward to telling Mum as I knew she'd also be pleased for him. It would be welcome news, as these days much of Mum's stories was basic and pretty dull.

Following this presentation, we all assembled in an offshoot of the Dining room, with comfortable Dralon type velvet armchairs.

Helen and Jayne joined me, and along with their partners, we spent the remainder of the evening talking to each other and of course about Jack and his unexpected but well-deserved reward. Also, Steve's kindness and generosity.

Jayne suggested that we should all meet up one night for

a drink at a pub within easy walking distance of us all. But just us three girls for a *girly* night out.

Taking the lift to my hotel bedroom, I so regretted not having Brandon by my side; still, there was hope he would soon contact me.

Although we had to vacate our rooms by 10 am, it was now 9.45. I had initially woken much earlier but must have fallen back to sleep. I was still exhausted and feeling not only a little bit bloated but also more than a little bit tipsy.

Chapter 41

I rang Cabs4U and told all the stand-in drivers were currently occupied. It wouldn't have been right to call another cab company, so I decided to take a slow walk home.

The journey along the A33 took me much longer than expected, and the car fumes along this busy roadway didn't make me feel any better; in fact, I now felt much worse than I did when first leaving the hotel.

The straight dual carriageway also made my walk seem to be never-ending, and on occasions, I would have appreciated a seat to rest my weary limbs, so it was a wonderful feeling to arrive home finally.

Elsa welcomed me, confirmed Mum was ok and then casually informed me that Brandon had rung. "I explained where you were Alice, and told him I didn't expect to see you until later today. Anyway, he said he'd tried your mobile, and there was no answer but if you were free today, would you fancy going out somewhere. If he doesn't hear from you, he will call back sometime this evening."

Typical, why couldn't he have rung just a few hours sooner, well maybe, a day earlier!

At this particular time, all I wanted to do was sleep. Although I did want to talk to Brandon, at the moment, I was in no mood for dating chit chat and anyway he'd told Elsa he'd call me back later.

When I told Mum Jack's news, I realised I was right in thinking how pleased she'd be.

"I always told you he was my favourite cabbie!"

Feeling exhausted and much too tired to continue the conversation, I walked to my bedroom and climbed onto my bed; I just collapsed on top of the covers and burying my head in the pillow; I must have immediately fallen asleep.

I don't remember anything else at all until Elsa screamed my name from downstairs. "Alice, it's Brandon." Looking at my watch, it was 8.30 pm!

Our phone conversation wasn't a long one, and he explained, if he'd been able to contact me earlier, it was a beautiful day, and he would have liked to take me on a boat trip along the Thames.

"I have a friend who owns a nice boat, and I thought you might have enjoyed the boat ride."

Considering the state of my stomach, a boat trip, was the last thing I'd have enjoyed today. Still, I replied positively "Thank you, Brandon, it sounds a great idea, but it's too late now, so perhaps another time."

"Ok Alice," he replied as though I was trying to put him off, "So how about meeting up for a meal one night this week, I know a few good restaurants around here; do you like Curry?"

"I'd love to meet up for a meal, but I've gone off Curries,

thank you," I replied remembering it was David's favourite meal and we had spent a great deal of our time in curry houses!

"Ok, so how does Italian food sound?" Brandon said, desperately attempting to find a cuisine I would like.

I didn't want my answers to sound as though I was playing *hard to get.* A tactic I considered abominable.

"Yes, it sounds fine, thank you; anything would be good. Except for Curry!" I replied. "Please let me check my diary. How about Wednesday evening as Wednesday's my first early shift this week, and I'm free all evening."

"That's also good for me, it'll be my second-day tiling at a new wine merchants store, but I reckon I'll have finished the job by then; I'll pick you up at 7 pm if that's ok for you?"

"I'll be finishing work earlier than you Brandon, so how about you, booking our restaurant table for Wednesday night and I'll come to meet you; it'll give you more time to shower and get ready. I've kept your contact details, and your home isn't far away."

"Thank you, that's very nice of you; I look forward to seeing you on Wednesday. Bye for now, Alice."

Behind me, a voice echoed, "Sounds good Sis; not that I was listening."

Grabbing Elsa by the waist, I cuddled her and said, with a big grin "Of course you weren't listening," Elsa naturally grinned back at me.

It was only a fleeting moment, but while cuddling her, in some ways I was sad; Elsa was no longer that little sister of mine but had now developed into a young lady, a mature woman.

A Dose of Insulin

However, she still watched over me and always considered whatever I did and precisely who was accompanying me.

Arriving at Brandon's house, at the agreed time, his front garden looked a bit of a mess. He opened the front door, and I was surprised he didn't invite me inside.

Brandon was wearing his overcoat, and we left immediately for the restaurant; he must have booked an early table.

The Italian restaurant is busy, and a smartly dressed employee, dressed all in white, guides us between the different tables to the seats reserved for us by Brandon.

Brandon steps in front of the waiter and withdraws my seat from the table and courteously invites me to sit.

The waiter lights the candles arranged on our table and then asks whether we would like to look at the Wine list before selecting our choice of food.

Brandon has a look and recommends a wine called Treviso Garbèl.

"It's a light, sparkling wine, produced in the North of Italy by *Adami*: their wines are always highly rated, so let's try a bottle.

Anyway, we can imagine it's champagne and celebrate our first date!

Incidentally, the smell of this wine should be of ripe fruit such as pear, apple and melon, but all I can smell is alcohol!" Brandon said with a laugh.

Looking at the menu, I asked Brandon what Antipasto meant; something that had puzzled me.

"It means *before the meal,* and it's an Italian platter

of cured meats and various cheeses," Brandon confirmed knowledgeably.

I commented, "You seem to know quite a bit about Italian food and drink."

"Yes, my Grandmother was an Italian, and she used to show me how to make Italian food, like Bruschetta Fungi and Gorgonzola."

"It sounds revolting to me," I said.

"Nonna always said Italian food was the best food in the world; anyway it's lovely, she made the Bruschetta with mushrooms, different herbs and sourdough bread.

I'll make you some when you come round to my house sometime."

"Your House?" I questioned.

"Yes, although it's a little derelict at the moment. I bought it shortly before me, and the lads went to Bournemouth, and I have been renovating it ever since we returned.

I've just finished erecting all the plasterboards and am now onto the tiling; how about you coming over and doing a little painting?"

"But I've never done any painting before," I said and then realised this was all part of establishing our friendship.

"Oh, it's easy, and you'll soon get the hang of it, Alice."

Brandon continued to talk about the plans for his house and then, about his Tiling business.

Now well into our main course, the wine bottle was empty, so Brandon ordered another.

"I told you it is a fantastic tasting wine; one of the best!" He said.

Talking about the trip to Bournemouth, Brandon mentioned how well it had turned out for Chris and Penny.

And then, *out of the blue*, Brandon said "I also fancied Penny, but she chose Chris instead of me. Oh well, that's life."

Brandon immediately realising his mistake, then said: "I'm not complaining as I've met you, and you are such a gorgeous woman."

"A brilliant recovery Brandon!" I said with a hearty laugh.

I wasn't too sure whether to take his comment as a compliment, but overall I was happy with the evening and agreed on a time and date to help with the painting at his house.

Brandon paid the bill, saying that I shouldn't worry about contributing as this evening, was at his invitation and anyway, he'd offset the cost, on his list of company expenses.

As I arose from my seat, Brandon halted me as he wanted to finish the last drops of wine left in the bottle. "Don't want to waste any of this brilliant wine!"

I waited but also realised that I'd only had one glass from this second bottle, and it had only been a tiny glass of wine.

Brandon walked me home and as we parted, this time Brandon's kiss was more than just a peck on the cheek, and his firm cuddle made my heart pound.

I couldn't wait to see him again, and before I knew it, I was dipping my large paintbrush into a five-litre can of white paint.

Considering the work, he must have already completed, his house looked a lot better than I had imagined, certainly the paintwork looked fine, but then again I guessed Brandon was a perfectionist.

During the next few months, our relationship grew much stronger, and all my free time is spent with Brandon, most of it helping him with odd jobs improving his home and the front and back gardens which were in genuine need of serious attention.

Overgrown hedges, weeds everywhere, many brambles and a collapsing garden shed, all this in addition to a concrete pathway which was long past its best! I was by myself as Brandon was working on one of his contracts.

After bending up and down to clear weeds and other garden rubbish, my back told me I should take a rest. Sitting down with a cup of coffee, I switched on Brandon's large panoramic TV. I was going to make the most of this short break from the gardening.

The screen came to life, and I couldn't believe what was showing. It was a repeat programme; of the Carribean and San San Andrés. Typical I thought, any repeat and it had to be the one to remind me of David Wilson and my missed opportunity in San Andrés.

I switched the TV off, washed my dirty cup and returned to the garden, hoping this new friendship would be so much better than the last.

On several of these occasions, I'm working by myself as Brandon is on a contract somewhere or other and sometimes late into the night.

Whatever it's most enjoyable knowing I'm doing

something positive to help him when he is so busy working elsewhere.

He is hardworking, runs his own business, is well mannered and extremely considerate towards me. A perfect relationship, what could go wrong? I asked myself.

Elsa welcomed my relationship with Brandon but commented that "Like your time with David, Brandon often leaves you alone in the evening as he's working somewhere. He treats you well and seems a kind and considerate chap; just be cautious Alice!"

It was clear; she must have given my situation a great deal of thought when she told me of her heartfelt feelings.

"I'm so happy for you Sis; it seems such a long time ago since your bust-up with David. I know it hurt you so much and for a long time, Mum and I were so anxious about you.

Especially considering, the long-lasting mental effects of having an abortion.

Please understand, I'm not saying you have recovered from that awful experience." Elsa said with a look of concern.

Once again, it was times like these that I realised how special my lovely sister was and how difficult it would be for me to live my life without her; she was not only an exceptional sister but also a unique friend. It was impossible to explain the love I felt for Elsa.

Penny was also pleased that I had recovered from my earlier traumas and finally found someone I could care about emotionally.

My friendship with Brandon was different; not just the relationship itself but the fact that he was well known to one of my closest friends and also her partner, Chris, who had been friends with him since they were children.

Apart from complimenting me, Penny did say something I had already noticed although it hadn't registered in my brain as something that I would need to worry about as our relationship grew!

"He likes his drink Alice so please beware. That was the reason his wife divorced him."

I didn't respond to Penny's statement, but although Brandon had said his wife had divorced because they didn't get on together, he hadn't mentioned anything about drinking.

The only time I had witnessed him drinking was the cans of alcohol at Penny and Chris's Engagement party and a couple of bottles of wine at the Italian restaurant, which was our first date. Both of these occasions were special and therefore nothing unusual about having a good drink!

The thought of questioning him about this unrevealed fact did cross my mind, but who knows that was presumably his wife's version of events and if I asked him about it, there might have been an unnecessary conflict between Brandon and Me.

I wanted to accustom myself to the man I knew, not to the excuses of his first wife.

Whenever we did work together renovating Brandon's property, it was always good fun.

The mistakes either of us made, paint on his head, especially considering how much he loved, what he called his perfect hairstyle, taking *the mick* out of each other while we enjoyed a brief break in our work and his odd swearword each time a tile wasn't quite in the correct place or had slipped out of position.

Mind you; this was nowhere as bad as his language when he accidentally knocked one of his midday tins of beer from the trestle table!

Neither of us missed the opportunity to joke about each other.

Especially my gullibility when Brandon looked at me straight-faced after an exhausting day's work in the garden and quite seriously said: "I've gone off this house, and I've decided to sell it and buy another!"

I had grown to like this residence of his, and after all our hard work, and then working our other roles, me as an operator at Cabs4U and Brandon his tiling business, I had become much attached to the building as it became better and better.

Brandon held his straight face for as long as he could, and then, much to my surprise broke into laughter. I thought of Penny's gullibility and the suitcases immediately before our trip to Bournemouth!

I chastised him for his sense of humour, which I hadn't found the least bit funny, although he continued to laugh at my initial reaction.

And of course, I continued to complain about his original estimate when he'd told me the remaining work renovating his house would only take a matter of a few weeks.

Already it had taken several months with a great deal more to complete in the garden which he called his Outback!

Everything we had done, including bits of new furniture

and white-goods looked spectacular — a beautiful home to live!

It suddenly occurred to me that Bradon wasn't smoking? I remember when I first started work on his house, he would often take a break while he enjoyed a smoke; he had never seemed to stop.

When I questioned him about it, he said with a look of one-upmanship, "No Alice, you moaned so much about the smell of your clothes that I decided to try and pack it up!"

This thought was exceptionally kind of him.

I did consider that after the many months we had spent together like man and wife he might even propose to me. Much to my disappointment, there was no such proposal.

The best offer I received was an evening meal at his favourite Italian restaurant which, although disappointed I naturally accepted the offer.

Our favourite waiter, Valentino, greeted us and looking as pristine as ever, he took us to our usual table which was already prepared, including the first bottle of Treviso Garbèl, Brandon's favourite.

While initially, I had been unhappy with his reward for all my months of hard labour, the food, as always, was excellent and the evening itself most congenial.

Finishing my glass of wine, Brandon stopped me.

"There's something I want to ask you, Alice?"

Chapter 42

I waited with excitement and anticipation of his question and knowing precisely the question he was going to ask. "The work we have done to my house makes it look wonderful, but it does need a woman's presence."

I was most impatient and just wanted him to get on with it!

"So would you consider moving in with me?"

I was wrong, it wasn't the question I wanted him to ask me, but it was second best!

Whatever the question, I was never going to give him a straight 'yes'.

My answer was an obvious one but as Penny had often said, never give a man a 'yes' first time; keep them waiting just to let them know who's in control of the situation!

It did occur to me that this was as bad as somebody playing hard to get, but perhaps this was a different type of situation!

"It's very kind of you to ask Brandon, and it's a wonderful idea, but you've had time to think about this so, please let me have some time to consider the implications."

"Implications, what do you mean implications?"

He accepted what I'd said, but it was clear from his expression that he had expected an automatic and positive response. He certainly didn't understand what I was implying with the word *implications*!

Despite this, the evening went well, although I was looking forward to returning home and discussing the matter in a little more depth with Elsa.

It was late, but Elsa was still awake, and I could hear her talking to Mum.

Within seconds she was downstairs and by my side asking questions about Brandon and my night out.

"He's asked me to move in with him," I told Elsa.

I didn't have time to say more as Elsa immediately pointed out a few reasons I should think about before agreeing. Like Mum and her health and of course, me and the housework, and "I can't manage everything by myself, Alice."

"Oh, making me feel guilty is so unfair, Elsa!"

"I know Sis, but I love you so much and just don't want you to leave home, and I know Mum will feel the same as me."

Whatever Elsa said I discussed the matter with Mum, and whether Mum wanted me to leave home or not, she finally explained to me that I was now a grown woman and accordingly I must make my way in life.

"Of course I'll miss you, Alice, but we'll keep in regular contact as you'll only be living around the corner."

My workmates from Cabs4U, Helen and Jayne finally met up with me for our *Girlies* night out.

The Pub certainly was local, only a few minutes walk

from home, although I had never visited it before. It was located, down a side alley, and I was a little cautious walking down the passageway as I was by myself and the street lights had failed.

It was only a short walk, but in the dark, the shadows cast by the Pub's door lights seemed to be moving everywhere. At least I hoped these daunting shapes were shadows!

With relief, once inside, the Pub was quaint and had that friendly appeal about it.

There was nothing intentionally special about our night out, just a few beers in a local pub although Helen produced five twenty pound notes from her pocket and explained, "I told Steve, what we were doing tonight and he gave me this dosh and said have a drink and a bite to eat on him!"

"We're so fortunate to have a boss like him. We work hard and don't let him down or take the piss, and he rewards us. He's one in a million." I said, with great appreciation.

"The fact that we have kept the same staff for many years and those that have left have done so because of personal reasons of one sort, or another demonstrates how much everyone likes him as a boss," Helen remarked positively.

"Go on, Helen, tell Alice about your earlier life, she'll be interested," Jayne said with enthusiasm.

Helen seemed reluctant, but I confirmed my interest, although I had no idea what her story concerned.

"You'll be bored, Alice,"

Helen sounded reluctant to talk about her youth, so I decided not to question her further although it did make me wonder as Jayne had made it seem something of great interest.

We then discussed ourselves, and our current life; they asked me about Brandon. It was good to be able to tell them something positive and factual about my man and me.

"When you've settled into your new home, we should all meet up again with our respective partners, and the men can also get to know each other better."

Months move on, and I was now happily living with Brandon although his regular snoring wasn't something I had ever been used to while living with Mum and Elsa.

His snores reminded me of Penny and our time in Bournemouth! Although I did consider it was inconsiderate to compare Penny and her snoring with Brandon!

For a while; only a short while, he found my comments about how the windows rattled while he snored, as humorous.

However, it annoyed Brandon when I then stated his snoring was a result of his heavy drinking, which had become progressively worse.

Apart from this, his Tiling business was doing exceptionally well, and his accountant; Penny's partner and Brandon's long-time friend Chris, was delighted with the financial results.

Probably the thing I missed most, was my little sister, Elsa, knocking on my bedroom door each day. Although I have to keep reminding myself, she isn't *little* anymore.

Penny and I had arranged a convenient time to meet for an after-work update about what was happening in our lives. At least that's what I thought our chat was going to be about; we had chosen a local cake shop, which also served hot drinks.

It was a small establishment, and we hoped there would be a spare table where we could sit and rest our limbs while enjoying our chosen victuals.

Their cakes were homemade and the feather-light Choux buns gorgeous but never good for our waistlines, I reasoned. We had only been seated a few seconds, and I was sinking my teeth into the first bite of my delicious looking bun when Penny announced, "I have something special to tell you Alice; I'm pregnant!"

Another case of Deja Vous, only this time it was Penny. I prayed her relationship with Chris would be different from my disastrous experience with David.

"Chris and I are getting married as soon as possible and want you, my special friend, to be our chief bridesmaid. I do hope you will accept?"

This request was what these days they call *a no brainer.*

And, Penny continued, "I want Elsa to be a bridesmaid. You can tell her about you being the Chief Bridesmaid, but Chris and I will send Elsa an official invitation."

"Can I tell Brandon?" I asked inquisitively.

"As you know Chris and Brandon were meeting up this afternoon to discuss Brandon's accounts for his year-end returns and so Brandon will almost certainly know by now. Incidentally, Chris is going to ask Brandon to be his best man.

Anyway, how's everything with you and Brandon now you've moved in together?"

"Fantastic Penny but as you know his snoring often keeps me awake during the night; sometimes he goes out for a drink with his customers, and when he comes home he collapses on the kitchen table and snores the night away instead of coming to bed.

At least I get a better night's sleep when he does that."

"Oh, Alice, I'm so very sorry, but I did warn you about his drinking!"

"Yes, you did Penny, and I'm a little bit worried about tomorrow night, as Brandon and I are going out for a drink with Helen and Jayne and their respective partner's."

"I wouldn't worry about it, Alice, if he snores during your time with Helen and Jayne and their partner's, just deal with it." She said with a chuckle.

Overall, the following evening went well with the men mostly chatting amongst themselves, about Rugby, Reading's football team, Brandon's tiling business and probably much more, although now and again Brandon, most courteously, talked to Helen and Jayne and occasionally me.

It was apparent Brandon found it easy talking to new acquaintances which in turn pleased me.

One evening, Brandon was away on what he said was a business meeting, and Elsa joined me for Dinner. It was most enjoyable, talking the night away with my little sister.

"Incidentally Sis, Mum said to me that you should beware of Brandon; She'd noted signs that worried her."

"She's said nothing to me Elsa; what signs?"

"She never said what the issues were, but you know Mum she never wants to cause upset! People have to find their own way in life; I think that's her expression!"

"I understand Elsa, but that's what I'm doing; making my own way!"

Suddenly Elsa's mood changed, and she asked whether I'd heard any comments about her and drugs?

"You mean your Diabetic drugs?"

"No, drugs like Pot, Coke and Heroin!" She stated with exasperation.

"Oh no, Elsa, not you!" I pleaded.

"No, not me, you fool; A few days ago I was walking home from work at the Care-home, and a scruffy chap stopped me and said, 'I hear you sell top gear.'

Now honestly Sis, the only Top Gear I've heard about is the car magazine and the TV Programme.

He was after drugs and somebody had told him I was *a dealer*."

Sympathising I said, "Don't worry Elsa he's mistaken you for somebody else!"

"No Sis, he knew my name, Elsa Edwards, and it gets worse. The week before that, I had been called into the HR Manager's office at the Care-home and questioned.

Somebody had phoned them and said I was *dealing*. It's such a load of fucking nonsense, and when I asked HR who it was, they said the individual didn't leave their name and hung up.

The manager explained it was apparent the caller had tried to disguise their voice when phoning HR.

Who's behind this and more importantly, why?" Elsa said with anger in her voice.

"You should have told me about this before Elsa?" I responded with more than just a little frustration.

"I didn't, because number one, it's an absolute load of

cobblers, and number two, we've got our worries with Mum and telling you such news wouldn't make anything easier."

That night, after Elsa's return home to Mum, I continued to worry about our discussion; unquestionably I trusted Elsa's version but couldn't stop worrying about who was behind this rubbish and as Elsa had asked with concern, *Why?*

Time moved on, and my worry dissipated.

On a later occasion, she caused more concern when phoning me at work. She said: "I don't want to worry you." A phrase that automatically puts my mind on the edge!

"But you must come and spend a little more time with Mum; she isn't well, and although she not that old, with her heart condition you never know how long she's going to be around!" There was nothing out of the normal to worry about at this moment in time, but I could tell Elsa was tearful.

Her blunt statement shocked me, and I decided that as Brandon was often out of an evening, I would spend longer at home with Mum.

Brandon arrived home, and he was reasonably sober.

"Are you coming home early tomorrow night?" I asked.

"Not sure darling depends on what the hell happens."

"Well, if you don't mind I'm going to see Mum as Elsa says she's not that well. I might even stay the night."

"OK, that's fine. I'll eat out somewhere and see you later." He replied sympathetically.

Despite his late nights out and his regular snoring, Brandon was certainly a considerate companion, or so I believed.

A Dose of Insulin

Work was more hectic than usual, and I wondered when I'd be able to get out and buy a lovely bunch of flowers for Mum. She was always more of a flower person than chocolates.

I was taking over from Jayne was on *The Switch* today as Helen had a day off and was going to visit Covent Garden in London with her husband and from what she had previously told us about that part of London; it sounded a most enjoyable visit. I thought it would be a lovely day out for Brandon and me some time.

Jayne kindly offered to remain on *The Switch* until I had bought a bouquet for Mum. "There's a florist just around the corner which I've heard people recommend so have a look there Alice."

The spray of flowers was superb with white Lillies, red and yellow chrysanthemums, and blue Iris, along with plenty of greenery, which made the flowers pronounced.

Jayne agreed they looked spectacular, and while looking at the flowers, she asked me how I'd enjoyed the other evening with them and their partners.

"Great thanks Jayne, it was something different and a most enjoyable night out."

"So how long have you been going out with Brandon?" Jayne asked.

"Not that long; why do you ask?" I questioned.

"Nothing Alice, he's a nice chap, it's just that Helen and I noticed he has the *gift of the gab*! That's all."

I had previously noticed how well Brandon mixed with others and thought Jayne's comment a little crude. He's a fantastic partner for me, so I thought no more of Jayne's feedback, whatever she might have been saying.

Thanking her kindly for allowing me to find flowers for Mum before I commenced my shift she commented: "Oh, by the way, Alice have you heard the news, Steve's hired a new *switch* operator, and she starts next week.

Hopefully, we'll now be able to work regular hours, and Helen and I might get more time driving the Cabs!"

Jayne kindly took the flowers from me and placed them in a water jug as we had no vases in the cab office, saying they would still be fresh when I took them home to Mum.

Work was uneventful, and my shift dragged.

That evening I walked home to my old haunt and arrived indoors before Elsa.

I shouted up to Mum and then made her a cup of tea and placed the flowers in Mum's favourite vase; I guessed she was having a late rest.

As I walked through the bedroom door, flowers in hand, the smile of pleasure on Mum's face was exceptional; possibly, the happiest look I had seen for a long while.

"Oh thank you, Alice, they're so pretty; would you please put them by the window-sill as tomorrow they'll look spectacular in the early morning sunlight."

I gently held Mum's feeble hand. "I'm pleased you like them, Mum, anyway how are you feeling today?"

"Well, sweetheart, I'd like to tell you everything's fine, but just recently I've been feeling weaker and sometimes just getting to the bathroom is a struggle.

Apart from that; you know how we all know our bodies, well, I know mine is different from what it was a year ago, and something's telling me I'll be lucky to see Christmas out!"

"Oh, Mum, you mustn't talk like that; have you spoken to Dr McArthur?" I asked.

"Not recently and I think I've bothered him more than enough. I'm not even sure there is a prescription for old age.

I'm unable to explain it, but somehow, I know!" Mum said as though she was resigned to her fate.

"And please say nothing to Elsa as I want to have that conversation myself."

Completely lost for words; just what do you say in such circumstances. I looked away from Mum and saw the vase of flowers elegantly sitting on the window sill and wished I had bought something other than white Lillies.

It was getting later, and Elsa still hadn't arrived home. Must be working a late shift, I thought.

I cuddled Mum as best I could and reactively told her "You'll be ok Mum, you know you're so much stronger than you look.

How about one day soon we get a Taxi, take your Wheelchair and have a day out at The Farmers' market? I know you'd like that."

"I know I would Alice, and it's very kind of you, but at the moment I don't feel up to it, perhaps another time when I'm possibly feeling a little better.

Anyway, are you enjoying your job?" She asked, changing the subject entirely.

We chatted on about our lives, history and anything of interest which immediately came to mind.

Although it was pleasant talking to my dear Mum, I

couldn't help but worry whether Elsa was ok as now, it was even later.

With relief, I heard the front door open, and a loud voice shouted up the stairs "Hiya Mum, Hiya Sis!"

Mum tried to reply, but as with her body, her voice was also feeble.

"I'm going downstairs to have a chat with Elsa and get you something to eat Mum; what would you like?"

"Whatever you choose, thank you, Alice."

As I moved away from the bedside, I could feel Mum's hands clinging to mine for as long as they could manage; that act was emotionally upsetting.

Downstairs, I heard talking and realised it wasn't just Elsa. I walked into the kitchen and it was Gabby. Elsa gave me a warm hug and asked how Mum seemed.

"Reasonably ok but a little tired," I said, being somewhat economical with the truth.

"Anyway Elsa, your late!" I said.

"Yes and guess where I've been these last few hours?"

"No idea, so surprise me," I remarked with interest.

"Well I had another visit to the Police Station and whoever it is, is at it again! Even worse, the Police initially arrived at the Care-home and asked to see me.

Think I can probably say goodbye to my job. The Police had no proof, but *somebody* had also informed them I was a *dealer*. HR told the Police they'd also received such a call although it was insincere, although I did wonder if they were beginning to suspect there was something in these different tales!

The Police didn't have the name of the informant either

but said, in the Public interest, they had to investigate. After a few frustrating hours, they let me go.

Anyway, Gabby was kind enough to come with me as she thought it would also be an excellent opportunity, not just to comfort me but also to come and have a chat with Mum.

"Gabby's has been here on a few occasions now, and Mum enjoys her company; unfortunately Gabby's soon moving to Manchester. She has applied for a job up there and will now be the one in charge of a care home. I will miss her!

And Sis, what about Brandon, how's everything going with your *live-in-lover*?"

"Fine," I said somewhat apathetically as at this particular moment, the thought of Mum was the essential thing in my head and of course whatever the problems some idiot is causing for Elsa!

"And what does *fine* mean Alice; something not right is it?" Elsa questioned knowingly.

"Well Elsa, he's a great guy, but it seems he's drinking more and more as time moves on; sometimes he comes home and falls asleep, snoring on the kitchen table, even when I've placed his evening meal before him.

Our sex life is almost non-existent."

For the first time, I felt confident in telling everything and continued.

"Also, of an evening and sometimes weekends, he's often out somewhere, having a meal or a meeting with a business client and I'm left at home by myself. As the days move on, I seem to be spending less and less time with him keeping me company."

"For Christ's sake Sis, this isn't good; you've got to discuss it with him," Elsa remarked sensibly but definitely with more than a little anger in her voice.

Chapter 43

The date for Penny and Chris's wedding was set and had arrived before we even had time to think about it!

Chris and his Best Man, Brandon, was standing at the front of the Church as the well-rehearsed sound of *Here comes the bride* rang out from the Church bells.

As I walked down the aisle with the other bridesmaids, including Elsa, Penny looked fabulous in her pure white wedding dress and escorted by her Foster-Father Ted, who had travelled to Reading with Molly, his wife, from their home in Devon.

It must have been a burden for them as Penny had told me, they are both in their late seventies, and they travelled on three trains and had to use several taxies.

Everything went well, and Chris and Penny signed *the banns*, and we all made our way to the reception hall, situated behind the Church.

Outside the Church, I noticed a dark car, parked in a layby and a couple of customarily clothed men sitting in the front seats and attempting to look inconspicuous; I wondered who they were and what they were doing. I preyed Elsa hadn't noticed them!

The Reception Hall had many wooden beams supporting the roof, and a Tudorish look about it; It was most enchanting and could have been hundreds of years old.

Fortunately, the Reception hall was warm, and many of us exchanged our outer garments for a receipt as we stopped at the cloakroom.

As expected, Brandon and I sat at the main table with Chris, Penny, their Parents and the other Bridesmaids.

Penny's Foster-Father, Ted, was a friendly man and told me, "When Molly and I lived in Bracknell, Penny was always talking about you, and also after we moved to Devon.

Whenever Penny and I speak on the phone, she continues to mention you as her special friend.

Is Brandon, your boyfriend?" He asked.

"He's my partner; we live together," I replied.

"Well I knew him and Chris when they were a couple of little scoundrels; always up to mischief of some kind or another. Mind you; they were just youngsters growing up, not bad boys!

As they reached their mid-teens, Brandon was the one who always attracted the pretty young girls; but I can see he's finally met the woman of his dreams."

Ted smiled and clinked my glass.

"Anyway, this time I'm going to beat him to it and ask you for the first dance! Would you like to waltz?"

Considering his age, he made an excellent effort guiding me from corner to corner of the dance floor. He was an accomplished dancer, and before we knew it, the dance floor was full of other dancers.

By late evening, I had danced so much that I needed to sit down and rest. This reception was the first time I had danced since injuring my back. I thoroughly enjoyed the experience but began to worry what it would feel like in a couple of days!

Penny joined me as she must have danced with everyone.

"Hi Alice, enjoying yourself? Anyway, when are you and Brandon going to tie the knot?" She asked with amusement, if not a little bit of devilment.

"This time, I want to make sure I have the right Guy! But yes, Brandon's a good man! So who knows?" I replied.

"He's certainly fit for his age, or should I say energetic; he hasn't stopped dancing since we finished our Dinner. Penny commented. I think he must have danced with all the Bridesmaids, in fact, all the women except for me so now I'm going to grab him immediately he finishes this dance with Elsa."

Walking across the dance floor, Penny asked Elsa to excuse her and without waiting for a reply, took Brandon's hand from a somewhat bemused Elsa!

After completing several dances with Penny, Brandon also sat down for a rest alongside me at the table. I couldn't resist a bit of humour, or should I say mischief when I mentioned Ted's remarks.

"Penny's Foster-Father's a nice chap; he was telling me about you and Chris as naughty youngsters and what you were both like as you grew older," I said to develop the conversation.

"Did he mention his favourite memory about us as

young men and how we attracted all the girls?" Brandon said with a grin.

"It's such a coincidence that he knew Chris and me when we were kids, and he's Penny's stepdad! Whatever, Alice don't take too much notice of him!"

Brandon didn't take the bait, so I continued the conversation with sincerity hoping he'd ask me the critical question! After all, we were at a Wedding reception; what better place to ask, although my enquiry wasn't quite as direct as Penny's question had been!

"I'm so pleased for Penny that's she at least kept in touch with Ted and Molly; it was great to have him here to escort her down the Aisle. Incidentally, Brandon, earlier Penny asked me how long you and I had been together as she had forgotten."

His reply still wasn't the one I wanted when he said: "She's got a bloody awful memory; maybe she's suffering the early stages of dementia!" Brandon responded with a loud laugh.

Without even trying, he'd terminated my verbal approach to provide an answer to the ultimate question I wanted answering; was it intentional? Whatever, I daren't ask the actual question outright.

I made one last attempt to obtain the answer I wanted when I commented, "Ted says he thought we make a very nice couple."

"That's nice of him." was Brandon's minimal response to my enquiring statement.

For a brief instant, my memory returned to David Wilson; it wasn't easy. I began to wonder whether evading the question

A Dose of Insulin

was the usual response from men when they reach this stage in their relationship with a woman.

Anyway, I had made several attempts to obtain the question I wanted answering and decided tonight wasn't going to be the night!

As the evening moved on, it was clear Brandon had drunk sufficient alcohol as he slurred his speech each time he lost his footing and bumped into others on the dance floor.

My mobile pinged, and it was a message from Robin, telling me he was waiting outside in his Cab.

Brandon and I said our goodbyes to everyone and must have kept Robin waiting for at least another 20 minutes; Brandon added another £20 to the fare as an apologetic thank you.

Indoors, I was so pleased to sleep but not quite so pleased when I received an eight am phone-call from Elsa!

"Sis, it's Mum, come quickly she's not well at all! I think she might have suffered a heart attack."

I ordered a Cab while Brandon and I rushed to get ready. Robin was still on duty and arrived without delay. He could tell from my expression that all wasn't well. I explained, and he put his foot to the pedal, ignoring the many 30 mph speed signs as well as other drivers and pedestrians who verbally complained about his manner of driving.

Elsa had left the front door open and was sitting beside Mum in her bedroom. "I've called Dr McArthur, but he's not available and a stand-in Doc is coming.

Mum initially complained of pains in her chest, but

since then she's just laid on her bed and appeared lethargic; she hasn't spoken at all."

No sooner had Elsa finished the sentence than another voice shouted from downstairs; it was the stand-in doc.

He asked Elsa and me to wait outside, so he had sufficient room to check Mum, although I knew he thought Mum was bad and the Doctor didn't want us in the room in an emotional state and distracting him from what he needed to do. I just hoped nothing was as severe as it seemed.

While waiting, Elsa and I sat on the stairs, and hardly spoke a word. Mum looked far from good; probably worse than when she'd recently attended the Hospital as a casualty patient!

Mum's bedroom door eventually opened, and it was clear from his facial expression that the news wasn't what we wanted to hear.

In a sincere but a well-rehearsed manner, the Doctor explained, "I'm sorry to tell you, but your Mum has passed away. She has died from a heart attack."

Tears were flowing down our cheeks, even before the Doc had finished his sentence.

Brandon, who had been waiting downstairs, walked up the stairs to console us. Naturally, he was the most composed, he wrapped his arms around our shoulders but said nothing.

Dealing with our emotions as best we could, the ambulance men eventually arrived to transport her body to the mortuary.

They respectfully carried Mum's shrouded body from her bedroom down the stairs and placed her into the

Ambulance. As they drove away from the house, taking Dear Mum's body away, once again it brought Elsa and me to our knees.

Neither of us could explain how we felt; our intense feelings were so very mixed. It was the end, and we'd never see Mum alive again.

That wonderful woman, who never complained about anything and whose only purpose in life appeared to be us, Elsa and me.

"She only 54, not even 55 yet. It's too young to die!" Elsa wailed in her emotional upset.

My attention was drawn, to Mum's room and the flowers I had bought her a few days earlier; these were still in the jar on her windowsill.

They were dead!

The following week was one I wished to forget; everyone at Cab4U, Elsa's Care-home and immediate neighbours were most supportive, as were the Undertakers.

Daily, Penny was by my side and did her very best to provide individual comfort and support to Elsa and myself. She had offered to help me with the preparation for Mum's funeral, and while I appreciated her offer so much, I knew it was something Elsa and I had to manage by ourselves.

The day arrived, it was early morning and a bright day with the Sun's rays casting an eerie shadow of the Hearse and the top section of Mum's Coffin as well as the various flowers onto the footpath. Elsa and I were still inconsolable.

Mum had never wanted anything fussy, just a cheap cremation; She had often told us she didn't want people wasting their time, visiting and tidying her grave, 'a cremation will do me fine.'

Intentionally, the funeral was a small one, only attended by myself, Elsa, Brandon, Penny, Chris and one other.

Gabby, bless her, had travelled from Manchester for Mum's funeral and rather than stay with us, she had stayed locally with another old friend rather than cause, what she considered, an additional complication for Elsa and me.

Mum had always been clear about those in attendance, how she wanted to be remembered and exactly where she wanted her ashes to be scattered. Although I think she would have forgiven Gabby for making an effort to attend the funeral and pay her last respects!

The crematorium's service chapel was reasonably large with sufficient seating to accommodate whoever might have attended. When considering the limited attendance, everything seemed unnecessary.

Mum's coffin was laying on what appeared to be a dark coloured table at the front of the chapel, along with a single wreath of flowers from Elsa and I. Again, it was how she wanted it.

As we waited for the service to commence, Penny passed paper tissues to Myself and Elsa.

The suitably attired Funeral Celebrant, with his notes and Bible in hand, entered the Chapel through a side door and commenced the Service.

We repeated the *Lord's prayer,* and Mum's coffin slipped quietly behind the curtain. I always remembered this part of her funeral as the most emotional time. It was the final parting; both Elsa and I acknowledged our beloved Mother.

She had struggled as a single parent, to raise us as kids and then later in life; Both of us accepted that we could have done so much more for her while she was alive!

I knew she would never be forgotten by either Elsa or me or indeed anyone who knew her.

In my spare time, what little there was, between her death and the funeral, I had contacted various people and relevant institutions, informing them of her death.

Between us, Elsa and I had obtained and completed a regulated Council form requesting that Elsa become the authorised Tennant of Mum's house.

The responding letter, printed on the Council's, letter-headed paper, confirmed that Elsa could stay but only for a few weeks when she must vacate the premises. The letter provided no understandable explanation of why she must leave.

Accompanying Elsa to the Council offices, it became apparent that she wasn't entitled, even as the Tennant's daughter to take control of the premises we had lived in for the last two and a bit decades. She would have to find lodgings elsewhere.

"Fucking unbelievable!" Elsa commented.

It wasn't often I heard Elsa swear, and it told me how angry she was at a time of such despair.

As the time approached when Elsa had to leave the premises, nowhere suitable or even affordable was found for her to live. Everything became so very tense.

Chapter 44

I had thought of an idea but not mentioned it, holding the idea in mind until the last possible moment; but, I needed to say nothing as Brandon suggested to me that Elsa, could rent one of his spare rooms. My initial solution.

Elsa was grateful, and during the time available, we packed her belongings and transferred them to Brandon's house.

There was a significant excess of Mum's clothes and shoes which had built up over the years, Elsa decided she would take many of these items, to the local charity shops where they would be purchased cheaply by the needy.

Brandon gave Elsa the choice of two rooms, one on the same floor as us and the other on the top floor. Elsa had always liked the loft-type elegance of the upper level, with its wooden beams and sloping roof it was compact and warming.

The only limitation was the lack of storage space - only one small cupboard.

"Never mind, I can sleep up here where I'm not in your way and store the majority of my clothing in the cupboards of your spare room; if that's ok with you Brandon."

Looking out of the Dormer window, Elsa watched people happily striding up and down the street, walking their dogs, making their way to the shops or just walking. None of these individuals realising she was watching their exploits. She said, "It's an interesting view. Thank you again, Brandon, it's so much appreciated."

Once again, living in the same house with Elsa was a joy and brought back special memories from our times of previous years.

After a while, it did occur to me that since Elsa had moved in, Brandon took an even greater opportunity, to stay out with his various friends instead of spending it with me.

Despite this, Elsa and I would talk about many things of interest although I couldn't help but wonder why Brandon and I were living together, but not like a loving couple.

Elsa enjoyed her time living with me at Brandon's house but astounded me when she said she was going to look for a flat. "Digs somewhere," She said.

"Why Elsa, aren't you happy here?" I asked.

"It's ok Sis, but I just need to be the one in control of what I'm doing."

"Is it me, have I upset you somehow?"

"No, you've done nothing Sis; anyway if you don't mind I don't want to talk about it!"

"Why not Elsa?" I questioned knowing there was more to this situation than she was telling. As sisters, we were so very close, so it had to be something exceptional.

"Oh please Sis, let it drop!"

Again It was time for Cabs4U's annual party, reminding

me that it was approximately a year since Brandon and I had been dating. This time he would be accompanying me as my guest, and maybe he might think seriously about our future together.

One evening, Elsa assisted me in preparing the evening meal.

We were chatting when Brandon arrived home, he was carrying a bottle of beer in his hand and had obviously, drunk more than enough already.

He fell through the front door and into the kitchen, where he collapsed on the table. Elsa placed his cooked meal in front of him.

He was still snoring over his uneaten meal when Elsa and I climbed the stairs to our bedrooms, a good while later.

The following morning, Elsa mentioned to me how she was now witnessing the regular event of Brandon, and his snoring after what had become typical drinking sessions somewhere or other.

She also said she had believed I was exaggerating a little but now agreed it was a regular occurrence.

However, there were some evening's when he appeared sober but still arrived home much later than he should have.

The phone rang, and when I picked it up, the line went dead?

Elsa laughed when I told her I didn't have anything to wear for Cars4U annual dinner and needed to go shopping for something suitable.

"Have a look in your cupboards Alice; you're so like Mum, bless her. It's one of her habits you'll always have.

With all the clothing and footwear you possess, you could open a second-hand shop and make an absolute fortune!"

Later that evening, I mentioned the same thing to Brandon, and his response was the same as Elsa's.

Thinking about their comments, I attempted to justify what I wanted to do; after all, I did like shopping for quality clothing whatever was in my cupboards.

I was so pleased Elsa had decided to move in with Brandon and me as it brought added company. She was there to chat along with me when Brandon wasn't, and this was often!

"I'm so surprised Sis, Brandon never seems to be around of an evening, surely it can't be me. She questioned. I've certainly done sod all to upset him!"

"No, it's not you Elsa; I think he's gone off me and prefers drinking time with his buddies!"

Elsa didn't reply to this particular statement.

"Alice, at Penny's wedding reception, I noticed how well he got on with the other woman and at the time I just thought he was sociable. Could it be there's another woman? I've also noticed his reactions elsewhere."

Recently I had noticed that sometimes Elsa's reactions to Brandon and any comments or questions he asked, was a little less than friendly; not like Elsa at all, as she was usually polite and friendly with everyone.

"Just because he gets on well with other women doesn't mean he's having an affair with them Elsa; It's a good thing, some people find it easy to associate with others; some don't!"

The phone rang again, and this time I was close enough to answer immediately. "Hello?" I answered.

Again there was no answer; strange I thought.

Opening my wardrobe, it was unfortunately clear that both Elsa and Brandon were right.

I checked several of my clothing options and eventually settled on something they both agreed looked suitable for the Cabs4U occasion.

The more time moved on, the more I became concerned, not about the time I spent with Elsa, although I did feel I was getting in her way and preventing her from living the life I believed she should, but the lack of time I was spending with Brandon.

Ted's comment about Brandon as a youngster also crossed my mind; had he changed since his youth had departed him – perhaps not!

It wasn't just weekdays, as he now found regular excuses for working almost every single weekend.

I knew he worked hard, keeping his business afloat as more and more Europeans moved to the UK and competed financially with us Brits. I also knew he liked a drink or two but, I'd never considered another woman!

Despite her meeting with the Diabetic specialist, Elsa continued to suffer issues with her blood sugar levels.

"It's not the specialist's fault; I've got to be doing something wrong!" Elsa said in exasperation.

Tonight my shift on *the Switch* was a late one; another 7 pm to 7 am, session.

After arising from my afternoon sleep after such a long shift, I needed a hot drink. Walking downstairs, I picked up a couple of letters; one handwritten to Brandon and marked private and confidential and the other from a power company. Almost certainly a bill!

I opened the Electric bill but left the other in the letter rack for Brandon, although I did wonder what the letter was about, and specifically, who had sent it.

As arranged, Penny and baby daughter, Tina, arrived for lunch although that was putting it somewhat grandly as lunch was a couple of cheese sandwiches with a little bit of salad and a drink for Tina.

And after my long overnight shift, getting up after only a few hours sleep was a struggle.

Penny knew I was going to ask for her opinion of the clothes I had selected for the annual party, and I was extremely pleased when, like Elsa and Brandon, she complimented my ultimate choice.

I talked to Penny of Elsa's remarks regarding another woman in Brandon's life although I didn't have to say much.

There was a pause before Penny said with an awkward look on her face: "Chris, told me not to say anything Alice, but he also believes Brandon might have another woman in his life."

Shocked, I immediately asked, "Who?" not able to deal with Penny's statement in a resourceful manner.

"We think she's the wife of a man Brandon once did work for; a woman called Sandra. She runs a Café not far from the Bridge."

Elsa's comments were a possibility whereas Penny's appeared to be factual.

Was any of it right or was it all, just wild guesses. What was going on?

Later that day, I was deciding whether or not to question Brandon and thought more about the mysterious handwritten letter marked Private and Confidential.

What's this about? After the conversation with Penny, I had my suspicions; whoever it was had sufficient confidence to send this letter by post, knowing I lived here with Brandon!

I waited anxiously for his arrival and hoped he would be reasonably sober.

Fortunately, he was, and after a positive greeting, with impatient interest, I pointed to the letter.

Sitting down at the table, letter in hand, rhetorically he asked who could have sent it?

He opened the envelope carefully with a letter opener, slicing the horizontal edge and withdrawing the letter, he read it. Then with a questioning look on his face, he reread it.

He said nothing, so enthusiastically but a little nervously, I asked what the letter said?

Brandon still said nothing until he passed me the letter and in a much louder voice than usual said: "Read it!"

The envelope was handwritten, but the letter itself is type-written; As expected, no name or address.

I was exceedingly interested what it was about but not too sure I wanted to read it, just in case, I didn't like what it said!

Whatever, curiosity got the better of me, and I read the letter. Like Brandon, I was shocked and read it more than once; if only to ensure I had correctly understood what the letter said.

"That's nonsense Brandon; I've never cheated on you! You believe me don't you?"

His response was almost aggressive; not physically, but the nature of his voice sounded threatening.

Whatever I knew this wasn't the time to question Brandon about *another woman*! Well not yet anyway!

"And what about Elsa?" he asked.

"Well, you know she's not into drugs; you'd soon know if she was! Anyway, it has to be this head-case who's been causing her grief. Now, they're picking on me as well, not about drugs but making ridiculous and exaggerated claims!"

"Ok Alice, I'll tell you what we're going to do. First, we'll talk to Elsa about this letter and see what she has to say, and then we're going to the Police. This fuckin idiot is dangerous and needs stopping!"

The discussion with Elsa was excellent and indeed not as ferociously denied as I'd expected, although while agreeing wholeheartedly with our sentiments she did say, "If I find out who this bastard is, they're going to get a big dose of fucking insulin."

She did laugh it off as a joke when I criticised her dreadful intention and indeed her foul language. Nonetheless, I was also angry at whoever it was sending this letter.

Elsa was working a later shift tomorrow, so we all agreed to visit the Police Station first thing in the morning and explain everything. Accordingly, I phoned Cabs4U to notify them I'd be late.

In Brandon's absence, Elsa said something which I

found unbelievable and I was utterly confused as to why she'd have thought it in the first place!

"Alice, please think about this; the letter was typewritten, and it wasn't signed. Could Brandon have sent it?"

"Brandon? Whyever would he have sent it?" I asked — not so much a question but perhaps more of an annoyed reaction.

"I don't know, but perhaps he might want you and me out of his life Sis, and he sent this letter, so he has a reason to make things difficult for us; irrespective of whether it's true or not! Maybe it was him that phoned the Police?"

This particular discussion continued for a short time longer, but then I became irritated. Elsa realised how I was reacting and ceased this specific conversation.

Elsa and I collected Mum's ashes from the Chapel, and we knew where she had asked us to spread them. They were in a shiny black Jar, but it didn't feel right to dispose of them straight from the Chapel.

Taking the ashes home, we placed them on the kitchen table, irrespective of what Brandon might have said. Elsa and I spent most of the evening remembering Mum and what she's done for us since we'd first been born. We talked as though Mum was present, even asking her rhetorical questions.

When I awoke, Brandon had already left the house, although he hadn't told me where he was going. Thankfully he hadn't moved Mum's jar of ashes from the table.

In front of each seat were three hot cups of steaming tea.

"Bless you, Mum," Elsa said.

Like the previous evening, we continued to chat about

her, and our conversations were as though she was sitting at the table alongside us.

Nearly everything was a repeat of what we'd said the previous evening, but to us, that wasn't a concern of any kind.

Elsa and I finished our cups of tea, although she refused to empty the tea from Mum's Cup.

She washed and dried our crockery but left the full cup of tea at the side of the sink.

"I can't pour Mum's Cup of tea away, Sis!"

"I understand Elsa, anyway, shall we lay Mum to rest?" I asked as I placed the black casket into the larger of my handbags.

As we were about to leave, the phone rang. It was another of those creepy calls; the caller hung up. Who the fucking hell was it? There hadn't been any for a while, and I'd hoped these types of calls had ended!

Equally mystified Elsa asked. "Incidentally, Alice. Who is it that keeps phoning and then hanging up when one of us answers? What's the point."

The journey to her final resting place was a short one. Once again, it was a calm and sunny day. We stopped at a suitable spot, overlooking the Island nearby, and Caversham Bridge. Carefully I removed her jar of ashes from my bag.

I wanted this day to be special, although I did consider whether, without official permission, what we were doing was legal.

Elsa replied with authority, "It's what Mum wanted, so it's what's she's going to get!"

Jointly, we slowly emptied the jar's contents over the

edge of the Island wall and into the River Thames; all this in full sight of Mum's favourite Bridge.

When talking about Mum, we recalled her saying *'Whenever you're next to the water, wherever it might have flowed, I'll be there.'* That was such a pleasant thought!

We had bought a wreath of different flowers, every one of them coloured white, and dropped the wreath into the river immediately after her ashes.

The wreath landed in the slack water beside the Island and for some while, drifted slowly, around and around in neverending circles. Eventually, a passing barge created a tow and accordingly the wreath travelled downstream.

"It's as though Mum didn't want to leave us!" Elsa said tearfully.

Individually we said a private prayer and left.

Arriving at *The Switch*, Helen was awaiting her first job of the day while sitting on the tattered old couch.

The new employee, Justine, was vacating the switch role for tonight and wished me well as I took her seat.

I did think that finding an extra *switch* operator was so we could work shorter shifts, but now Helen and Jayne were working full time as cabbies. There were still only two *switch operators!* Me and Justine! Maybe Steve intended to use Helen and Jayne in rotation; one on *The Switch* and one as a Cabbie; whatever he was such an exceptional boss that I wasn't going to complain.

After Justine had left the business for home, I naturally discussed my possible concerns about Brandon with Helen. Also about the mystery headcase, and how they were now targeting me as well as Elsa. And of course, our visit to the Police Station and the formal complaint.

"I'll keep my ears to the ground Alice; it's surprising what we hear when our punters are talking amongst themselves.

Anyway, you will remember, after what you had said a few months ago, Jayne and I discussed our thoughts about Brandon. He does sound a great guy and until you have proof of something, don't rely on what people tell you, Alice.

Often there is another explanation; perhaps they're regular friends, and he's unsure about telling you just in case you are jealous; after all, that's understandable.

Just because somebody tells you he's seeing somebody else doesn't mean it's a relationship or even that the story's right!"

"No, it doesn't Helen; what Cabbie shift are you on?" I asked, satisfying myself that Chris and Penny had been wrong.

That evening Brandon was in one of his recent grumpy moods.

"What's up, Brandon?" I asked with great concern.

"Was that letter right, Alice?"

"Brandon, you know Elsa's never been involved with drugs."

"No, he shouted, about you having it off with somebody else!"

"Don't be so fucking stupid, Brandon!"

Immediately Brandon jumped up from his seat, hands raised and shouted: "Don't you ever call me stupid or else!"

I was frightened and said nothing in reply, although I realised he still questioned my loyalty based on some creepy letter!

"You haven't answered my original question; what about your boss Steve? You are always saying what a wonderful man he is and the two of you seem to get on very well! Anyway, you often tell me he's taken you out to lunch. I know something is going on between you."

"He's only taken me to lunch twice, Brandon, and he's just a nice guy; everybody likes him.

Anyway, of an evening, I'm rarely out anywhere; All I do is sit indoors waiting for you to come home!"

Chapter 45

It was that time again, and after a great deal of thought about who I should invite to the Cabs4U dinner and dance, I decided that despite everything said about him, there wasn't an inkling of proof and so my partner had to be Brandon.

After over an hour and many of Brandon's complaints about the lack of time before the dinner was due to start, I eventually opened the bedroom door.

Whatever, irrespective of the time I had taken to prepare, I was upset that Brandon made no compliments about my dress-code. I then thought maybe I was unfair as it was possible, he had previously seen me dressed in the outfit and complimented me accordingly at the time.

Mind you; he still could have said my clothing looked nice!

Apart from that, we arrived at the location in plenty of time, and we were probably one of the first couples to reach the hotel, irrespective of Brandon's earlier comments about the lack of time and how late we might be.

As expected Steve was already present, and welcomed Brandon and me to the evening. As two men continued to talk, Helen, Jayne and their partners walked through the door, shortly followed by Jack Harrison and his wife.

It wasn't long before the reception area was crowded by members of staff holding their Champagne glasses and waiting for Steve to make his customary speech. Quite naturally, I was wondering who would be the Employee of the year.

Whatever, I wanted Steve to hurry up with his toast to the lucky winner as I felt in desperate need of a taste of my champagne.

For the previous few weeks I and several of the staff had discussed their length of service and who might be favourite for this year's award and the weekend trip to Europe.

Some of us had written off our chances as our employment at Cabs4U was less than a couple of years, but it would certainly be interesting as since his award and his trip to Barcelona with his wife, Jack's talk of his journey had sounded most desirable.

On this occasion as a result of *woman pressure*, Steve had seated Me, Helen, Jayne and Justine on one table and next to each other with our respective partners. I had met Justine's boyfriend a few times before when he collected her from work.

He was nothing special but friendly with a great sense of humour. For a chap, he had exceptionally long hair; a throwback to the sixties Justine had previously told us with amusement, although he didn't wear the *bell-bottom* jeans from that era.

I could have put money on it; Brandon was the first to

open the wine although he didn't miss the opportunity to complain, as usual, about the quality!

It was time for the *Employee of the Year award,* and everybody waited patiently and in silence for Steve to make the announcement.

This year there didn't appear to be a large brown envelope, and I wondered whether Steve had scrapped the whole idea because of cost.

Steve stood and remarked about last years award to Jack Harrison and the reasons behind his decision on that occasion. It soon became clear there would be another year's award but this year, for an entirely different set of achievements.

I thought about what I had achieved during my time working at Cabs4U and then realised nothing at all!

Anyway, Steve was about to tell us who the lucky winner was, so with interest, everyone focussed on his announcement.

"Since joining Cabs4U, this individual has taken no time off sick. Not one single day! Also, you know how, from time to time, we all moan about unacceptable customers, I've never heard this person ever complain about anyone, well certainly not without worthy cause." Steve sniggered.

"As always, our customer's view is paramount, and for this reason, I have employed a third party business, to contact our customers face to face and establish their preference. Our customer's response put this particular person top of the list."

Everyone looked at each other with expectation as the

choice could be any member of staff. It was such a great crew!

Steve continued "And I'll let you know the result later!"

'You make it sound like a bloody TV quiz show Steve!' someone shouted.

The humorous comments resulted in massive groans, mingled with laughter.

"No, the delay's unfair," said Steve "so let me tell you, the winner, this winner also makes a great cup of tea. Congratulations, Alice Edwards!"

Everybody clapped and cheered. It was so unexpected, and I had absolutely, no idea what I should say.

Brandon clasped his arms around me in genuine applause and then whispered, "So where are we going Alice, I hear Rome's nice at this time of year!"

I didn't have time to reply as Steve took a small envelope from his suit pocket and called me to join him.

He passed me the envelope and whispered in my ear that these were the contact details of the firm arranging my trip, although this was really for public display as I would find the details again on my email at work. Also, a little cash paid into my bank account.

It was only after the general disruption quietened a little that Brandon's suggestion sunk in.

Long before tonight, I had thought how much I would like to visit the charms of Paris on a warm Summer's day, but Brandon had never suggested taking me anywhere further than Bournemouth, and even that was an exception.

My choice would have been to take Mum as I always remembered her talking about a trip to Paris, the beautiful shops, the wonderfully designed clothes and looking at the French Capital from the top of the Eifel Tower. With great regret, this was no longer possible.

Brandon's remark was quite an understandable one, but when I thought about it and Mums historical comments about Paris, I experienced an unrealistic and unfair level of annoyance towards him.

For the remainder of the evening, despite his earlier complaints about the lack of quality, Brandon drank several more glasses of wine, and did nothing other than talk about the long weekend in Rome, as though I had already booked the trip to Italy.

Rather than suffer a fall out in public, I told Brandon I didn't feel well and would rather discuss the matter when I was a little better.

Whether he believed my excuse or not, for the time being, he stopped talking to me although as the evening continued, he did ask whether I was ok.

Brandon and I must have been one of the last couples to retire to the pre-booked bedrooms; pre-booked for everyone by Steve.

Earlier, we had deposited our clothes, and the room still looked welcoming.

Whatever, Brandon didn't miss the opportunity to moan about the traffic noise entering from the busy road outside.

Chapter 46

At home, it was an awkward situation as I wanted to tell Elsa, about my award but with Brandon in ear-shot, I knew that would have been a wrong decision; mainly if I talked about a visit to France.

As much as I wanted to tell her my news, I believed it better to discuss it the following morning when Brandon wasn't around.

Elsa said "By the way Sis, we had another of those crazy phone calls tonight. I wonder whether it's the same person, or people, that are spreading the tales about drugs and the one about you cheating on Brandon?"

"Who knows Elsa, I still don't know why, whoever it is, is doing it in the first place!"

Just considering the drug stories about Elsa, the lie about me cheating on Brandon and now these odd phone calls; it was getting me down.

Now, in Brandon's absence, was the time to tell Elsa about my award, "Do you remember me telling you about Jack Harrison's award last year?"

"Something about a weekend in Europe wasn't it Sis? Has the lucky bugger won it again?"

A Dose of Insulin

"No Elsa, I have!"

"Wow, Sis!" was her initial response. "I bet Brandon was excited but why didn't you tell me last night?"

I explained the whole story of Brandon's expectations and my feelings on the matter and how it could have been a trip of a lifetime for our dear Mum.

"Can you imagine the look on Mum's face when I told her, also her excitement when we arrived in Paris?"

"Oh Sis, She would have loved it! Throughout her life, she never had pleasant surprises like that, and if anybody deserved them, she did!" Elsa said with the utmost sincerity. "Anyway, you said you and Brandon were going to Rome?"

"No Elsa, I said Brandon had decided we would go to Rome! I've decided I'm going to Paris."

"So what will he say about Paris?"

"I don't know Elsa. Anyway, I've been thinking, and I can't take Mum, bless her, so how would you like to join me."

"Me? Wow, that would be fantastic Sis!"

I continued to ramble on, but Elsa was noticeably quiet. "What's the matter, Elsa?" I asked her.

"I'd love to visit Paris; but thinking about it Sis, on such an event, there is no other choice, you must take Brandon. You don't have an alternative; your relationship is over unless you take him, whether you want it to end or not."

Ultimately I knew this was the correct answer and trying to justify the decision. I told myself that whatever doubts I might have about Brandon's commitment to me, this trip could only make our relationship stronger.

In reality, Rome did sound an exciting destination, and

as it was clear Elsa felt awkward about accompanying me to Paris, then I wasn't particularly bothered where I went; just that the experience would be a good one!

"Anyway, Elsa, I'm going to the Bridge for a few moments, just to tell Mum my brilliant news."

Caversham Bridge is busy with Road traffic and people walking from one side to the other. I stopped, looked over to the water below and apologised.

"Hi Mum, I'm so sorry I can't take you to with me. I know you would have loved Paris."

It was refreshing to have these type of chats, which I did whenever I crossed Caversham Bridge, or even when I wanted to discuss something personally with Mum. Bless Her!

When Brandon arrived home, fortunately in one of his more sober moods, I waited for him to settle down and then asked him what he had planned for our trip to Rome.

Elsa knew we needed time by ourselves to discuss various matters, so thoughtfully, she retired to her bedroom, taking a book and a couple of magazines to read.

His amazement was not what I had expected. "Nothing is planned at all, because of your reaction last night, I believed you didn't want to visit Rome, and I had put the thought of going anywhere completely out of my mind. Whatever, if you want me to, I'll ask around, and we can think about it."

Brandon's mood was good, so I took the opportunity, as Elsa had recommended, to also discuss why I wanted Brandon to spend more of his time with me; that is if he cared.

The following evening Brandon was absent when Elsa

arrived home, and understandably she asked. "What did he say last night, Sis?"

"Well, Elsa, in short, he said that since I'd moved in with him, I'd been more like a Mum as opposed to a girl-friend. I complained about his drinking. I complained about his sleeping at the kitchen table. I complained about his friends. I complained about almost everything. He didn't feel it was his home any more."

"So what else did he say, Alice?"

"Nothing, however, he was pleased about the trip to Rome and said he would explore some ideas about what we could do while there."

"Did he say anything more, Alice?

"OMG Elsa, what is it you want to know about?" I asked in exasperation.

"Nothing Sis." Although she did mention, she still believed there was a concern in my mind about Brandon and his loyalty.

"No, he's obviously not seeing another woman when he's drunk Alice, and every night he's sloshed, well most nights anyway," Elsa said with a grin. "Anyway, as I've said before, you must talk to him about your concerns; Don't let them build up as you know it's not good for you."

Again Elsa was right. I must talk to Brandon about the lack of time he spends with me; me, his live-in partner.

Chapter 47

At work, I also talked about our decision to visit Rome and received enthusiastic feedback from a couple of staff who had been there. The more I heard about Romulus and Remus and their foundation of the City of Rome, its culture and the places to visit, the more I became enthused. Brandon was right after all.

When I mentioned this matter to Helen, she said nothing; unlike Helen, her body language suggested she was not paying attention and thinking about something else.

I touched her shoulder, and suddenly she jumped to attention.

"Oh, I'm so sorry, Alice, but I was away with my dreams!"

"Dreams? What dreams?" I asked.

She didn't respond immediately to my question.

"Come on, Helen, whatever you were thinking about, it must be exciting."

"Exciting's not the word Alice, do you remember, shortly after you joined Cabs4U, Jayne asked me to tell you about my interesting years as a youngster, and I didn't want to

A Dose of Insulin

talk about it, well Rome was part of that story, or rather my Family's story!"

"Interesting Helen, go on," I asked with great interest.

"It wasn't interesting either, Alice, it was terrifying, and for several years I lived in fright of my life, and to some degree, I still do!"

That one comment shocked me, although I wanted to know more!

"You see, we lived in London, and my Father was an investigative journalist working with one of the National newspapers in Fleet Street. As a result, he had many connections with the 'underworld', and he was working on this particular story about a bullion robbery.

Anyway, the closer my Father got to the truth of the story, the more excited he was, we all were. He kept telling us about how his story would be a 'Front-page No1.'

Then he received various threatening messages telling him to drop his investigations or else!"

"I guess the sort of messages you don't take lightly," I stated.

"No, they weren't, but the threats continued. Then Mother was warned her life was in danger, also mine! The hostilities they threatened were so bad that none of us could sleep at night or even during the day.

Dad reported these threats to the Police; they suggested we changed our names, and over a couple of years, we moved into several different houses around Britain in the hope that these gangsters would lose touch!

Whatever, wherever we moved to, we still received threats. This Alice is where Rome comes into my story.

Mum complained to Dad that at any moment, anyone of us could be killed so with the help of his Newspaper, we ended up living in Rome. Dad became a secretive source of European information for them."

"Sounds great," I said before realising that under the circumstances, it wasn't the right response and almost certainly there was more of this tale to come!

"Dad told us all he had finished with his gold bullion story although Mother asked whether he had ceased to investigate the story or whether he had finished his gold bullion story? There was a big difference between these two questions.

Moving abroad was a massive transition in our life, but living in Rome was wonderful. The culture was so very different from that in England, and at first, we all lived a most relaxed lifestyle.

We'd lived like this for a year and had become used to the lifestyle and culture of this beautiful city. The history of threats was behind us!

Or so we thought!

We were sitting alongside the river Tiber, Mum and Dad enjoying a glass of wine and me a cold soft drink as we watched the river flow over the pebbles on this section of the river. Although in many instances we couldn't understand what they were saying: it was apparent people passing our table were also enjoying this pleasant day.

A scruffy middle-aged man with unruly stubble on his face, stopped, faced Dad and in a clear English voice said: 'Don't forget, Mr Tyler we warned you!' and then he disappeared."

A Dose of Insulin

"Tyler, but your name's Evans, well before you got married it was Evans!"

"Evans was the name the Police suggested we use, I have never told anybody of my original surname."

"I understand Helen, but you now live in Reading, why didn't you stay in Rome; it sounds beautiful?" I asked with interest.

"After the day the mysterious stranged confronted Dad despite this mans comment, nothing happened," Helen continued with a troubled expression. "For several weeks, as you would expect, we were all troubled, especially as somebody had now found us in Rome. Dad suggested that we should return home, and without delay, He and Mum made preparations."

"So that's why you returned to England," I said, thinking I was stating the obvious.

There was a long delay in Helen's confirmation. "No Alice, I was the only one to return to the UK; shortly after this verbal confrontation, there were several nighttime disturbances which came to nothing, although at the time they caused an immense amount of worry for us all.

Ever since we moved to Rome, my Mother had collected me from School. One particular day she didn't turn up, and after waiting in the play area for about 30minutes, one of the teachers took care of me and after an even longer wait she took me to my home.

My Mum wasn't there, so the teacher took me to the local Police Station. I was extremely worried as I could only believe that Mother must have involved herself in an accident; although while I waited, I was most anxious about Mum, at least once Dad knew what was happening, he would collect me from the Police Station.

I waited, one day, two days and more; I've never seen either one of them since.

Incidentally, Alice, Joyce is a kind woman but she does talk a lot, so I have never told her the complete details of this sorrowful tale; only that I travelled to live in Italy when I was a youngster!

Anyway, to continue, I was still a youngster, and apart from my anxiety and upset, which was endless, I lived under the watchful eye of a woman and her husband living in Manchester. They never told me, but now I know they were Police officers, married to each other.

These days I try to act naturally, but I don't think you will ever understand Alice how this hurt has travelled with me mentally all these years and continues to do so.

Considering her story, I thought of my family and realised how very tragic her life must have been; by comparison, I wouldn't dare to compare my misfortunes.

Chapter 48

For hours I couldn't help but think of Helen's astounding story, and then it occurred to me I hadn't checked my email from Steve and the trip organisers details.

In some ways, I wished Helen had won my award, but then again, I didn't think, considering her history, any good fortune would improve her memories!

I even felt guilty about my good fortune winning this trip, although I was interested to know how much Steve had paid into my account.

The Bank answered my initial call much sooner than expected. Still, when they attempted to put me through to my account manager, those words *'We apologise for keeping you waiting, but your call is important to us!'* continually frustrated me.

Eventually, my account manager politely answered my call personally; however, checking my recent deposits with her, nothing had changed, my bank balance was as it was generally at this time of the month!

There was a delay in the transaction process.

Should I wait a few more days? Should I contact Steve?

Should I ask my account manager to review my account details again?

I chose the latter option, but the result was the same. Discounting the conversation with Steve, I decided to wait until next week and check again.

One evening Elsa asked whether I had heard from the Police about our complaint and I hadn't heard anything at all. Brandon, in a liberal state, suggested that we revisit the Police Station before our trip to Italy, to discover what was happening?

Elsa and I were both busy with our work so Brandon offered to attend alone, although the Police news wasn't surprising. He informed us; 'They were continuing with their investigations!' or as Brandon put it 'They'd discovered sweet bugger all!'

The closer the time approached for our long weekend to Rome, the more excited I became. Brandon had done a great deal of research, and from what I had heard from others, there would be so much to see and learn.

Just a few hours before our flight, I remembered I hadn't called my bank to check that the money from Cabs4U, was paid into my account.

The phones were continually engaged, so I gave up and hoped.

We boarded a twin-prop aircraft at London Gatwick airport. And I was sitting next to the window I had a minimal and somewhat worrying view of the airport, as the plane's speed increased along the runway. Was it travelling fast enough to take off; would we end up in the field across the road?

A Dose of Insulin

I tightly grabbed hold of Branson's hand.

We eventually climbed into the sky, and the view was sensational. Below us, was the odd cloud, thousands and thousands of tiny houses, playing fields, a motorway and dual carriageways stretching for miles. All were becoming smaller and smaller, the higher we climbed.

Shortly after takeoff, everyone is notified by the co-pilot's tannoy system, that it's safe to switch our cabin lights back on.

We climbed higher into the sky, and within a matter of minutes, I witnessed the English Channel and could even see a few boats travelling the waves.

Before we had even reached the coast on the other side of the English Channel, another tannoy announcement warns us of turbulence. As informed, we lock our seat belts, and without time to digest the comment, above us, a few of the lockers fly open, and their weakly secured contents fall everywhere.

The remaining flight is comfortable with, the exception of a few air pockets when the plane dropped from the sky and left my stomach touching the ceiling! I asked myself whether it would have been any different travelling in a Jet aircraft; probably not!

The flight attendants, women and one man who regularly pushed the trolly with food and drink, were polite and reassuring whenever they needed to be.

Brandon didn't fail to mention how pretty the women attendants are. "Bet that's rule number one for employment in this job; Beauty." He said with a laugh.

The trolly approached with food and much to Brandon's

delight, drink. Not just soft drinks but alcohol and not only one glass, as during the journey, he was also delighted to be asked for his choice several times.

After about four hours, we approached Fiumicino Airport, otherwise known as Leonardo da Vinci. The pilot announced that our landing time was within expectations and the weather was reasonable for the time of year. It all sounded good!

Looking out of the window, we were almost touching the landing strip. Feeling nervous, I once again grabbed Brandon's right hand tightly as the aircraft seemed to skid a short distance. Gratefully our plane, all in one piece, successfully docked at the terminal.

Many people arose and unlocked their seat belts and then hurriedly opened the lockers above them; some belongings tumbled out and in one instance dangerously so. It was a bottle of alcohol, presumably purchased from the inflight trolly! Fortunately, it wasn't ours!

Our Hotel room was as expected. Brandon unpacked his case first, and while I carefully hung my clothes on an assortment of coloured hangers, Brandon read me the places of interest we were to visit tomorrow and Sunday.

Eating Dinner in the hotel restaurant, I suddenly remembered Brandon's love of Italian food and now guessed why he had perhaps recommended Rome in the first place!

Back in England, Elsa was preparing something to eat for her dinner when a knock on the front door took her by surprise. Cautiously she asked who was calling before she opened the front door.

"Elsa, it's Penny," she shouted.

A Dose of Insulin

Elsa opened the door, and Penny apologised for interrupting her evening meal.

"I know Alice and Brandon are in Rome, so I thought I'd check you were ok and whether you needed help with anything."

Elsa invited Penny to stay; they shared the meal and spent the whole evening chatting about various things but mostly about Alice and Brandon and their wonderful trip to Rome and especially how jealous they both were.

Penny asked Elsa about feedback from the Police about the false accusations made against her.

"Nothing Penny, Brandon visited them to enquire just before they left for Rome."

"It must be worrying you, Elsa. Who do you think it might be doing this?"

"I've no idea Penny; I've considered people at my work, although they are all wonderful people and wouldn't even consider doing something like this. Also, people at Alice's office as she's now involved, but I can't think of anybody who dislikes us that much! And, I don't know anybody who's that sick in the bleedin head!"

"Ok Elsa, so why don't you make a list of all the people you know or have known and you have upset them, or they have upset you.

Against their names put the reason why and grade them 1 – 10. One for least likely and ten a definite concern; don't forget I'm a 10," Penny said with a laugh.

"That's a great idea Penny, but you'd have thought the Police would have gone through a similar structure with me; but maybe not! Anyway, I'll give it a go sometime. Thanks!"

"So Elsa, tell me, have you seen anything of Tim recently or his nut case ex-girlfriend?" Penny asked.

There was no response for quite a few minutes.

Slowly waving her hands backwards and forwards in front of Elsa's face. Penny said, "Hello, Elsa, the lights are out!"

Suddenly Elsa responded "That it; *Brotherton*! Fiona Brotherton, Tim's ex, the cow, she's gotta be number one!"

"Well done, Elsa. That's great; you've already started thinking about it. I'll get you a pen and some paper.

Now continue thinking of anyone else you suspect and put them on your list. Don't forget to state why and again grade your suspects; 1 -10."

Else's fingers clamped the pen tightly, but there was another long pause. "Well, Elsa, anyone?" Penny asked.

"I can think of a few people from my school days, but they were just a result of kids' school arguments and fall-outs; you know the type of thing. Not something you'd put on a list like this!"

"Elsa, put anybody on the list that comes to mind, even if they're unlikely but only mark them with a low grading!" Penny said with enthusiasm as Elsa was getting there.

Elsa scribbled a few more details on the notepaper but graded each entry between 1 and 3, so maybe not a decent selection after all.

She was in the process of writing another name, looked up at me, stopped and stared.

"What is it, Elsa? Have you thought of somebody else for the list?"

"Certainly somebody else who might fit the bill."

"Well go on, write it down!" Penny said, "just in case you forget their name!"

"No, not this name Penny I won't forget this one!" Elsa said woefully.

"Elsa, how many more times, if you want to trace this gutless individual, then you must consider everybody and write their names down on the paper. So far the only number 10 you have is the Brotherton woman. Who are you thinking about now?"

"Well, this person's a potential number 10 although I'm not going to write the name on the paper or why!"

"Ok, Elsa, in that case just tell me!"

Chapter 49

Discussing Rome in greater depth, it was clear either Brandon already knew a lot about it, or he had spent significant time investigating. Whatever his conversation, it made our Dinner most enjoyable.

"I've already discussed the various selections for tomorrow's viewing, but I think you should make the choice in which order we visit them, Alice," Brandon said.

I was most appreciative of his offer, but he had a much better idea of the highlights, so I asked him to choose the order.

"Ok Alice, I will write what I think is the best order for the whole weekend, and over breakfast tomorrow morning we will agree between us, to make sure we don't keep changing our minds."

"Very organised of you." I laughed but with sincerity.

Checking Brandon's list, the City of Rome was teeming with historic buildings, spectacular scenery and places of interest to visit, such as museums and palaces.

Its many streets are adorned, by spectacular monuments and the most notable landmark in Italy, the Coliseum.

"Well, Alice, do you like the choices?" he asked.

"Everything looks brilliant to me, Brandon, so let's just go, and you can enthral me when we arrive wherever it is you have selected!"

"Ok then Alice, the first choice will be the obvious one, somewhere that everybody should visit!"

"Where?" I asked in wonder.

"I'm not going to tell you now so you must guess; it'll add to the fun," Brandon said with a big smile on his face.

We hadn't been walking for long when our destination became apparent as a result of the many signposts, all pointing towards St Peter's square and the Vatican City.

It was costly to book our trip around the Vatican, St Peter's Square and the Basilica itself but it was certainly worth every penny of our money, or should I say Lire.

Although like most people, I had heard of the Vatican City, I never realised how much there was to see. Despite the lengthy tourist queues everywhere we looked, it was a treat to behold.

The climb up the 230 odd steps to the top of the dome, seemed effortless for Brandon, but it exhausted me, and I had to stop several times for a brief rest.

However the panoramic view of Rome was undoubtedly worth the effort; wherever I looked the sight was incredible, and when I loosely closed my eyes, squinting, I could so easily imagine stepping back in time a few thousand years.

The semi-circular collonades surrounding the Square and the cobbled spaces, definitely took my imagination back several centuries.

We checked Brandon's list once again. We agreed that we would need at least a week, possibly longer, to make the most of our visits to St Peter's Basilica, the Vatican Museums, Michelangelo's Sistine Chapel, the Vatican Gardens and the Grottoes containing the tombs of former Popes.

There was all this, and of course, we both wanted to enjoy an Italian coffee for two, sitting at different locations as we overlooked the River Tiber.

All of a sudden, I stopped in my tracks.

"Is anything wrong, Alice?" Brendon asked with concern.

"No, I'm ok thanks, Brandon." Although in reality, the thought of a drink sitting alongside the River Tiber bought back memories of Helen's young life. I know I had absolutely no reason to feel like it, but temporarily I was frightened!

Brandon told me that somewhere under the Colonnade, there is the Vatican's own Post Office where we can buy stamps and send our cards directly from Vatican City. "You can send a card to Elsa as well as Penny and also your friends at work. Imagine what it must be like to receive a card with the Vatican City stamped on it."

During Saturday and Sunday, we also visited other highlights including the Arch of Constantine and Palatine Hill which Brandon told me is the centremost of the seven hills of Rome and one of the most ancient parts of the City.

Tomorrow was Monday, our final day and Brandon said there was somewhere special we were going to visit.

"I never wrote it down as I wanted it to be a surprise for our final day and it's another place of interest, every tourist should visit." He said.

Mind you he had said this about most of the places in Rome!

During dinner that evening, I did everything I could think of, to prize the details from him, but he kept laughing and telling me to have more patience. Also, he kept dropping different clues to make me respond even more.

Our Monday flight, home to Gatwick was late evening, but Brandon had still set our alarm for 5,30am so we would have as much time as possible to appreciate our final day and the surprise visit he had planned for me.

Sleep for me had been challenging, as I kept wondering what Brandon had planned, although I knew it would undoubtedly be something exceptional.

Today was similar to our Vatican visit as Brandon believed it was better to surprise me, rather than tell me what he had planned!

Wherever it was, the scenery was beautiful as were the spectacular homes in this part of Rome. Once again, I sadly remembered Helen telling me about it and then some of the glamour disappeared for me.

We were walking through a lane which connected to a square.

Before we reached the end of the passageway, Brandon suddenly placed his hands over my eyes and said: "Keep walking Alice and trust me, we're almost there."

I walked for what seemed ages with both of his hands clamped firmly over my face. Gingerly, I stepped forward, one foot in front of another.

Appreciating my anxiety, Brandon attempted to relieve

it when he said: "It's going to be worth it, we're nearly there; ok now open your eyes."

In front of me was an enormous concrete building, approximately 90 feet tall and 60 feet wide. Water gushed into a pool with life-sized granite statues either situated on the edge of the pool or peering from the building overlooking the fountain itself.

I had read about this particular site and immediately guessed this was the famous Trevi Fountain. Brandon confirmed my belief, telling me that, legend holds that a coin thrown into the fountain by ancient Roman's made the Gods of the water favour their safe journey wherever they were travelling.

"Apparently if you're seeking love you throw in a second coin." He said.

I listened but didn't hear one coin thrown into the fountain, let alone two!

Listening intently to Brandon's interesting comments about the fountain and Rome itself, I realised how knowledgeable he was. I recognised his research before our visit had been worthwhile.

The entire weekend had been fabulous and queueing at Fiumicino Airport for our flight home; I realised how much I was in love with him, irrespective of his taste for a beer or two! Mind you, I had noticed for some reason, Brandon had drunk hardly any alcohol while we'd been staying in Rome; maybe it was his mates' that influenced him after all!

The flight home seemed much quicker as he occupied my attention, telling me about Trevi Fountain and the other beautiful sights we had visited.

"Trevi fountain was built at the end of the aqueduct, at the junction of three roads. These three streets, *Tre vie*, give Trevi Fountain its name, the *Three Street* Fountain."

Ordinarily, I could have been bored senseless, but I found his knowledge extremely interesting. Not only that but his different descriptions painted so many memorable pictures in my mind.

However, he was embarrassed when I asked him why St Peter's Square was circular and yet it was called a square. Brandon, who seemed to know the answer to everything about Rome, obviously hadn't researched this question.

Our return flight was much better, although, much To Brandon's disappointment, the distribution of free alcohol was less generous than when we flew to Rome.

The conversation had dwindled during the flight.

I noticed he hadn't shaved. It must have been the early morning rush, but I couldn't help mentioning it. At least it created conversation.

"I've decided to grow a beard as I think it would look good on me!" He replied.

"Yes, I can see that, and it would certainly make you look more masculine!" I laughed.

"More masculine, eh? Well thank you so much, Alice, I rever realised what a complete and utter wimp I looked. Oh, I might even join the Gym and add some muscle to this sad looking body!" He said.

I smiled but wondered whether he was serious. Mum's historical and dubious thought's and her opinion of David Wilson returned!

It was late Monday night when we arrived home to be

greeted by Elsa. "Was it a good weekend Sis," she asked with much interest. "Tell me about it?"

Everywhere inside the home was neat and tidy; as both Brandon and I knew it would be. Brandon took the words from my mouth when he said with genuine appreciation "Thank you very much indeed, Elsa,"

Considering our early rise and busy day, the door to door journey from Rome to Caversham had also been a tiring one; we sat on the sofa and told Elsa what a special place it was and everything about our weekend and the different sights we had seen.

Looking at my watch at least an hour and a half had passed since we had started to tell Elsa about everything; both Brendon and I were exhausted and apologising to Elsa, we made our way to bed.

"Tell me more tomorrow," Elsa said. "Goodnight and sleep well!"

Not surprising Elsa hadn't received my postcard sent from the Vatican; it had only been a couple of days since I posted it.

To recover after our long weekend to Rome and back, I had booked an additional day off work and knew I could spend a few more hours relaxing in comfort. Brandon had another contract to start; unlucky I thought!

Thoughtfully Elsa had also taken a day off work just in case there had been problems of any sort during the weekend or whether I might have needed assistance in any way.

"So how did you get along with Brandon; any problems?" Elsa asked with concern.

"No, he was the most perfect of company and Rome was unexpectedly brilliant; Any doubts I might have had about taking him before the trip, disappeared entirely. He is still the man I fell in love with all that time ago."

"Much happen while we were away Elsa?" I continued.

"Not much;" said Elsa and then remembering, "Oh yes, The Police!

Penny got me thinking about whoever it might have been causing us all those crazy problems before you left for Rome.

I visited the Police and told them of my theory, Fiona Brotherton."

"Fiona Brotherton, you mean Tim's Ex?"

"Yep Sis, that Bitch! They took me into a backroom, accompanied by two people, a woman officer and most likely the Officer in charge of our complaint and what do you think I found out?

The Police already had their suspicions because of their records and the history between us."

"So it was Fiona Brotherton," I replied without much thought.

"Oh yes, and it gets worse than that Sis! There was also somebody else behind it!"

"Who?" I exclaimed but now with keener interest.

I knew Elsa was enjoying teasing me. "Apart from that bitch, think about who else I have pissed off this last year or so!"

I thought seriously for a while but had to accept defeat and asked Elsa to tell me.

"Tim, remember I dumped him for defending Brotherton

when she attacked me, and I clouted her with that metal ball you bought for me at the market.

Anyway, they're back together again; Boyfriend and Girlfriend. The Police told me Tim had admitted the charge, and it was initially his idea, a laugh he thought! Although Brotherton typed the letter, they were both involved in making the different phone calls."

"Oh Elsa I can't believe it; and what did the Police do."

"I don't know Sis; possibly, they were both charged for wasting Police time when they accused me of being a dealer. And of course, you will remember that like me, Brotherton was under an earlier warning, not to harass or cause each other problems, remember?

As for Tim, the bastard, I've no idea why he would think it was fun! I hope both of them rot in hell."

"Yes I can understand how you feel Elsa, but why me? What had I done to them? Whatever we can both set the record straight with Brandon. Mind you. I hope this solves his recent aggressive approach's towards me. Although I'm pleased to say, there was no such response during our time in Rome; he was a real gentleman, a completely different person!"

"Oh, one more thing Alice, I've had a few more of the dodgy phone calls; you know the ones that hang up when we answer. That was after the Police got hold of Tim and his fucking girlfriend, so I'm guessing it's not them!"

"Then who the hell is it?" I asked with concern!"

Chapter 50

Elsa was home when Jayne knocked on the door. "I Apologise, you're Alice's sister Elsa aren't you?"

"Yes," Elsa replied, "Can I help you?"

"I wanted to talk to Alice," Jayne answered. "It's something personal. I'm Jayne, one of the Cabs4U drivers."

I was wondering and even concerned at Jayne's visit when thankfully Alice arrived home with bits and pieces of shopping she had collected on her way from work.

Jayne took Alice to one side and made a brief comment. Alice was far from happy and somewhat argumentive with her friend Jayne.

"What was all that about?" Elsa asked with curiosity.

"I'll tell you indoors." Alice briefly replied.

As Jayne drove away, Elsa and I moved back inside the home to help me prepare dinner.

"So Alice, what was that all about?" Elsa questioned, knowing there were only two options; I'd tell her or I wouldn't.

"Recently, I told Helen about comments Penny had made about Brandon, and she then told Jayne. As a result, whenever either of them drove past they have been keeping an eye on the Café where Penny thinks Brandon might have a lady friend.

A few times, they have seen Brandon enter the shop. Such as today!" I said with concern.

"A few times, Alice. What once, twice, five or six, what's a few times Alice?" Elsa questioned.

"I know what you're saying Elsa, but in reality, I'm not too sure either.

It could have been to do with his work; couldn't it," Alice stated hopefully, "Or even that's where he stops for breakfast or to buy sandwiches; who knows?

Anyway recently and especially in Rome, he's been the perfect boyfriend. We've got on so well that at any time, I wouldn't be surprised if he proposed to me, so why would he even think about another woman? Penny and Chris have blown this story out of all proportion!"

"Hopefully you're right Sis and as I said, what's a *few times*? Think about it, because of your concerns you put the idea of his infidelity in Helen and Jayne's head and because he stops at a Café a couple of times because he's hungry and wants to buy something to eat, a couple becomes a *few times,* whatever that might mean. Soon that will become *loadsa times*!"

Again, I dismissed all the negative comments about Brandon. His drinking even seemed to improve, and on some occasions, he returned home sober, although sometimes it was still exceptionally late.

I started to question myself, why would Chris have made any such comments to Penny, unless it was the truth?

Thinking deeper could it even be that Chris knew Brandon

had fancied Penny and perhaps Chris believed Brandon might still be interested.

Chris, telling Penny, about Brandon's *other woman* and knowing what good friends Penny and I were, just might put Penny off Brandon, if there was ever a chance she was 'on him' in the first place.

It was a possibility, but at times, I continued to torture myself. Then in a moment of reality, I questioned the positive side of events and without reservation, once again told myself how much I was in love with him.

Should I tell Penny about Brandon's historical view of her and then mention my conclusions about why Chris had told her about Brandon?

For a long time, I realised I must have this particular conversation with her, but the time never seemed right, and apart from that, I knew it was likely to destroy our close friendship, once and for all.

Fortunately, Penny was still there for me; sometimes to nullify any concerns I might have about anything, in particular, It was even better when we had her wonderful daughter Tina to amuse us.

Her curly hair had grown quite strongly, a natural blonde and she was developing individual characteristics such as liking sweets, wanting her own way, liking shoes and of course loving her Mum without reservation.

Playing with Penny's makeup, if she could get her hands on it, was also pretty high up on the list.

She was a typical youngster!

I so wanted a child of my own!

Since Brandon had talked about his complaints of how

Elsa and I had treated him since we moved in together and complaining about everything, Elsa and I had successfully managed to reserve any comments we might have had.

Although in reality there hadn't been anything worth mentioning.

Yes, this approach had seemed to work, and as a result, the three of us found living together much, much better.

One evening we were all eating our dinner of Beef Goulash, cooked skilfully by Elsa, the recipe learnt when watching the cooks preparing meals at the Care-home.

Brandon said "Don't cook dinner for me tomorrow night, or yourselves, as I'm taking the two of you for a meal at the Italian Restaurant. I've already booked the table, Alice."

It was a great surprise for me because, after our beautiful meals in Rome, and our local restaurant, Italian food had now, without a doubt, become one of my favourite cuisines. However, I wondered with great interest, whether there was a particular reason for this specific night out?

Elsa also thanked Brandon as following our descriptions, now and again, of how enticing Italian food was, especially the most recent stories, she was grateful to be asked.

The following evening Elsa arrived home from work before Brandon, and while she had the chance, she questioned me about all the thoughts which must have continually crossed her mind while working at the Care-home.

"Why all three of us, why not just you and him? Has he got a surprise for both of us and if so, what is it? Is he finally going to propose to you or perhaps even propose to us both?" She said with one of her mischievous giggles!

Similar thoughts had puzzled me throughout the day,

but I managed to distract Elsa enough when I mentioned that Brandon would soon be home and me and Elsa had limited time to prepare ourselves for the evening at the restaurant.

Brandon arrived, asking whether we were ready, although the answer to his question was an obvious one and he knew it!

At the Restaurant, Brandon apologised for our late arrival, and Elsa mumbled something of an apology saying it was all her fault, not Brandon's or mine.

The food, the drink, everything about the meal was fantastic, but Elsa's expression was not quite what I had expected. For some reason, I noticed an expression on her face which puzzled me.

The three of us chatted accordingly, and there were no negative approaches from Brandon so clearly the evening must be leading up to something more positive but then again if it was, what?

Also, I still wanted to know why he had invited Elsa to join us?

Although it was a good night out, Brandon had made no statement of intent or asked me any specific questions.

I was mystified; however Brandon had more than enjoyed his consumption of wine, and it was fortunate that Elsa and I were fit enough to help him home through the dark streets, especially those even darker ones where the light bulbs had failed.

It had started to rain quite heavily, and on a few occasions, Brandon made the gentlemanly effort to pull us all undercover into either a shop or house doorway.

However, his thoughtful efforts created more problems than they resolved, especially on the occasion when he slipped on the wet surface and crashed into a household door. At least the damp pavement was his excuse!

In the local Reading dialect, the householder called us all *a load of down and out drunks who should know better than disturbing those that rested after a hard days work!* Or words to that effect.

Whatever, it did give us all something to laugh about, although it was Elsa, my considerate sister, who backed the householder's complaint and said she could hardly blame him for his comments; after all, it was our fault, and we were making a loud din!

Me, I was still asking myself the reason for this night out.

Chapter 51

During the next week or two Penny and I met up, always accompanied by Tina but on each occasion, it appeared Penny mentioned Brandon, less and less.

It did occur to me that as Brandon was once again in my good books, it was better and more enjoyable for Penny to talk about Tina.

Especially when she started crying about nothing in particular and then smiling at me when Penny turned away from us; Tina wanted something!

"Anyway Alice, I'm pleased you and Brandon are getting on so well, especially since your dear Mum departed you and Elsa, it's good you have Brandon by your side."

Was this the time, should I ask Penny about Chris's comments of Brandon and another woman?

I took the cowards approach and asked her what she thought about Chris's remarks about Brandon; were they realistic?

Unintentionally Penny sidestepped my question when she said: "He appears to be treating you well, but Chris knows Brandon better than most, so he's the one you should question; anyway why are you asking?"

Aggressively I replied, "I'd have thought that was obvious, Penny!" And then I realised why I'd had the original concern about discussing this particular matter with Penny. "Sorry, Penny, It's just that I'm not sure exactly where I am with Brandon."

"You mean, whether there's another woman or whether he will ask you to marry him?" Penny asked me earnestly.

Immediately it became clear; Penny's different questions were one, and the same. Would Brandon marry me if there wasn't another woman in his life?

I could see how easily this conversation could develop the wrong way, so I didn't ask more questions but focussed on baby Tina.

Irrespective of me changing the subject matter, Penny said, "Chris didn't say Brandon was having a relationship with another woman, just that he was seeing another woman!"

Now, Penny was playing with words, and I regretted asking the initial question so very much.

"Anyway Alice, Brandon's certainly a much better partner than David Wilson ever was. I even recall you saying that!"

Penny seemed to be protecting Brandon, and for a brief moment, I wondered about the possibility of a friendship between the two of them. I knew what Brandon thought of Penny; No, surely not!

Rather than ask Penny to forget about Brandon, and Chris, I continued discussing Tina and how well she looked.

Thankfully it worked, Chris and Brandon and any other related questions evaporated, or so I thought!

Before Penny and I parted company, Penny said: "Alice, remember when you and Brandon were in Rome, I stayed the night with Elsa; well I think you should ask her what she honestly thinks about him."

"Why, what did she say?" I asked; just that one statement of Penny's was oh, so mysterious.

"You must ask Elsa."

"Penny, we're friends. Please tell me?"

"Well, I suppose Elsa didn't say this part of the conversation was in confidence; after witnessing your situation following the break-up with David, she's become so concerned about the potential effect of a bust-up with Brandon. We are both concerned, knowing how traumatically it affected you last time. Whatever Alice. please talk to Elsa!"

"What more is there to talk about?" I asked Penny.

"There's more Alice, but please talk to Elsa but make sure there's just the two of you."

"So why haven't you talked to me before about this Penny?" I asked more out of interest than wanting a specific answer.

"For the same reason as Elsa, and also because I don't want to upset Chris any more than I already have when I told you about the Café shop woman and Brandon."

"So what are you saying, Penny?" I asked with a high degree of frustration and what was now anger.

"What I'm saying Alice is you must wait, during what you consider a suitable time, outside a particular café and I'm saying nothing more about this specific matter apart from talking to Elsa; and I mean seriously talk to her."

"About what?" I asked now earnestly worried by the statement and the authoritative tone of Penny's voice.

"I'd like to tell you, Alice, but she told me something else, and that was in extreme confidence; you remember when you and Brandon were in Rome, you asked me to check that Elsa was Ok. Well, she talked to me about the creep that was telling stories about Elsa and drugs."

"You mean Brotherton and her old boyfriend, Tim?"

"Yes, Alice, but there was also another possibility at the top of her list."

"And that was?" I asked.

"That's my problem, Alice. Elsa was most reluctant to talk about it. When I persuaded her to tell me who it was, it was conditional that I told nobody; this my friend is why I'm saying you must talk to her if you want to know the answer."

That evening Brandon was late home from work, and I thought, nothing changes, even if I had believed things might be better after our return from Rome.

Before even thinking about visiting the Café, I knew things weren't right; just the tone of Penny's voice had told me everything I needed to know. And then her mysterious conversation telling me to ask Elsa?"

Penny could have told me more, I just knew it, but perhaps her idea was if I found this woman myself, in Brandon's presence, it would be so much more comfortable for her and Chris, than if Chris found out that Penny had informed me about this woman and the relationship.

Those traumatic feelings I had experienced with David were once again growing out of control. I was hearing

A Dose of Insulin

stories from others, and at the same time wishing, I could discount them. After our fantastic trip away, the fact that I even doubted Brandon was seriously confusing.

I had booked a day's holiday from work and, I stood in a closed shop doorway, marked *Premises for lease*, across the road from the Café.

A few people visited the Cafe, and after a short while, the same people left but no sign of Brandon entering or leaving.

It was 4 pm, and there had been no sight of him.

I reassessed everything Penny, Elsa and Jayne had said, and perhaps I was even grateful that so far, I hadn't seen him entering or leaving the Café.

A notepad I had intentionally purchased for the visit, so far, only bore today's date. There were no comments worth writing.

On several occasions during the day, I convinced myself this exploration had been a complete waste of time and considered returning home for a nice hot cup of coffee and a comfy chair. Still, something kept me waiting outside my observation post.

This puzzle of mine was stupid. I wanted to know the truth, but then again, I certainly didn't want to find Brandon with another woman!

I had given up when the Café door opened and out walked Brandon; he must have been there for the whole day. Surely not! I was shocked.

I left it a good few minutes before I followed Brandon home and then stopped off at a shop to buy some ready-made meals, something quick to prepare for tonight's dinner although a couple of times I did ask myself why I was even bothering? Whatever, it was a habit!

By the time I arrived home, I was an emotional wreck!

As I unlocked the front door, Brandon asked me where I'd been today?

I was so angry at his question but replied: "Nowhere really, only out to buy us all something to eat for our dinner. What about you, what have you been doing?" I asked him with anticipation, wondering what his reply would be.

"Working, of course."

"Whereabouts," I asked, once again, interested to hear his reply.

"What is this, a fucking quiz show?" He answered aggressively.

"No, I'm just interested in your business and your day in general."

"Well it's a job I'm just finishing in Bracknell," Brandon replied without a flicker of guilt on his face. He was sober, so I know he couldn't even try to use drunkenness as an excuse for telling a blatant lie!

"So when will you finish this Bracknell job?" I asked while trying to commit him to this dubious explanation.

"Another couple of day's, maybe more depending on what additional work they want doing."

Brandon moved upstairs for a shower, and I called Penny on my mobile, quietly explaining my day and the lies Brandon had told me.

"Is he nearby?" Penny asked.

"He's upstairs and having a shower, and for once he's sober," I replied.

"Good, now what I'm going to say is only a suggestion, Alice, it's what I'd do in your position. I'd confront him."

"Yes, Penny that's an obvious conclusion, but I thought we were getting on so well together, and if he denied it, it would solve nothing and just create a massive fallout between us!"

"Please let me finish Alice instead of watching him from across the road. I'd follow him inside the Café and confront him there; in front of her! Whichever way you deal with it, eventually there will be a fallout – like it or not."

"You're right Penny. I might as well deal with it sooner rather than later. Anyway, I can hear him moving upstairs, so I'd better go for now, but as always I'll keep you in touch with what's going on."

Shortly afterwards, Brandon came downstairs and collected two cold cans of beer from the fridge, also explaining he wasn't hungry so I shouldn't cook him anything to eat; "I'll eat when I'm hungry, thank you."

"So I guess you've had something decent to eat today, Brandon," I stated knowingly.

He said nothing but carried on drinking from one of his cans of beer.

When arriving home, Elsa's question after question routine was no different.

After today's revelations, I wanted to tell her but knew the conversation would continue for hours and most likely involve Brandon to an unacceptable degree if he heard us talking; an almost certainty!

Also, Penny had said I needed to talk to Elsa.

Even then, if I could talk to Elsa in private, I wouldn't tell her about Brandon being in the Café for the entire day.

I decided to say nothing about what I had planned for tomorrow as it might complicate my tactics if Elsa disagreed or thought I should deal with matters differently. I knew her ways of dealing with this particular matter definitely wouldn't be mine.

Before saying anything to anybody, I wanted to be 100% sure I was right.

Chapter 52

Awaking, the following morning, I waited for Elsa and Brandon to wash and prepare for work before I dressed.

They had both left home when I phoned work; Justine answered my call and passed me through to Steve. I explained I had a few personal issues and needed to take a couple of extra days holiday.

Being the individual, he was Steve didn't ask any questions, knowing that if I had something to say I would tell him when I was ready.

Now, I had a few more days off work, and I thought about what Penny had recommended but decided to watch the Café for another day before confronting Brandon in the shop.

My legs were tired, and after waiting opposite the Café for another whole day, I desperately needed a women's toilet, but I daren't move from where I was in case I missed Brandon either entering or leaving the premises.

My suffering continued until *the girlfriend* locked the shop door and I guess made her way home; this, was the first time I had seen her, and she was nothing exceptional. I wondered why Brandon would have chosen her over me.

There was not any sight of Brandon; perhaps he was genuinely working in Bracknell! The whole day had been a complete waste of my bloody time!

I told Elsa of my concerns about Brandon, his visit to the Café when he had told me he was working in Bracknell a couple of days ago, and my plan following the conversation with Penny.

"Well Alice, Penny was right; at some time you are going to have to deal with it, so I suggest you do what she said and confront them both in the Café.

Please let me help you, as I'm sure I can ease the pain and certainly be there just in case either of them starts on you; it must be terrible for you dealing with it all by yourself." Elsa said with sincerity.

"Perhaps there is something you can do to help me, Elsa; Penny suggested I talk to you about something you told her while we were in Italy."

"Oh no! Elsa exclaimed I told her not to tell anybody, especially you."

"What do you mean *especially me* Elsa?" I asked with concern.

"Well Alice, it was that other No1 at the top of my suspect list for whoever might have been saying I was a drug dealer and causing me problems with the Police.

It is something I'm going to deal with in my own time," Elsa remarked like somebody who had everything scheduled. Her reply was most strange, and I wanted to know the answer!

"But you still haven't answered my question Elsa, why *especially me*?"

"Because Sis, the other person I had at the top of my suspect list was Brandon!"

"Brandon!" I confirmed with alarm. "Are you going to tell me why?"

"It doesn't matter now Sis, Tim and that bitch Brotherton were the quilty ones so please forget about Brandon."

"I understand that Elsa, but Brandon, my partner, was on your list. Tell me why!"

I was upset that Elsa wouldn't tell me more as I couldn't remember a time when either of us hid a secret from each other! Was the strong bond, Elsa and I possessed since childhood, disappearing? Was there more to this story than she was telling me?

"Whatever Alice, you know I'm here for you and please, please don't get into the state of mind you did with David. And if you do, as I've told you before, you must talk to me immediately."

Brandon continued to drink his beer throughout the evening. As usual, he drank a lot and eventually fell asleep in the armchair while watching a film on the TV.

The atmosphere between Brandon, Elsa and I was most strange; it seemed as though everybody knew something, but nobody said anything.

Elsa walked to her bedroom as she typed something on her mobile.

I switched the TV off, and unlike most times, there is no automatic response from Brandon telling me he is listening to the programme, even though he is snoring.

He is asleep.

My mobile phone pinged to tell me I had received a text message; it was from Penny and just said 'R U OK?'

Before contacting her, I walked upstairs to the bedroom and deliberately left the door open to make sure I could hear Brandon walking up the stairs if he awoke from his snores.

I phoned Penny and explained my day's activities. Also, my surprise that his shop *girlfriend* was quite ordinary and not the sort of woman I'd have expected Brandon to find of interest.

"But Alice, that's why I text you; I wanted to know how you were and also to tell you that the woman in the shop today wasn't his girlfriend; apparently, the girlfriend took a day off work and went on a Thames boat trip with Brandon.

Her name's Sandra. At least that's what Chris told me the night before. Now that's twice he's told you he was working in Bracknell and twice he wasn't."

Right, I was going to confront them both, Brandon and his *bit on the side* and rethought my plan of attack; the Café with other witnesses to hand just in case it developed into something nasty, was the best location.

Also, as Brandon had already told me he was working in Bracknell, he couldn't then deny he was in Reading!

I didn't tell Elsa of my plan as I didn't want her to become involved but again waited for her and Brandon to leave for work and then prepared myself for another Café visit. It was a windy morning, and even my thick overcoat with the woollen hood didn't stop the cold.

Using my small umbrellas was impossible as the wind kept blowing it inside out. I just hoped the hood on my coat would manage to keep my hair in respectable order.

A Dose of Insulin

During my walk to the Café, it occurred to me that Brandon actually might be working somewhere today as he had to earn money somehow. Again, was it going to be a complete waste of my time?

Then again, if he was going to visit her, at what time would it be. It would look unusual for me to spend the whole day sitting in the Café, occupying a table all by myself.

I decided to look in from outside, and if I couldn't see him, I'll make the best of my time and look around the shopping centre, maybe even visit the Station's coffee shop and think about Mum and days past.

Religiously I followed this plan, but there was no sight of Brandon, although now and again I could see an energetic woman, clothed in a white apron, either serving or cleaning the tables.

After another tiring day, I returned home with absolutely no positive result. Mind you, I now had a rough idea of what this woman looked like, and she was prettier than her stand in the day before.

Not a lot, but she was better looking with beautiful shoulder-length black hair.

Irrespective of what Brandon was going to tell me tonight, tomorrow I was going to follow him, at least for a short distance, just in case he did go to the Café, and then I would confront them both.

Brandon eventually arrived home at 10.45 pm, and alcoholically, he was past the point of having a normal conversation. I wondered whether he might have turned up at the Café after I had left and taken her for a few drinks?

Or maybe he'd even met his drinking pals and taken her along with him?

Whatever, wherever he's been and with whom, he'd certainly had a great deal of alcohol to drink.

The following morning as soon as Brandon leaves home, I follow him, walking a considerable distance behind. Was today the day I'd catch them together?

No matter the possibility, and not knowing what to expect was frightening.

Immediately I realise he's not going to Bracknell as he doesn't head towards the Railway station and therefore he must be heading towards the Café. Excellent!

After he entered through the front door of the Café, I waited a few minutes before boldly walking in; there was no Brandon. I rang the counter Bell, and the women I now believed to be his girlfriend stepped from the back room and asked me what I wanted.

In a voice quieter than usual, I asked for a cup of black coffee and took it to a seat out of sight of the side-room where she had returned.

In the background, I could hear a heated exchange of voices; the most expressive was Brandon's!

He steps from the side-room followed immediately by *the girlfriend.*

Walking over, he asks "And what are you doing here?"

"I could ask you the same question, Brandon, you said you were working in Bracknell!"

"Yes, I am, and I've popped in here for Breakfast."

"But I could have cooked breakfast for you, or you could have eaten something at the Railway Station before you got the train to Bracknell. Why come here; it's in the opposite direction of the Station?"

The girlfriend interrupted aggressively.

"Fucking hell Brandon, stop fooling about and tell her."

"Please, Sandra, don't create unnecessary problems!" Brandon said with authority.

"Now Alice, you go home, and I'll explain later!"

"What, explain the fucking obvious about you and this bitch, you bastard?" I raged.

On the way back home, although pleased, I had tracked him and his girlfriend, I was far from happy about it. I was puzzled why Brandon had ushered the girlfriend back into the side-room and told me to leave immediately without saying anything further. I had discovered them; why not admit his relationship?

I rang Elsa on her mobile phone, confirmed what had happened and asked her to meet me at home urgently as I was concerned about what Brandon might do whenever he got home. I then sent a text to Penny confirming what had happened so far and that I would update her after I'd heard Brandon's response.

A short while later, Brandon returned home, and understandably he was stone-cold sober.

With Elsa standing by my side, Brandon's first words were "Right, sit down, both of you! Alice, what was today all about?"

Immediately Elsa interrupts, "You know what it was all about Brandon, you cheating bastard!"

"A cheating bastard, eh? You brainless piece of shit,

you've got no idea what you are talking about, now sit down, shut up and let me speak!"

I was about to say something in support of Elsa and call him much worse than she had. I opened my mouth to speak, and Brandon said: "Don't you dare say anything, Alice; I can probably guess what you're thinking!

No, I haven't been working in Bracknell, and yes, I've been spending all my time recently in the Café with Sandra. Is that what you want to hear?

I initially worked for her and her husband when they got married a few years ago. And yes she's a kind woman, and I like her a lot. I guess that mouthy friend of yours, Penny has stirred you up with all this shit!"

At this point, I was afraid Elsa was going to attack him as it was clear she was so outraged and once again, I attempted to intervene.

Chapter 53

"No, Alice, let me finish. Rightly or wrongly, for some while now, I've got the impression that you wanted more out of our relationship and marriage is something I've never really contemplated before.

Still, I did want you to know how much I care for you, even more so, after we both spent that fantastic time in Rome."

Once again I wanted to say something, but I only got as far as saying "But…." when Brandon raised his right index finger.

"Do you remember Alice, telling me when you started working at Cabs4U that it would be good for us all to run a family business of our own? You, me and Elsa!

Well, this was it! Our café with plenty of room to live. Sandra told me she wanted to pack it in and move back up north with her husband and settle near their respective families.

Approaching the landlord, he told me he would continue to lease it as a business or sell it as a going concern. A great deal of work needed doing to the property, so we agreed a deal.

I would do the necessary maintenance work, it was pretty much simple and easy jobs like woodwork, decorating and tiling, and when finished, I'd have the first choice of buying the business for us all. Alternatively, I could lease it for you to run as your own. And that is why I been spending so much time at the Café.

Whether we buy it or lease it, the choice would be yours. All I wanted to do was show how much I care for you and all I get is a pile of shit!

Finally, if we didn't buy it and decided to lease, he would offset my renovation costs! Although I would also ask you to consider the amount of savings we'd possess after selling this home and buying the Café!

We would be able to have regular holidays, plenty of cash to do what we wanted to the Café and a lot more besides!" Brandon opened his arms wide and said, "Now it's your turn so over to you, Alice."

There was absolute silence, and Brandon still facing me but with his outstretched arms now lowered by his side, asked: "Well, haven't you got anything to say, Alice?" The silence continued so turning to face Elsa he said: "You had plenty to say a few minutes ago Elsa, so what do you want to say now?"

Suddenly Alice walked closer to Brandon, said nothing but wrapped both her arms tightly around him and kissed him.

Elsa then joined them in a silent group cuddle.

I felt so very guilty but didn't know what to say and exactly how we could all recover from this exceptional misunderstanding.

Understanding the reason for Brandon's *white lies* and his regular visits to the Cafe: It wasn't a simple matter explaining why, under such circumstances, any woman would have believed the same as me.

Brandon listened intently to my explanation.

Elsa backed up my reasoning and also made her apologies.

It wasn't clear whether Brandon had accepted our apologies or indeed the explanation as the evening moved on with only a few more words spoken between us. No doubt caused by extreme embarrassment.

Fantastic, I was overwhelmed at the thought of owning my own business.

However, none of us wanted to eat, or even drink, although the silent and upsetting atmosphere didn't stop Brandon from consuming his prescribed level of alcohol!

My brain was bursting, and I had to talk to someone, so naturally enough, I called Penny on her mobile. She apologised as she was in the middle of feeding Tina.

I was in such a state of confusion, that although she offered, I didn't want her to hang up and call me back later.

In the background, I could hear words and then a baby's cry as Chris had taken Tina from Penny.

I repeated what had happened; my visit to the Café, the accusations and subsequent explanation from Brandon. There was a silence between Penny and me.

"Please say something Penny," I said with frustration at the lack of reaction to my incredible news.

"I don't know what to say Alice other than if it's true,

what a pleasant surprise it is for you. Certainly, Brandon's a very thoughtful guy!"

Her reply upset me "What do you mean *if* it's true?" I said cantankerously.

"Did you speak to Elsa following our recent conversation?" Penny asked inquisitively.

"I did, and she mentioned Brandon, but as the case was solved, she didn't see the necessity of talking about him any further."

"Ok." was Penny's only comment.

I noticed that not once, did Penny mention Chris or any of his upsetting comments made about Brandon during these last few months!

After Penny's brief comment, the silence returned. I made my excuses and ended our conversation, once again wondering whether our friendship would ever be the same?

I was awake early morning and made Brandon sandwiches, each with different fillings, although it was more of a gesture as I knew he still had some work to finish at the Café and I was confident he would eat there.

That night was another 'Vampire shift' for me, but I so much wanted to tell the news to my friends at Cabs4U, and I knew Helen was working the day shift. I decided to drop in and inform her of my exceptional news and then return home again for a quick nap before returning to start my long shift.

At least running a café would be regular hours.

As a matter of courtesy, I had to tell Steve so he would have time to find my replacement. However, he was such a kind man, just the thought of informing him upset me a great deal, let alone ultimately leaving the business I had enjoyed so much.

I opened the Cabs4U door, and Helen was surprised to see me. "Want a Cab?" she said with a laugh.

"No thank you, Helen, I have some great news to tell you and Jayne, but I must tell Steve first."

"Ok then, place Jayne and me at the bottom of the list, Steve's out the back. I don't know what he's doing, but whenever he hears your dulcet tones he's normally out here like a shot!"

"Oh Helen, you know that's not true, anyway I'll make him a coffee, would you like one?"

"Is the Pope a Catholic?" she said with one of her sarcastic grins.

I walked into the back room and greeted Steve who was crouched over his table and spreading paperwork everywhere, presumably into some order, although I thought it would look tidier if he just dumped the lot into his waste bin!

"Hi, Steve, like a coffee?" I asked.

"Yes please, Alice and what's the problem!" He replied.

I told him the story, and just the look in his eyes and his body language told me how pleased he was for me.

"Congratulations Alice, I hope your replacement is going to be as good as you. A naturally reactive individual, in the best way possible! Anyway, I'm going to miss you so very much, as will your workmates and customers; have you told any of them yet?"

"Thank you, Steve. No, you're the first to know, but I'm going to tell Helen next as she's out the front."

"Ok, tell you what Alice, she can have a coffee break while you tell her and I'll cover for her on the switchboard."

Once again, that suggestion typified Steve.

I was looking forward to my afternoon snooze, but as you would understand, this morning had been problematic but incredible. I set my alarm in plenty of time for the *vampire shift*, curled under the covers and tried to sleep. I only managed in fits and starts as I was emotional about leaving my job; especially Steve and my other friends, Helen and Jayne.

Day by day, the relationship between everyone at home settled down with normality, although my calls to Penny and her visits with Tina became fewer and fewer. Something noticed by Elsa and Brandon.

"I notice that you are getting less involved with your friend, Penny, the little shit-stirrer; I'm so pleased that now we all know how trustworthy she is.

Incidentally, I changed my accountant today, so Chris is also history."

I could sense a moment of joy in Brandon's statements although I experienced a personal feeling of remorse which immediately took over from annoyance when I remembered Brandon and Chris had been friends from boyhood. I realised it must be like losing a member of your family!

As time moved on, Brandon's potential purchase of the Café appeared to sit on the back burner. Also any comments he might have had about his tiling business or any other type of work.

If I wanted to know anything, I had to ask, although when I did ask, the answers were minimal and confusing.

A Dose of Insulin

What was happening, were we going to put our house on the market, were we going to buy the Café or even lease it.

Since Brandon first unloaded this incredible news on us, he hadn't discussed it any further.

Our lack of conversation about the Café also made it difficult for Elsa and me to plan our working lives.

Elsa eventually made the decision, to tell Brandon we would be pleased if he sold the house, bought the Café and worked it as a family business.

At least we would know what direction we were heading in and could give the Care-home and Cabs4U plenty of warning about our leaving dates.

I still wanted to know what it was Elsa had against Brandon. Most days, their attitude towards each other was ordinary and spontaneous, so perhaps whatever it was, she had forgiven him!

This move, a total change in direction, was a massive decision for us all, so Elsa decided to cook a special dinner for the evening meal before we questioned Brandon.

As he walked through the front door, Brandon exclaimed: "Mmmm, something smells good!"

Elsa dished up and served the meal, and Brandon said, "What's up, this is Italian food? Something must be wrong, so exactly what have I done?"

"Nothing, well not yet anyway. We haven't eaten any Italian since we visited the restaurant the other week and I thought it would be good for me to experiment with an Italian recipe as I know how much you like it, Brandon." Elsa said with total innocence.

This Italian meal also confirmed my belief that both of them had resolved their historical issue.

He stared with that mystified look on his face whenever he knew there was more to come. "Ok, what is it?"

"Well," I said, "Elsa and I would like to know what's happening about the Café so we can start planning our lives."

Brandon didn't respond immediately, and I could tell his thoughts were ticking over in his head.

"Come on, tell us what's happening." Elsa ushered him.

"Sandra and her husband are having second thoughts about moving back up North, and She is, therefore, thinking about hanging onto the Café for the time being.

More than that I don't know, so at the moment, it's a case of waiting!"

Brandon's surprise statement left everything in disarray!

Elsa was the first to respond. "OK, Brandon but if the shop does become available, Alice and I have decided we do want to buy the Café as a business and move in as soon as possible. Not just rent it."

"Is that what you want, Alice?" he asked, for confirmation.

After my affirmative reply, we stopped discussing the Café and enjoyed Elsa's attempt at Italian cooking.

"Do you know Elsa, whatever it is you cook, it tastes great. Perhaps you should think about cooking for a living." Branded said as a glowing tribute.

It wasn't bad; Elsa was indeed becoming a good cook. Midway through our meal, she left the table, and from the fridge, produced a bottle of Treviso Garbèl wine and placed it on the table in front of Brandon.

I'm not sure whether his expression was one of excitement

or possibly amazement that Elsa had even thought about the wine.

"Drink up and enjoy as there's another bottle of it in the fridge Brandon." She said, pleased to be the perfect host.

Although there would be a possible risk of upsetting Brandon and ruining Elsa's wonderful meal I had to tell Brandon I had told Steve and others that I would be leaving Cabs4U to run the Café in the not too distant future.

"And did Steve offer you increased pay to stay on?" Brandon asked cynically.

"No, Brandon, Steve, as did others, commented on what a kind, thoughtful and loving person you must be and how fortunate I was to have met you!"

My comment pulled the plug on any more of Brandon's cynical remarks.

Elsa and I happily discussed several ideas for the Café and the living quarters' when they became available.

Brandon said "Right, whatever is happening with the Café, let's put this house up for sale now.

We could then move into the Café immediately it becomes available; in the meantime, we could think about another type of business to buy just in case the Café idea never happens. Cash in hand is always better when negotiating, whatever it is a person's buying."

"Great idea Brandon! Fantastic!" Elsa confirmed.

After our visit to Rome and now this dramatic change in our fortunes, I couldn't believe how fortunate I was to have teamed up with Brandon!

Brandon had finished both bottles of Treviso Garbèl,

although Elsa and I had assisted him by drinking a couple of glasses.

Sounding as though he was suffering the effects, instead of easing up on the alcohol, he walked to the fridge again and bought three cans of beer to the table so we could all continue our celebration.

It was a thought, but Elsa and I declined his offer with thanks.

"Ok Elsa, you're the most accomplished of us on the PC, so how about you finding the best Estate Agent to manage our house sale and then I'll manage it from there," Brandon suggested.

Elsa and I retired to our bedrooms in a positive frame of mind although it was certain Brandon would finish the three cans of beer and end up sleeping at the Kitchen table as he often did following one of his major drinking sessions.

If only I could persuade him to stop drinking alcohol; or even reduce his consumption!

Elsa told me that when she had climbed into her bed the previous night, she didn't go immediately to sleep, as she was so enthused about everything.

Elsa worked on her laptop and selected several Estate Agents for Brandon to choose the one he liked best.

Within a matter of days, the 'offers over' price and an excellent picture of our house are at the top of the Agent's window, with the notification 'All visits must be by appointment'.

Elsa and I decided to take a walk to The Island and Caversham Bridge and tell Mum about our exciting news. There was no difference; everything looked the same as it always does. We must have talked to Mum for about 20 minuted before we said our goodbyes and made our way home.

It was a new experience for us, as during the next few days there were several calls from the Agent's staff attempting to either lower the price for interested parties or organise suitable times and dates for genuine buyers to view the premises.

Whatever, keeping the house and furniture, dust-free and in perfect order was no small effort. And of course, the back and front gardens had to be maintained in the most respectable order.

As always, Steve was most accommodating when a viewing appointment was required, although I did involve him in the process of agreeing the time and date, convenient to him and his business and suitable for me.

There were only a few visits; some potential buyers wanted a smaller house, some wanted more bedrooms, some didn't like the bathroom, some the garden space but the one common reaction, they all wanted us to agree on an unrealistic price.

Everything about the property was shown on the marketing details leaflet and clearly explained by the Estate Agents, or so I thought despite regular buyer complaints.

You can imagine my delight when I received an Agents call telling me another potential buyer wanted to have a look round, and she wasn't going to quibble about anything.

She fully understood what was for sale and what was negotiable and what was not.

Although at the moment, it wasn't a sale, I felt so much happier as this viewing could be a much greater possibility.

"The woman is called Edna Morrison. She has inherited cash and wants to buy somewhere suitable where she can rent a couple of rooms. Not too many because of the extra work involved but enough to make money.

She also wants to visit as soon as possible so the date is up to you, although it must be, a weekday and a morning visit, preferably after ten." The Estate agent confirmed.

"That's fine if it's that urgent, how about tomorrow morning or the day after, say ten o'clock?" I replied with enthusiasm.

"No, I already know she can't make tomorrow, so how about the day after?" asked the grateful Agent.

The time and date were agreed.

Elsa and Brandon were pleased, even more so when I told them the woman, Edna, appeared happy with the house details and wasn't intending to quibble.

Brandon also smiled and mentioned that he had yet to meet a woman who didn't quibble about something.

"Sounds a great possibility, and Alice, you still have a whole day to tidy up before she visits!" Elsa contributed, with a giggle.

In a more serious tone, I said "Incidentally Elsa, tomorrow is your afternoon shift at the Care-home, so, you can help to tidy up in the morning and the following day is one of your midweek breaks!

If you leave anything dirty, you can then explain to this buyer the reason why!

And please don't try to kid me your not available to clean up as you've written your work details on the Kitchen Callender!" We all laughed with amusement, even Elsa.

Chapter 54

The morning of the Edna Morrison's visit, everything looked smart and tidy, Elsa had done an excellent job, and Brandon wished Elsa and Me all the very best with the sale. However, Elsa moaned for good effect that after all her effort to clean the house, she would now be spending her day off, trying to sell it!

I prepared some ground coffee, a pot of tea and some assorted biscuits and cake.

There was a knock on the front door, and it was exactly ten o'clock.

I opened the front door with a welcoming smile on my face and Elsa standing beside me, and before I could utter a word, the woman physically forced her way past us both into the hallway. This person wasn't Edna Morrison.

It was Sandra from the Cafe.

"What the fuck are you up to?" she screamed at me.

"I should be asking you that same question; now get out of my house, I've got someone visiting me."

"You mean the buyer, Edna Morrison. Well sorry to disappoint the two of you but that's Me! Now, I want to know the fucking truth, you bitch."

Elsa and I just stared at each other in disbelief.

Without waiting for a reply, Sandra asked, "So what's this terminal injury, you've been telling Brandon you've got, you sad old cow; you'd do anything to hang on to him!"

Elsa screamed at her, "Don't you dare talk to my Sis like that, or else!"

"Or Else what!" Sandra replied in full voice.

I was amazed and not without reason, frightened! I was pleased Elsa was by my side and wondered what Sandra meant when she said 'You'd do anything to hang on to him,' although it soon became apparent to me.

It was apparent she was here for a purpose!

I had to hold Elsa back as I could see a disastrous situation developing in my own home.

"Go on, let her go, and we'll see how tough the little creep really is," Sandra said as a genuine challenge.

I asked everybody to calm down as I was somewhat confused. "I've never told Brandon any such thing; I'm perfectly fit and healthy. The only conversation I've had with him was about you and your husband leaving the Café and moving up North."

"Is that what he told you, He must be full of shit fucking excuses! Well, let me tell you my husband and I, got divorced a few years ago, and I've no idea where he is now. Apart from that, I have no intention of giving up the Café and never had!

Anyway, why do you think he's selling this house, you stupid bitch?" She shouted. "It's so that he can move in with me! Cash and all!

Thinking about it, maybe it's you with all the crap

excuses; whatever I'll find out!" Sandra said believing she had won the round!

With that final insult, she slammed the front door behind her as forcefully as she could.

I was mortified and slumped onto a seat. Elsa sat beside me and hugged.

For a while, neither of us could say anything and tears flooded down my cheeks.

Everything around me just seemed a blur, and apart from my constant shuddering with anger and incredible upset, I sat motionless on the kitchen seat!

Elsa broke the silence when she passed me tissues and told me to wipe my eyes.

"The bastard I'll kill him!" she said as she exploded with a series of profanities.

I asked myself, should I ring Penny? It sounded as though Chris had been right after all. Knowing who to believe and which particular stories to rely on, I was pleased, Elsa was by my side.

Elsa waited some while before she felt it was ok to say something else. Placing a cup of black coffee in front of me, she asked whether I wanted to talk.

We both began to discuss this morning's horrific chapter and what we would say to Brandon. We talked about the sale of our home; "What if she was right, you and me, Elsa, we have no title over this dwelling." I stated with alarm.

We talked for hours, although I was still confused about what to say to Brandon. In Elsa's case, it was more about what she wanted to do to him!

The day and then, the evening dragged on at a languid pace.

I left several messages on Brandon's mobile phone, and I'd lost count of the text messages asking him to call me urgently.

There was no Brandon! At 11 pm, Elsa correctly suggested that Sandra had most likely told Brandon of her visit to see me, and he was too scared to come home!

In my misery, I had used all the paper tissues and climbed into bed holding sheets of kitchen paper towels; no matter what I thought, tears kept flowing.

Nighttime lasted an eternity, and I was relieved when morning finally arrived. It was only 5.30 am, and Elsa heard me arise and followed downstairs. She made us both a cup of coffee.

"It was apparent you had a disturbed night Alice so in a minute I'm going to phone Cabs4U and the Care-home and tell them we won't be working today."

"Thank you, Elsa, but I've already booked today as a holiday," I muttered in between bouts of tears.

"OK, Sis, now would you like something to eat with your cup of coffee; neither of us have eaten anything since before that woman arrived yesterday, and you must be hungry."

It was hard enough to enjoy the coffee as my tears kept falling into the steamingly hot drink, and for a brief moment, I became captivated by the perfectly formed liquid rings which appeared from my teardrops as they fell into my coffee cup. I thankfully refused Elsa's kind offer of food.

My eyes were extremely sore, no doubt it was a result of the constant crying.

Still dressed in my nightdress but no nightgown, I walked to the bathroom and looked in the mirror.

Bedraggled hair, smudged makeup, red eyes and untidy looking clothes, I was in a terrible state.

Downstairs Elsa tried to comfort me saying it didn't matter how I looked as nobody else was here, and it didn't bother her in the least.

It couldn't have been more than a few minutes after she had said that and there was a noise at the front door.

It was Brandon.

Instinctively Elsa and I arose from the Sofa.

Brandon looked specifically at Elsa and said "Don't say anything, but I want you both out of this house within the next two weeks; I've met somebody else, and once I've sold this place, I'm going to move in with her. Do you understand!"

"You mean that slut Sandra, at least you could have the courtesy to use her fucking name Brandon," I said with uncontrolled anger.

"Do you realise you've mentioned her name a few times when you've been drunk or asleep," I said with even more anger.

I knew the latter was untrue, although he wouldn't even realise I was wasn't telling the truth.

In future, he would always worry about what he might have said or better still might be saying in his sleep!

"So, we're not buying the Café, eh? "I know everything about your recent games, Brandon. You even told her I had an incurable disease; perhaps you'd like to tell me what it is I'm suffering from, you complete and utter arsehole!

Anyway, I suppose you're now telling me the truth, or some of it because she ordered you to tell me what's going on, as she did in the Café a few days ago!"

When he responded to our outburst, it was clear Brandon didn't give a damn about us or anything we said.

"Do you think I give a fuck and don't think you can wreck this place before you leave; I've already thought of that, and I'll be staying here until you're both out of the way! Also, I don't want either of you involved in the sale of this house. I know the tricks you would play." Brandon said with contempt and a feeling of total control.

Although I could see his heartless reaction coming, understandably I couldn't help but reply as I did.

"You unbelievable piece of dogs' crap, as though you could believe we'd do something like that. Anyway, I wonder how long it will be before you find another woman and kick Sandra into touch. Ha, bloody ha!"

As Brandon turned to leave, he said "Yes very funny Alice, now you can understand why I never really loved you; now start looking immediately for somewhere else to live but please don't forget at least I'm not kicking you both onto the street. I'll be back later."

"Oh Alice, he now thinks he's The Terminator!" Elsa said although I didn't detect, she meant it to be a humorous comment.

The front door eased to click shut behind him, and what now seemed to be a habit, Elsa and I said nothing. For a while, we just stared at each other.

A few minutes later Elsa said "Well Sis; It's what we would have expected so perhaps this is the best time to tell you my story about Brandon and why I put him at the top end of my suspect list when somebody was accusing me of being a *drug dealer*; it can't make anything any worse!

I know how upset you are, and this isn't going to make it any better, so it's your choice. Do you want to know?"

"Go on, Elsa; I agree, it cant make me feel any worse than I already do!"

"Ok Alice, the reason I originally said he might be playing around with other women is that I guessed that's what he did! And if you ask me how I knew, it's because he had already tried it on with me a few times! The bastard can't help himself." Elsa said most vehemently.

"Are you sure you want me to continue with this story, Sis?" Elsa said with a profound expression of concern.

Confirming I did, Elsa continued, clearly with reluctance.

"Well, it started a couple of times when you were conveniently out, either shopping or at work.

On one occasion he bumped into me quite severely. He knocked me to the floor and then apologised, saying it was an accident.

He picked me up by my waist, but even when I was standing up and fully recovered from the unexpected fall, he didn't let go of me. I know it sounds stupid of me, but the whole situation seemed strange. However, a while after I forgot about the incident."

"Well Elsa, that's innocent enough, what's wrong with assisting someone after an accident?"

"Absolutely nothing Sis but when almost the same thing

happens again a few weeks later, I started thinking again; a funny coincidence! Not only that but it was the look in his eyes; it was so strange, as though he expected a reaction from me and once again it happened in my bedroom when he said he was checking the electric points around the house and then again when you were absent. Think about it, Alice, he could have waited until I had finished what I was doing and I'd then have left my room!"

"As you said Elsa, a coincidence; they do happen!"

"Please, Alice, listen to what I'm saying; sexual assault is no coincidence."

"What, Brandon assaulted you?"

"Certainly, he attempted but failed to realise the reaction he'd get from me.

Sis, that look in his eyes. It's difficult to explain, but I don't think I'll ever forget it. Anyway, this is what I told Penny about a while back. I didn't go into explicit details then, and I'm not going to now; It's so distasteful.

Believe you me Sis; he didn't get what he wanted, and at some stage, Bandon's going to regret those actions and the way he's treated you.

For a long while, I have managed to convince myself it was an innocent accident, but after your recent experience, I'm convinced it wasn't.

Even at Penny's when I gave him 10/10, I still managed to convince myself I was wrong, thinking I'd only put him at the top of my mental list because Penny was pestering me to think of somebody other than Brotherton."

I was so upset for my dear Sister that I didn't know what

to say, and then it dawned on me; we were talking about Brandon – my boyfriend!

"Oh, Alice, I have been so concerned about telling you that story; I wasn't even sure you'd believe me."

"Bless you, Elsa. You must realise that this awful situation could have been so much worse. Whatever, you should have told me at the time!"

"However, Alice, as you say, it could have been much worse. I always attempt to remember the trauma of your time with David Wilson and I knew this would have caused great upset whether you believed me or not!"

Elsa and I already had our marching orders, but I would have liked to question Brandon about Elsa's statement; however, I knew whatever I said, he would have a definite explanation. Most likely he'd have denied it entirely and said Elsa was lying or possibly, that she even fancied him and it was Elsa that made advances.

After his different stories of the situation between Sandra and me, I knew there was absolutely no point in asking, despite how much I wanted to hear his excuses or incredible lies about Elsa.

Anyway, he returned home in his usual drunken stupor and collapsed asleep on his favourite kitchen chair; his head and arms were resting on the table so, it wouldn't have been a worthwhile discussion anyway.

"I couldn't say anything to anybody. At night I lay in bed and asked myself whether I just imagined everything. Was I going mad?"

"So, Alice, what are we going to do?" asked Elsa.

"About Brandon and you?" I enquired.

"No, Alice, don't worry about that, I've got it sorted; Now we both need to find somewhere else to live."

"I've no idea Elsa, physically and mentally I feel an absolute wreck; I haven't felt this bad since that other bastard, Wilson!

I sat in silence and thought. I couldn't return to work in this state of anxiety. At least Steve would be pleased I wasn't leaving after all.

For some unexplained reason, I didn't even feel comfortable talking to Steve, but I must let him know I was unable to return work immediately.

There was an uncomfortable feeling about walking to work and then telling someone what had happened, as I knew Steve would collar me and ask all kinds of thoughtful questions, and at this moment I didn't want to discuss anything in detail.

Instead, I asked Elsa to phone the Cabs4U number and if either Jayne or Helen answered, pass them onto me.

Helen answered.

I asked her to inform Steve I didn't know when I would next be at work and apologised accordingly. I tried to explain what had happened, but it was difficult as she talked to me between taking customer calls.

"What, the Café's not yours; Brandon's finished with you? Did you say he's been seeing another woman while he was with you! The bastard!

Whatever you can't stay there for the night; listen to yourself, Alice, you can't stop crying. Anyway, we have a spare room, so how about you and Elsa coming here for a couple of days at least until everything has settled down a little. Not that you can settle from something like this."

I was still feeling so bad, but despite my upset and concerns, I thought about Helen and what this poor woman had lived with; for her entire life!

Understandably I was most grateful as the thought of sleeping under the same roof as Brandon tonight, absolutely appalled me. I thanked Helen gratefully and explained I'd discuss it with Elsa.

Elsa had been listening intently to my brief conversation, and when I finished the call, she asked me to explain the outcome.

Our conversation continued for some while, and Elsa said "It's a kind and thoughtful offer Sis, but maybe I'll come over to Helen's tomorrow as there are a few things I want to do today as when I leave here, I'm never coming back. Please say thank you to Helen and tell her, maybe it's tomorrow night for me."

We enjoyed our comforting cuddle and accordingly, I rang Helen.

Feeling a little settled, I raised the courage to call Penny; it wasn't her or Chris's fault that Brandon was such a convincing liar!

By way of apology, I confirmed all that had happened today, and I was going to spend a few days at Helen's.

She wasn't surprised, and with genuine sympathy, she shocked me again saying "I'm so sorry for you, Alice, but I should have told you a long time ago, but Chris forbade me, telling me not to start more trouble.

Brandon's wife left him not just because of his drinking but also his constant womanising.

Do you remember what my Foster Father said to you at my Wedding, well he's never changed! Any piece of 'skirt' and he's in there if you'll excuse my pun! Whatever, I think you understand that now!"

I'm not sure how long we talked, but Penny said we must meet very soon as she missed our regular get-togethers and apart from that she knew baby Tina also missed me.

Elsa was busily working around me and said I had to pack my things for Helen's, preferably before Brandon's return.

I said goodbye to Penny, at least feeling more refreshed as I had sorted any personal dispute between us.

It took me ages making my mind up about what to pack in my suitcase although Elsa stopped me and said: "Sis, take the neediest things, those that will last you a few days, and in between, you can collect the remainder."

I took Elsa's advice and decided on the most needed items to pack.

Elsa had packed what she required at this moment in time, and while waiting for me, she returned to her attic room to read whatever book it was she was reading with interest.

At a time like this, how could anyone be relaxed enough to read a book?

Having packed, Elsa assisted me in taking my belongings to Helen's.

Chapter 55

Helen had finished her shift at Cabs4U, and she invited Elsa and me to sit down, take a rest and enjoy a hot drink and a piece of fruit-cake.

Our conversation envelops all the matters Elsa and I had discussed time and time again, and it was extremely late when Elsa said she must return home and finish what she was doing. "See you both tomorrow." She said while giving me a farewell kiss.

At home, it is lunchtime, and nothing had changed, and Elsa found Brandon, at the kitchen table, can of beer in one hand and an empty one laying on its side beside him with dribbles of lager spilt on the table.

As usual, he was snoring loudly.

His head was slumped to one side in an almost impossible position while sitting on the kitchen chair, an undesirable posture which you only see on kids TV comic programmes.

Elsa checked to see whether he was genuinely past his best.

Occasionally he mumbled words which drunks do and nobody else could understand.

Elsa stands for a short while, considering a few things;

she knows what to do as she had already planned her approach the day after Sandra had unexpectedly visited us and indeed when Brandon told us we were out of the house for good!

Brandon hadn't moved from the table and still lays in a drunken state; totally unaware of what's happening around him.

Elsa touches his shoulder, but there's no other reaction from him; only his continued snoring, interrupted by a few of his verbal mumbles.

Emotionless, Elsa locates the items she needs, stored in the fridge, where they are usually are. One more final check, to ensure everything is ok.

Brandon has settled over the table in his alcoholic stupor and is unaware of what's going on around him!

Elsa completes her task.

There is still no reaction from Brandon.

With her book and a cold drink, she walks to her bedroom, the sound of snoring still echoing behind her as she climbs the stairs to her room in the loft.

She sits in the tiny chair next to her bed, places her drink on an even smaller, collapsible table and sits down to finish reading her book; there are only two chapters to go, but without reading it, Elsa already knows the eventual ending of this book.

Was there any need to read on?

Maybe not, but overall, the book was a captivating read.

Completing the book, Elsa leaves it on the table, and climbs into her bed and comfortably falls asleep.

It is now very early in the morning. Elsa dresses, and

with immense anticipation, she realises sufficient time has passed.

Elsa quietly opens her bedroom door, walks downstairs and along the short passageway into the kitchen.

Elsa is relieved, his snoring has stopped.

Brandon remains slumped, face down across the table. A usual sight but this time there are no unpleasant sounds. Good.

She touches his left arm hanging awkwardly by his side. It is cold.

Places her hand on his forehead; also extremely cold.

Checking a second time, to make sure, Elsa then places six items in a black refuse bag and quietly leaves the house.

Arriving at Caversham Bridge, it is chilly but not cold. Elsa stares at the Island and remembers Mum.

Quietly she asks her, and perhaps Alice also, to forgive her!

Early morning mist hangs above the gentle flow of the Thames, and only one or two people are present as most are probably still asleep comfortably in their beds.

Elsa carefully reaches inside the refuse bag and drops the six items separately into the depths of the river; five empty syringes which had previously held quick reacting insulin and a book. The book she had been reading these last few weeks written by the much read authoress and TV playwright, Monika Lamb; *The perfect murder.*

Elsa thinks, David Wilson, you don't know how lucky you are to get away with distressing my lovely sister, and in an audible voice, she talks to herself. "And as for you

Brandon, now you know the result of messing with me and upsetting my Sister the way you did!"

She strokes the heart pendant hanging around her neck; *Always my sister, forever, my friend.*

Returning home, Elsa considers her next steps and top of her list, what exactly she should tell the Police; if indeed she decides to tell them anything at all!

About the Author

Since retiring from work, Keith C Payne has attempted to keep the grey matter working. Apart from freshwater angling, he enjoys watching documentary programmes and writing stories. He was born in London, moved to Birmingham with his family when he was in his late twenties and since then spent his last 30 plus years living in Berkshire.

Keith has had type one diabetes since the age of seven and writes this current novel from personal experience.

A dose of insulin is his third publication with Authorhouse, and he has another novel already planned; based on the effects of climate change.

This story focuses on the planet as it is today, and the potential impact climate change will have on our world many millennia after that.

Lightning Source UK Ltd.
Milton Keynes UK
UKHW041323120220
358590UK00009B/77